THE TAKEAWAY MEN

THE TAKEAWAY MEN

A NOVEL

MERYL AIN

Published by SparkPress, a BookSparks imprint,
A division of SparkPoint Studio, LLC
Phoenix, Arizona, USA, 85007
www.gosparkpress.com

Published 2020
Printed in the United States of America
Print ISBN: 978-1-68463-047-9
E-ISBN: 978-1-68463-048-6

Library of Congress Control Number: 2020901422

Formatting by Kiran Spees

For my grandparents and great-grandparents, who believed in the American Dream.

And for my parents, who defended and saved freedom and democracy as members of The Greatest Generation.

Until we are all free, we are none of us free.

—Emma Lazarus

PROLOGUE
AUGUST, 1942

———◦———

KIELCE, POLAND

WHEN THE TRUCK WITH THE painted Red Cross on its doors left Edyta off on the dirt road leading to her house, her neighborhood was already dark and quiet. Only the barking of a dog shattered the silence. The myriad silvery shining stars ignited the night sky like a pattern of delicate sequins and illuminated her path. Although she was exhausted and sweaty from her long day's work, and her nurse's uniform was damp and clung to her body, she could not help but reflect on the magnificence of God's creation. *But how was it possible,* she pondered, *that the barbaric Nazi destruction that was overrunning this corner of the earth—her town and her country—coexisted against the backdrop of God's masterpiece?*

Earlier that day, she had smuggled three toddlers out of the Kielce Ghetto and into the safety of the Convent of the Blessed Virgin Mary. The mother superior there had now sent her home with a small basket of bread, cheese, and apples for the two Jewish adults she was hiding in the attic of her father's house. She knew hiding Jews, especially in her own home, was a risky proposition and not within her comfort level. Her expertise was in rescuing small children, not grown-ups. But when

1

she was asked to smuggle two adults from the ghetto, one of whom she had known since childhood, she'd had no other choice. She knew full well that her decision was not without peril, particularly because her father, a Polish policeman, supported the Nazis in their hatred of Jews.

Despite her concerns, she convinced herself that this is what her late mother would have wanted her to do. Her mother had been a nurse, and Edyta's choice of a helping profession was no accident. Her mother had always been kind and caring, and had had a good relationship with her neighbors, including the Jewish doctor for whom she worked. Sometimes, as a small child, Edyta would accompany her mother to the office, which was located in the large stone house where the doctor and his family lived. She would fetch bandages and cups of water for the patients. As she got older, she became her mother's assistant, and was determined to become a nurse like her. The doctor had even offered to pay for her tuition at the nursing school in Radom when the time came.

Edyta had been infatuated with the doctor's son, Aron, ever since she could remember. He told her how he planned to become a physician too and go into practice with his father. As she got older, her crush on him grew. She had secretly dreamed of working beside him, and perhaps even marrying him one day.

But before Aron had an opportunity to apply to medical school, Jews were barred from higher education and from the professions. Hitler's invasion of Poland on September 1, 1939, and the ensuing chaos dashed Edyta's dreams of attending nursing school. She was forced to stay home with her widowed father, who had taken to drinking excessively and spewing forth anti-Semitic vitriol.

As she approached her street, she saw her small two-story house with its slanted roof and brown weather-beaten shingles. She was grateful for the cover of night because she could walk home without neighbors asking intrusive questions.

"Thank you, Jesus," she murmured as she crossed herself. But she was still nervous, thinking about her father. She became short of breath, and her heart started racing, as if she were being chased. The Jews had been in the attic for only a couple of days, and she was deathly afraid that her father would discover them.

Calm down, she thought to herself. *It is late; surely Tata is sleeping by now.* But as she got closer to the cottage, her fear intensified.

She opened the door gingerly, so as not to make a sound. As she looked around, she saw the telltale signs of a drinking binge—empty beer and liquor bottles were scattered on the floor and kitchen counter. And her father was awake. His eyes were glazed, and his clothes were disheveled. She could smell the honey and spices of the *Krupnik* on his breath. She could hear that he had been drinking for some time because he slurred his words as he screamed at her.

"Where have you been? What are you doing in your late mother's uniform? Up to no good, I'm sure. You belong in the gutter with the *Zhids.* I will kill the Christ Killers—and you too—before you get me killed."

He threw his drink at her, and the golden yellow liquid landed on her white uniform. The glass narrowly missed and shattered against the wall behind her, a shard lodging in her bare left leg. As it began to bleed, she ran upstairs to her room and locked the door.

While her father had been prone to angry outbursts in the past, he had never physically attacked her like this. *Was it the loss of her mother or the drink or the Nazi occupation that had turned him into a monster? Or had he always secretly hated the Jews, and Hitler's invasion had just given him license to express it?*

One thing was certain. He was a policeman with a prejudice, a gun, and a temper. With the encouragement and approval of the Nazi government, he was in a position to potentially inflict great harm. She shuddered to think about the evil her father might do.

She now knew for sure that neither she, nor the two Jews hiding in the attic, were safe from her father's wrath.

JULY, 1947

---◉---

OUTSIDE MUNICH, GERMANY,
IN THE AMERICAN ZONE OF OCCUPATION

"LET'S SIT RIGHT HERE, DYTA, under this tree," Aron said to his wife, who was out of breath and clearly struggling to match his brisk pace. Aron was always impatient, and in a hurry, and often he simply forgot that his petite, pregnant wife couldn't match the long strides of his six-foot two-inch frame.

"That's okay," she said. "I'll keep up with you."

She spoke in Polish, the language she found most comfortable.

Although his gruff and somber exterior matched his crotchety personality, he knew enough not to take his wife's words at face value. She would do or say anything to accommodate him. And he was not going to push her now, especially when she was three days into her ninth month, and she looked like she had swallowed a giant watermelon.

Yes, Blessed be the Name of God, he thought. It was as if they were literally recreating life in this waiting space, with its wooden barracks and sprawling green fields.

A former summer camp for Hitler Youth, they and other displaced Jews from throughout Europe lived in stone and wooden barracks in a treed, pastoral setting. Educational and religious life flourished in the *Warteplatz* Displaced Persons Camp, along with schools, synagogues, and adult education programs. There were classes that taught Hebrew and English to prepare the survivors for new lives in Israel or the United States. Dyta, especially, was a conscientious English student, hopefully preparing for a new life in America. She and Aron, like most of the survivors, had had enough of the graveyard that Europe had become for Jewish life. They wanted to leave the cursed soil. Staying in Europe was out of the question.

The crown jewel of the DP camp was a five hundred-bed hospital, provided by the American Joint Distribution Committee. It was staffed by Hungarian and Jewish doctors and American and Jewish nurses. And this was where Aron and Dyta intended for their baby to be born.

There was even a Yiddish newspaper, written and published each Friday by the residents, which Aron read religiously. Against all logic, he still scoured the weekly edition for news of friends and relatives who might miraculously be alive. After Aron helped Dyta sit down on the grass, he seated himself and picked up the latest edition of the newspaper, *Undzer Hofenung*

Although it revolted him in a raw and aching way, he also read and reread the horrific accounts of the survivors that were published each week. He kept his own experiences bottled up. But he was drawn to these narratives of others—addicted to them. They validated his melancholy, his frustration, and his anger. Like the dots in a pointillist painting, each word, each sentence, each paragraph was necessary to construct the whole picture. But unlike the pastel blues and greens in an idyllic Seurat landscape, the words of the survivors were black and bloody, painting a punishing picture of a world gone mad. These accounts he read to himself.

But the joyous news of the many *simchas*—weddings and births— he shared with his wife by reading them aloud. They occurred so frequently that it was as if the survivors were in a hurry to resume normal living in order to compensate for the years they had lost.

Their own wedding had been chronicled in *Undzer Hofenung*, along with the six other couples married by Rabbi Judah Zuckerman in a joint ceremony that day at Warteplatz. Each couple had been given two tickets for new clothes. Since the end of the war, these joint weddings took place on a regular basis among the shattered remnant eager to start new lives. And while very few children had survived the Holocaust, by 1947 more than three hundred had been born at the camp. As shattered and broken and traumatized as the survivors were, they were resilient enough to move on with their lives.

While the DPs sought dignity and normalcy, some chose to speak and write about their experience as part of their recovery. Many others, like Aron, found no purpose or comfort in sharing the unspeakable, and remained silent.

Aron knew full well that each and every Jew who perished, as well as those who survived, had a story. For him, his weekly pre-Sabbath reading ritual prepared him for a day of rest and reflection. As he read the account of Miriam Wolkowicz, a fellow Pole, his wife could see at once that he was being transported back to his haunted place.

Miriam wrote about her arrival at the Plaszow forced labor camp in 1942, when she and her whole family and several thousand other residents of the Krakow ghetto were marched there.

"When we arrived, the first thing we saw was three men hanging. The Gestapo barked 'Mach schnell, mach schnell!' at the marchers. Children and the elderly were forbidden to enter the premises, and they were shot on the spot. But some people had smuggled children into the camp anyway. There were inspections by the Gestapo, and they soon discovered the hidden children. They announced they were setting up a nursery for them. My sister, Marta, was relieved that her children would be cared for there, even though she had disobeyed orders by hiding them. But in a few days, we were standing for roll call and the

music was blaring. We saw from a distance an open truck with children. Marta was standing next to me with her twin girls, who were five years old. The Gestapo was looking for more children. The girls screamed to Marta, "Mama, the takeaway men are coming, they're going to take us away!" And they scooped up my little nieces, and the truck—loaded with children—drove off, and we never saw them again."

Aron's dark chocolate eyes always had a somber look to them, but as he read silently, his agony became almost palpable. It seemed to his wife as if three thousand years of Jewish suffering were contained in his sorrowful, otherworldly expression.

She had seen that expression far too often. In the long run, she was determined to heal him. For now, she would distract him.

"What do you think we should name the baby?"

Without hesitation, Aron replied, "I want to name the baby after my siblings of blessed memory, Yosef, if it's a boy, and Hannah, if it's a girl."

"I understand," she said as she tried to hide her disappointment, but then could not contain herself. "But my mother is gone too."

She saw the look of disdain that momentarily flickered on his face and her heart sank. She quickly caught herself.

"No, I'm sorry. I shouldn't have said anything. Your brother and sister deserve to have a name. They were such sweet, beautiful, innocent children."

That is what Aron loved so much about his Dyta. She was as soothing as an aloe plant, as flexible as a rubber band. She had even risked her own life for him.

"No, that's okay," he said. "Were it not for your mother, I would not have you—and I would be dead."

Suddenly, Dyta felt a huge rush of warm water bursting forth from her, soaking her underwear and her dress as it traveled down her legs onto the grass.

"Aron, I think my water has broken," she said.

"But it's too early; maybe it's just pressure on your bladder."

"No, I know what pressure on my bladder feels like; I think my labor has begun."

"But you're not due for another month."

"Tell that to the baby."

"Should we go to the hospital now? I want to make sure we get you to the hospital on time. I want a Hungarian doctor to deliver our baby."

"Why wouldn't you want a Jewish doctor?"

"They're out of practice. People here say you're better off with a Hungarian doctor. I want a doctor with recent experience."

Two hours later, instead of lighting Sabbath candles that evening, Dyta found herself in active labor in the camp's hospital. While Aron waited in the reception area, a Hungarian, Dr. Nagy, assisted by a Jewish-American nurse named Ruth, delivered a five- pound, three-ounce baby girl at 8:15 p.m.

And at 8:26 p.m., a second girl weighed in at six pounds, one ounce.

Dr. Nagy went out to the waiting room where Aron sat alone.

"Congratulations, Mr. Lubinski, you are the father of two beautiful baby girls—and two big ones at that! Twins delivered almost a month early are rarely this big."

"Two? What do you mean *two*?"

"Your wife has given you twin daughters. Would you like to see them?"

Aron was speechless. His life had been in jeopardy so many times in the past few years. He had lost his entire family. He thought of Miriam's piece in the newspaper about the twins taken away in the open truck. And now, there was new life. Not just one, but two new lives—and they were his.

Unlike death, new life has a pleasant smell. Moments later, Aron inhaled the fresh, milky, intoxicating fragrance of newborn babies as he marveled at his perfect twin daughters sleeping peacefully in the nursery.

Under his breath, he recited the *Shecheyianu* prayer.

Praised art Thou, Oh Lord, Our God, Ruler of the Universe, who has kept us in life and preserved us and enabled us to reach this joyous occasion.

❧

The next morning, which was the Sabbath, Aron went to the camp synagogue, as was his custom. Services were held in a large room that was also used for plays and concerts. A portable ark, which held the Torah, was at the front of the room. The same Rabbi Zuckerman who had officiated at Aron's wedding called him to the Torah and the babies were given Hebrew names: *Hannah Yosefa* and *Bracha Haya*, the daughters of Aron. Hannah Yosefa was named for Aron's sister and brother. And Bracha Haya was given a name that means Blessed Life in Hebrew. That's what he wanted for both his baby daughters—a blessed life.

This was the first set of twins that had been born at the camp. The entire congregation joined their voices in singing "*Siman Tov u Mazel Tov!*" There were few dry eyes; the thought that two future Jewish mothers had come from their midst made it a very special Sabbath indeed.

But just then a thought occurred to Aron, one he immediately pushed aside. He would not let that concern interfere with his joy on this day. But as the grandson of a rabbi growing up in an Orthodox family, he knew what Jewish law said about his situation.

After services, he followed the scent of gefilte fish, *challah*, and sweet red wine as he headed to the *Kiddush* in the back of the room. Once again, a sea of people fell all over him, congratulating him on the twins. The pangs of guilt he had experienced when his babies were named were now pushed aside. But Aron also feared that one day they would come back to haunt him.

Ruth, the American military nurse who had helped deliver the babies, greeted him as he entered an adjoining room.

"Again, a double *mazel tov*," she said, giving him a big bear hug. "You know, it's actually a triple mazel tov—your twins were born on a very special day—July Fourth."

"What's July Fourth?" Aaron inquired.

"It's America's Independence Day—a wonderful family day, and now you and your wife are starting a perfect Jewish family," she said. "I have to go now. We'll *schmooze* more tomorrow."

"Thanks for everything, Ruth. We'll see you tomorrow. Good *Shabbos*."

When Aron returned to the hospital to visit his wife and baby daughters that afternoon, Dyta was sitting up in bed, wearing a drab gray hospital gown, and looking exhausted. He pulled over a chair right next to the bed and reported what had happened in *shul*. He shared the great joy that was expressed by the congregation. He mentioned July Fourth. But he omitted the pangs of guilt. She was pure and innocent; she had no idea that he had committed a sin.

~

Ruth was a warm, caring, person. She was also an accomplished nurse, not only perky, but professionally proficient and dedicated to the DPs. But there were those who accused her of being a *yenta*. They whispered that she was not a person who understood the importance of boundaries. But that never stopped Ruth from getting involved in other people's lives.

So it was when she went to visit Aron, Dyta, and their twins in the hospital on Sunday, July 6.

"Mazel tov!" How is the beautiful mother of the beautiful twins today?" Ruth said.

"I'm okay,"

"Maybe it's none of my business," she said. "But have you given any thought to giving them English names besides the Hebrew names they got yesterday? You know, the Americans run Warteplatz, and you will likely end up in the United States. I told Aron I think it's an omen that they were born on July Fourth."

"Do you have any in mind?" Aron asked.

"Well I was thinking you could combine Yosef and Hannah, reverse it, and make it Joan or Joanne. Those are popular American names. And Bracha could be Barbara in English."

"How about Johanna?" Aron asked. "Is that a name in America, Ruth?"

"I think it's a little old-fashioned, but sure why not? You can always give her a nickname."

"Okay then, Johanna and let's name Bracha Barbara," Aron recommended.

"Johanna is fine, but I want to use my mother's exact name, Bronka," Dyta said as she began to tear up. She was less than thirty-six hours removed from the birth of the twins, hormones racing and emotions flaring. She began to weep. The thought of her mother and her family in Kielce touched a raw nerve.

"Fine, but Bronka is a Polish name, not an American one," Aron said.

As the words came out of his mouth, he realized that he didn't care. If naming the baby exactly after his beloved wife's mother would make her happy—even if her mother's husband was no good—that was the least he could do. The Passover hymn, *Dayenu,* came to his mind, but he used the tune to put his own words to the song.

If she had given him hope in a hopeless place. Dayenu
If she had saved his life. Dayenu
If she had loved him and married him. Dayenu
If she had given him two children at once. Dayenu.

She had already done more than enough. If she wanted the child to be Bronka, then Bronka she would be.

"Sounds good to me," said Ruth. "I was meaning to ask you, Dyta. Is your name Judyta or Edyta?"

"Just plain Dyta is fine with me."

"And did the two of you grow up together in Kielce?"

"In a sense," she said.

JANUARY, 1951

---◀◉▶---

NEW YORK CITY

ARON AND HIS FAMILY WERE standing on the deck of the ship as it neared New York Harbor. The voice of the captain boomed over the loudspeaker:

"We'll be docking within the half hour. We're now passing the Statue of Liberty; be sure to take a good look on the starboard deck so you can see her. Everyone in the world yearns to see Lady Liberty because she represents hope and opportunity for all who seek a better life in America. Look at her raised hand holding the torch. It's a symbol that America is a refuge, and all are welcome here to live in freedom. Welcome to the United States. Welcome to New York."

Soon, there was a big commotion as the boat full of refugees shifted to the right to see Lady Liberty. For a moment, Aron was almost afraid that the boat might tip over as everyone ran to one side of the boat.

"Look at the Statue of Liberty, look at the lady with her hand up," people started yelling in numerous languages—in Yiddish, German, Polish, Hungarian. As eyes filled with tears, many hugged complete strangers.

Aron lifted one twin and Dyta the other in order to give them a better view.

"We'll remember this day always," Aron said. "You will remember the day you were welcomed by Lady Liberty. It's the first day that we are truly free. We must thank God for rescuing us and bringing us to America."

When the ship docked, it was a clear, cold January day—about thirty-six degrees. As the captain raised the American flag, Aron put his right hand over his heart. He was free at last. Aron watched the wild waving and throwing of kisses as those on the boat and those waiting for them on the dock were overwhelmed with joy. During the long voyage, he had often come on deck to look at the ocean. He reflected on how beautiful and endless it was, especially on partly cloudy days when the sun occasionally peeked through the soft puffs of cotton clouds and provided a fleeting glimpse of a blue sky.

How foolish for man to try to control things when it is the Almighty with ultimate power, he thought. But then again, he told himself, *Within parameters, man makes choices.* Aron had made his choices, but he knew that it was God who wanted him to survive. Life and death were God's domain. God had given Aron and his family a new chance in America. It was now up to them to live their lives in a way that would please the Almighty. He would do his best, he vowed.

Throngs of people on the deck were there to greet the new arrivals. As Aron and his family walked off the boat with the other refugees, he saw some ahead of him kiss the ground, crying with emotion. Aron then spotted a bald, stout man in his sixties holding a white cardboard sign that said simply, "Lubinski." Next to him stood an elegant-looking woman with silver gray hair rolled up into a bun, neatly covered with a hair net. She wore a black Persian lamb hat and coat. Over the coat was a mink scarf wrap, which showcased the heads and tails of the animal.

"That must be Izzy and his wife," Aron said to Dyta and the twins, who, at three-and-a-half, were quite overwhelmed by the tumult.

"Izzy, Izzy, is that you?" Aron called out.

"Yes, Aron, it's Izzy and Faye," a deep, soaring voice yelled back.

Encumbered somewhat by their oversized rucksacks and each holding the hand of a child, the newly arrived Lubinskis could not run as fast as their hearts told them to. But the older couple started racing toward them, and in seconds Izzy and Faye were embracing the family as if they had known them forever.

"Such pretty girls," chirped Faye. "They look so alike, yet each is beautiful in her own way. Are they identical or fraternal?"

"Fraternal," Aron replied.

In fact, the most obvious difference between the twins was their coloring. They both had perfect little circle faces and bowlike scrumptious strawberry lips. But, on closer inspection, Bronka had delicious licorice eyes, while Johanna's eyes were dark blue flecked with gold. Bronka's face was framed with luxurious mahogany ringlets, while Johanna's curls were blond.

"Look what I have for you," Faye said, holding out two identical pink teddy bears.

The bewildered twins remained silent.

"They are a little bit stunned," Dyta explained in the halting English she had learned at Warteplatz. "It's been a long trip, and this is all so new to them. Thank you very much."

"We can speak Yiddish, if that's easier," Faye suggested.

"No," Aron said emphatically, almost snapping. "We all need to learn English better. My wife's been taking English classes, and she's been trying to teach the girls. But you'll see, they speak their own language, a combination of Polish, Yiddish, and English. So the more English, the better; the faster they'll learn."

"Okay then," Izzy said. "But don't be so hard on them, Aron. They're tiny girls. They'll learn soon enough. And at home you're welcome to speak Yiddish or whatever makes you comfortable. By the way, I can understand Polish too. Now since you're going to be staying with us, I want to get everyone's name straight."

"My wife is Dyta," Aron said. "The girls are Johanna and Bronka."

"Dyta for Judyta," Izzy surmised. "You're in New York now. I'm going to call you Judy."

Not wanting to get into a discussion about names, Aron said nothing. And that is how Dyta became Judy in America. It suited everyone's purpose.

～

Izzy's huge personality matched his large frame. At six feet tall, he had a booming voice, which sounded very authoritative, especially when he was giving his opinion on any number of subjects—names, the price of flour, the trial of Julius and Ethel Rosenberg, the treatment of Jewish refugees—or his favorite topic, his rabbi, or to be more exact, his former rabbi. But Izzy's kind heart matched his size, and when he had heard from Aron Lubinski, even though he had never met him, he'd stepped up to the plate.

In Izzy's eyes, Aron was, after all, family. Family he had never met, but family nevertheless. Izzy was a first cousin to Aron's father, David. Izzy's father, Tuvia, and Aron's father had the same grandparents—Necha and Hirsch Lubinski. Rabbi Hirsch Lubinski had been revered throughout Poland for his knowledge and his wisdom. People came to him from miles around for his learned opinion. Having him in the family carried with it *yichus*, pedigree, status. Yichus meant something in Poland. Unfortunately, not so much in Bellerose, Queens, where Izzy and Faye lived. But Aron remembered his father talking about large family *seders* presided over by his grandfather, at which the children would play under the table during the meal. He also recounted stories of helping his siblings and cousins put up and decorate his grandparents' *sukkah*, the temporary hut built during the festival commemorating the Jews wandering in the desert. Izzy also had fond memories of those special family holidays, and the sight of Aron, and his resemblance to Izzy's grandfather, brought back a rush of nostalgia.

In 1951, Izzy was sixty-three years old. He had fled the old country in 1908, when his parents, under the supervision of his grandfather, had chosen a wife, Malka, for him. He was twenty; Malka was seventeen. She was the pious daughter of another rabbi, and both families thought Izzy, because he was so quick and bright, would follow in the footsteps of both his grandfather and his father-in-law.

While Malka was sweet and attractive, Izzy was not ready to settle down, especially to a life that would be lived in a goldfish bowl. Izzy was brash and adventurous and did not want to be tied to an existence consisting solely of prayer and study. Despite his father's and grandfather's explanations and exhortations and his mother's tears and tantrums, he had left Poland for the United States—never to return, and never to see any of his loved ones again.

Although he was a headstrong man, he had loved and missed his family throughout the years. He had married in the United States, yet he frequently second-guessed his decision to leave the old country. Of course, all of the second-guessing stopped when the world learned what Hitler wrought. But the guilt and heartache never ceased— instead it got worse. Izzy believed that the entire Lubinski family had been consumed in the crucible of World War II. So when he learned that Aron and his family were alive and coming to America, he was elated. He would channel his grief and his guilt into generosity toward these young cousins.

"Let's head to the car," Izzy said. "You must all be exhausted and hungry. We'll eat and catch up when we get home."

They headed to a large black Lincoln Continental, and Faye insisted that Aron sit in the front with Izzy.

"I'll sit in the back with Judy and the girls so we can get

acquainted," Faye offered. But minutes after they got into the car, Bronka, Johanna—and Judy—were sound asleep.

Aron looked out the window at New York City for the first time from his front row seat. He had been told that in America the streets were paved with gold. He could see that this was not the case. In fact, he noticed that the streets were dirty, and there was even garbage littering the roads.

"You know," he told Izzy, "in Europe, people think the streets are paved with gold."

"Yes, I heard that rumor before I came here too," Izzy said with a laugh. "America accepts people like us and gives us the chance to get ahead on our own merit—that's what's golden about it. Look at the tall buildings, Aron. Bet you never saw anything like those before."

"Never," said Aron, wondering how buildings could be built so high.

"And in America, the minute you get here, you're free to have dreams as high and mighty as those buildings," said Izzy. "And people who dream and also work very hard, no matter who they are or where they come from, all have a shot at making those dreams come true. Look at me. Came here with nothing, and now I'm driving a Lincoln."

While Judy and the twins slept, Izzy and Faye filled Aron in on the family and the business.

"We've been married five years," Faye explained. "Edna, Izzy's first wife, died ten years ago of breast cancer. My husband, Milton, was Izzy's business partner in our Flushing bakery. He had a massive heart attack six years ago. He was working in the bakery at the time. He was DOA when he got to the hospital; Izzy rode in the ambulance with him. I fell apart. Izzy was amazing the way he comforted me and supported me. We stayed in touch, what with the business and the fact that we were both alone. It was *bashert*. We bought our house when we got married. And we just opened a second bakery on Union Turnpike in Floral Park."

Aron listened intently, his curiosity piqued by the seamlessness of their relationship. It appeared to be a marriage, not only of companionship, but also of comfort and convenience. He wondered whether he would describe his marriage to Dyta as one of comfort, companionship, or convenience—or all three.

"We even finished the attic in the hope that our children would come and visit often," said Faye. "But I only have one child—Rebecca—and she's living in Israel now, helping to build the new Jewish state. Izzy and Edna had one son, Henry, but I'll let him tell you about that."

"We named him after my grandfather, Hirsch," Izzy said, picking up the narrative from Faye.

"Edna was sickly and had trouble conceiving so we were thrilled when he was born. He's a dentist, a smart boy; he graduated from Queens College and then from NYU Dental School. He's part of a big practice in Cincinnati, Ohio. He got married four years ago to a girl he met here while he was in dental school. She's a teacher, her mother's a teacher too, and her father owns a candy store. Very comfortable family, pleasant people," Izzy said, but Aron could hear a *but* in his voice.

"But they're not Jewish," Izzy's tone dropped to a stage whisper. "Patty would've done whatever Henry wanted. But my son didn't push. Don't even ask me what kind of ceremony they had because they told me about it after it was over. Can you imagine? Then I started talking to Patty about converting before she had a child so the child would be Jewish. But then she got pregnant, and Henry just didn't take a strong stand. They had a baby boy, named him Edward after Edna. Yeah, he was circumcised in the hospital. Very good looking and smart child. He's two now.

"Then they started talking about bringing up the child with religion. Well, Patty thought there should be religion in the home. She's a really sweet girl. I sent her to my rabbi, Pulkowitz, to talk about converting. Not only was I a regular there, but I always opened my pocket every time he asked for money for the shul. I delivered cake and challah there every week, dirt cheap, because it was my rabbi and my shul.

"So, what happens? Patty goes to speak to him, and he has this very superior off-putting attitude. That's who he is, but he was particularly arrogant and snotty with her. 'Why do you want to convert, young lady? You know it's much easier to be a Christian.' For Christ's sake, she's married to a Jew and wants to raise her son Jewish—why else would she want to convert? Wrong answer. Not good enough for him! Yeah, I know, that's probably what my grandfather said in Poland too, but this is the United States of America halfway through the twentieth century—after six million Jews were killed in Europe! You'd think we'd want more Jews. So he did everything he could to discourage her—and then he threw in the clincher.

"'It wouldn't be enough just for you to convert,'" he told her, 'even if I accepted that you have a sincere desire to become Jewish, which thus far is not apparent to me. Your son would have to convert too, because he was not born to a Jewish mother. So that's something that would also have to happen. We can discuss that if I decide to accept you. But so far, you have not convinced me.'

"Patty walked out of his office, crying hysterically all the way home until she fell into Henry's arms. He told her she didn't have to convert, in fact, he didn't want her to if that's the way our rabbi was going to treat her. She said she wanted to move back to Cincinnati to be near her parents, where they would be respected. They did, and Henry joined a big dental practice there. Then they became members of the Presbyterian Church her parents attended. Henry was welcomed with open arms, and no one ever even suggested that he should convert! But Henry says since the baby is not considered Jewish, there's no point in observing Judaism. So they go to church, and celebrate Christmas and Easter. I'm sure Edna is turning over in her grave.

"And if that's not bad enough, His Eminence, Rabbi Pulkowitz, took away my High Holiday honor. I always had the third *aliyah* on Yom Kippur. And soon after that, the shul stopped ordering cake and challah from me."

"Do you see your son and his family?" Aron inquired.

"Of course, he's still my son. I'm not going to sit *shiva* for him—especially after the *Shoah*. And Patty's a nice girl from a nice family. And little Eddie is a sweet little baby—very well fed. We see them about once a year. Faye and I drove there in the summer. But it's a heartache, Aron. Can you imagine?"

"Actually, I can imagine, more than you know. I'm sorry you had to go through this, Izzy."

"Thanks, Aron. It's just one of many reasons why we are so happy to have you and your family here with us."

Aron lowered his eyes and looked the other way, feeling uncomfortable with the conversation as he thought about the choices he had made. Yes, he had taught his wife to be Jewish, and she was functioning as a Jew. She had eagerly sought and absorbed Aron's lessons about the religion and could even recite a number of the prayers by rote. During her four years surrounded by Jewish refugees at Warteplatz, she had picked up many Yiddish words and phrases, as well as a basic understanding of the Jewish dietary laws. But a rabbi had not officially converted her. The birth of the twins sealed his secret. *Bronka and Johanna were the future of Judaism. Why look back? And from what Izzy said, conversion was complicated here too—but he also said dreams could come true here. It was time to start a new life in America—with his Jewish wife and Jewish children*, Aron told himself.

JANUARY, 1951

BELLEROSE, NEW YORK

B ELLEROSE, IN NORTHEAST QUEENS, IN 1951 was as close to paradise as the twins and their parents had ever been—except, of course, when it wasn't.

With its rows of identical brick bungalows sitting on manicured forty-by-hundred-foot plots that were formerly potato fields, the neighborhood evoked a stability that was comforting in the postwar era. In winter, snow coated the homes, lawns, and trees, giving it a pristine, clean aura. In the spring this gave way to green grass, yellow daffodils, and pink and purple tulips. Summer trellises showcased red and white roses while backyard fruit trees sprouted apples and peaches. In autumn, the leaves on maple trees turned red and orange and gold. In every season, it looked, smelled and felt new, fresh, fragrant, and favorable.

The entire upstairs floor of Izzy and Faye's bungalow would be the newcomers' home for the foreseeable future. While many of the homes on the block had unfinished attics, the older Lubinskis had added a dormer and finished the space in the hope that they would have frequent houseguests.

The vacant finished attic provided ample room for the newly

arrived refuges. It enabled Aron and Judy to have their own bedroom with a double bed, as well as a blue bathroom with a sink and bathtub with a shower. There was no need to share the downstairs facilities. Faye had quickly and artfully created a warm and cozy pink bedroom for the girls out of the remaining attic space. There was a chest, newly painted pink to match the walls and the slanted ceiling. Two twin beds, arranged side by side, were covered with white chenille bedspreads, on which two matching dolls and the identical pink teddy bears made their home. This was a far cry from the barracks-like accommodations at Warteplatz.

To welcome the newcomers, Faye put out a spread on her yellow Formica and chrome dinette table that would have delighted David Ben Gurion, so Izzy said. Lox and cream cheese, pickled herring in cream sauce, egg and tuna fish salads, chickpea salad and olives, and the specialty of the house, the bakery items—onion rolls, bagels, jelly doughnuts, and blueberry muffins. Faye was glad she had added a leaf to the table; it both accommodated her houseguests and showcased the food. Faye's heart and her tiny eat-in kitchen were full.

"How do you like those baked goods?" Izzy bellowed, not waiting for an answer. "We make the best products in Queens." He took a bite of a cheese Danish.

"The timing works out perfectly," Izzy gushed between bites. "I'll teach you the bakery business from the bottom up, Aron. Before you know it, you'll be managing our new bakery on Union Turnpike. And when you have a chance, you can help out too, Judy. Faye does the books and even waits on customers behind the counter from time to time. That's when she's able to fit it in between her Hadassah meetings."

Working in a bakery sounded like a walk in the park after their wartime experiences. The couple nodded and smiled. The Lubinski family was busily engaged in eating the freshest meal they'd had in years. The twins were intrigued with the jelly, which squirted from the powdered doughnuts, and in picking the blueberries out of the muffins. They had never before seen a blueberry. While Johanna practically inhaled the egg salad, Bronka could not get enough of the lox. No sooner had she finished one piece then she said, "More loxy please" as the adults laughed.

"You better watch out, Aron," quipped Izzy. "A child with expensive tastes."

"Tomorrow we will take all of you to see the bakery. You better save your appetites."

"Yes, and I also want to give you a tour of the community," said Faye. "This is a great neighborhood for the girls. It's safe and it's clean. And I'm going to introduce them to some other children who live right here on this block.

"My friend, Jennie Mandelstern, and her husband, Harry, are in the house directly across the street. They live with their daughter, Lenore, and her daughter, Mindy, who's a little older than the girls, maybe a year or so. That family has had a lot of *tzuris*. Jennie and Harry lost a son in the war, and another died from polio as a child. But they are such good people; they take wonderful care of Mindy, and they are cheerful in spite of their woes.

"The daughter, Lenore, is another story. You'll see her in the morning about eight o'clock walking to Union Turnpike to catch the bus. She gets the subway at Kew Gardens and goes into Manhattan, where she has a very big job as an executive secretary for a *machar*, a bigshot in a huge company. Makes deodorants, which Jennie tells me is going to become a huge business. Women are very concerned about body odor in America."

"Lenore not only smells good, but she is a sight for sore eyes," added Izzy.

"Stop it, Izzy, you're old enough to be her father," Faye continued. "Anyway, she does make a pretty picture—with her auburn curls, blue eyes, black mascara, and bright red lipstick. Not to mention her fancy suits that show off her curves in all the right spots. Oh, and did I tell you, the high heels, I'm not really sure how she walks in them—or looks so good at eight o'clock. She must get up at five thirty."

"Nah," said Izzy. "She's a natural beauty."

"She may be a natural beauty, but she's sure not a natural mother," added Faye. "The earliest she gets home is seven after Jennie has fed and bathed Mindy. Sometimes she doesn't even come home; such an important job, she has to stay in the city."

Judy's curiosity was now piqued. "And where is Mindy's father?"

"I understand he died when Mindy was a baby," said Faye.

"Well it looks like Mindy can use two new friends," said Judy, reeling from all of this gossip. She was beginning to realize that privacy would have to be zealously guarded on this street.

"Yes," said Faye. "She's really a sweet little girl. Her grandparents are doing the best they can. So it will be nice for Mindy to have the girls so close by.

"I also want to introduce them to the Rosen girls. There are three of them—Victoria, Christina, and Antonia. They call them Tori, Tina, and Toni. I think Tina is the same age as your girls, but they're all very close in age."

"Christina Rosen?" Aron wondered aloud.

"Her mother, Concetta—or Connie as everyone calls her—is just the sweetest, kindest person you could ever meet," Faye said. "She is actually a *gezuntah* Catholic, very devout. She's one of eleven children. Her brother, Antonio, is a priest. They call him Father Tony. He visits from time to time. And her mother, Mrs. Mariani, who is very old school Italian, lives in a basement apartment in their house. Her name is Antonia, even though we all refer to each other by our first names, everyone calls her 'Mrs. Mariani.' She's got a thick Italian accent and she's always cooking Italian dishes in the downstairs kitchen—spaghetti and meatballs, homemade sauce, bracciole."

"What's bracciole?" asked Judy.

"Oh, it's an Italian dish that is made with thin sliced beef or pork. It's stuffed with breadcrumbs and cheese, rolled, and baked in tomato sauce." Faye explained. "I don't think they even use the kitchen on the first floor. Smells great when you walk past the house. Not sure if you keep kosher out of the house; if so, stay away from the meatballs too—her secret recipe includes pork."

"I'm kosher," said Bronka.

"Me too," added Johanna.

"See, the girls know already how Jewish they are," said Aron.

"Of course, our home is strictly kosher," Faye reassured them. "But to be honest, we eat everything on the outside." She neglected to mention that they also brought in Chinese food and ate it on paper plates. She made a mental note not to do that in front of their houseguests.

"Is a house kosher or a person kosher?" asked Bronka, commingling the three languages.

"That's a very good question, Bronka," said Aron in English, smiling at his precocious daughter. "Bronka talks *tachlis*."

"Yes, I can see she gets right to the heart of the matter. She's very literal and earnest." Izzy smiled as he patted her head. "And a *shayna maydela* too. Such a pretty girl.

Faye was now eager to change the subject from the status of her kitchen and the contents of her stomach.

"Oh, and did I tell you that Mrs. Mariani also helps Connie with the girls because Irv is on the road so much," Faye added.

"Is Irv Jewish?" Aron, now curious, asked.

"Not sure," said Faye.

"He started out Jewish," added Izzy.

"What do you mean?" said Aron.

"He's got a Jewish mother in Miami Beach, and his father is buried in Mount Hebron. I know he has a Jewish sister, who is married and lives in New Jersey. He met Connie at Fort Belvoir during the war. He was a staff photographer for the newspaper there, the *Belvoir Castle*, and she was a secretary. They married and had Victoria, right when the war ended. Get it? Victoria for victory. The two other girls followed within a couple of years.

"Now, Irv has a great job as a photographer for *NewsTime*, the popular weekly magazine," Izzy explained. "He goes all over, taking pictures of famous people. He has a darkroom in the basement, and I've seen some of those photos—General Eisenhower, Mrs. Roosevelt, Ingrid Bergman. Is he Jewish? Well, his wife and mother-in-law don't think he is. Kids are being raised Catholic. But between us, he likes lox as much as Bronka, and he's sneaked into *Yizkor* services on Yom Kippur more than a few times. So, I guess it's between him and God. Look, I say live and let live, who cares? I'm not in a position to judge; look at my own son."

"This is a very mixed neighborhood," Faye added. "About half Jewish and the rest mostly Italian and Irish. There are a lot of returning veterans, so everyone has the war in common. We all get along. No one cares or minds anyone else's business."

Judy and Aron almost gulped in unison. What was she talking about? The preceding conversation hardly indicated that anyone on 253rd Street minded his or her own business. Would these vets ask questions about their war experiences? Would their wives be snooping around in their business? They were four thousand miles from Poland, but could there be someone who would raise questions about Judy's background and heritage, especially her father? As lovely as their new neighborhood seemed to be, it appeared that the discipline and discretion they had learned in the war would come in handy. So would their halting English.

That night, even though the twins each had their own bed, they snuggled together in one. They reviewed the pleasant things they had experienced in "Amewika" as they called it—blueberry muffins, jelly doughnuts, and lox. Despite the changes they had experienced in their short lives, they knew that they shared a special bond and could always count on each other. They soon drifted off to sleep, comfortably cuddling their soft, pink teddy bears, secure in the knowledge that no matter where they were, they were together.

∿

Izzy and Aron were out of the house before the sun rose. Izzy wanted Aron to see the business from the bottom up, and that meant checking on the bakers who had been there since four o'clock. But Aron insisted that they stop first at the morning *minyan* so he could pray.

Izzy was less than delighted with this detour, but he knew that his young cousin would not be deterred.

"We'll go to Rabbi Herbert's shul," said Izzy. "It's a Conservative synagogue, meaning there's mixed seating, maybe a couple other differences; I'm not sure. But he actually has Orthodox *smicha*. So people call it *Conservadox*. It's kind of a combination of the two movements, but mostly Orthodox, as that's how he was ordained. He's a nice, young guy and they have a daily morning minyan. I'm sorry, but I won't step foot in my old Orthodox shul after the rabbi drove my kids away."

"*Vas iz* mixed seating?" Aron asked.

"There's no *mechitza*," Izzy replied. "Men and women sit together."

"As long as there are ten men there, I can *daven*," said Aron in Yiddish. "The label doesn't matter to me. And I have to say *Kaddish* for all of my family members on my first full day in America. Since I don't know when each of them died, I'm going to observe this day as the *yahrtzeit* of all of my family members who perished at the hand of the Nazis."

Initially, Izzy felt he had to humor Aron, and figured this going to the daily minyan would be a one-shot deal. But once the service got started, he saw that this was serious business for Aron.

The small chapel doubled as a classroom, with chairs and tabletop desks moved out of the way for the minyan. A map of Israel hung on the wall, along with a poster of the Hebrew alphabet. Aron donned the *tefillin* and wrapped a *tallis* over his head, both of which he had brought from Poland.

Aron prayed with an intense fervor, which surprised Izzy. He seemed to know the Hebrew by heart, chanting rapidly, and swaying to his own rhythm. And when he recited the Kaddish, tears streamed down his face.

Izzy was amazed. *Aron looked like a man who was one with God. How could that be after all he had endured? Why hadn't Aron lost his faith after what he had suffered? After all, where was God when all of the horrors took place? On the other hand, Aron was clearly not a cheerful, serene person. His expression was grim, and his eyes were sad. Aron was complicated,* Izzy thought.

While Izzy and Aron were at shul and checking out the bakery, Faye let the rest of the family sleep late. She was more than delighted to have this young family to take under her wing. Izzy was a workaholic and, as Faye saw it, she needed close relatives in her orbit because she was alone much of the time. Her friends had children and grandchildren nearby, and she was determined to make sure that her new surrogate family adored her. Ever the planner and the manager, she was happiest when she was directing. She knew exactly how she wanted the day to go. Let them sleep as long as they wanted to, so they would have energy for the day's activities.

Bronka and JoJo, to use Johanna's newly adopted American nickname, slept until eight thirty, whereupon they roused their mother. At about nine o'clock, they all went downstairs.

"Let's have a leisurely breakfast," said Faye, "and then we'll walk over to the bakery in an hour or so. I want to show the girls the bakery and also let you see the neighborhood. We can come back and have lunch, and then in the afternoon, we'll go across the street and meet Mindy and Jennie and Harry."

As they walked down 253rd Street, Faye pointed to house after house and described the opportunities that awaited the twins.

"It's such a great block for children," she said. "When the kids get to be about five years old, they ring each other's doorbells and call for each other to come out and play. Connie told me the kids staged a fashion show in the backyard last summer, and all the girls on the block put on special dresses. The mothers came and watched them as they paraded in their outfits, and then everyone had punch and cookies. The next day, the same girls dug up some worms, dismembered them, and had a funeral. Children nowadays are certainly creative. The bigger kids occupy themselves with Red Light, Green Light and other street games. The boys play softball in the middle of the street. The drivers know to slow down, and the kids know to stop the game when cars drive by."

Once on Union Turnpike—the main thoroughfare—they passed a brick two-story library.

"On another day, we can go to the library and you can pick out some books," Faye said to the girls. "And I'll read them to you."

They continued walking and came to a newly built brick Conservative synagogue, which Faye said was where she and Izzy now belonged. She noted that it housed classrooms for the Hebrew school. And a block away, Faye pointed out Izzy's former Orthodox congregation, which was housed in a small, one-story shingle house.

A quarter mile away, they passed a small Catholic church with a white steeple that Faye said had been built two years ago. There was a white front door with a large cross affixed to it.

Soon they reached a commercial strip.

"Here's where we shop; isn't this convenient? It's all so close," said Faye.

Judy and the girls were intrigued with Dan's Supreme, a full-service grocery store. So Faye took them in for a tour. They marveled at the aisles of fresh produce, boxed cookies, and canned goods, not to mention an appetizing counter with smoked fish.

"This is where we shop for staples," said Faye. "But of course, we don't buy our meat here, but from Morty, the kosher butcher—he's right next door to the bakery. We'll stop and say hello to him when we're finished at the bakery. And I'll pick up some chicken for Shabbos."

As they left the supermarket, Faye pointed to the store next door.

"Here's Jonny's Candy Store, where Izzy buys the newspaper every day," she said. "Maybe we'll stop there and get a treat some time."

They passed a Chinese restaurant, which Faye couldn't decide whether she should mention. But of course, she couldn't just ignore it.

"A number of Chinese people have moved into the neighborhood since the Communist Revolution and opened up restaurants and laundries here. So you see, Judy, the Jews are not the only refugees who have come to America.

Moments later, Faye explained, "And here's Luby's Bakery. We thought of using another name but decided to give it the same one as our Flushing shop."

Luby's bakery was small and narrow, but it was loaded with more goodies than the twins—or their mother—had ever seen.

Izzy greeted them with big hugs. "Welcome to Luby's."

On the left wall, breads and rolls, muffins and Danish and jelly doughnuts were displayed in hanging baskets. Beneath the counter were glass cases of cookies, little ones with colored sprinkles and jelly and chocolate, and big black-and-white and chocolate chip ones. There were cinnamon and chocolate and raspberry *rugelach*. There were chocolate, apple, and marble cakes, and apple and blueberry pies. On the right wall was a refrigerator case with chocolate mousse cake, strawberry shortcake, and three kinds of cheesecake—plain, marble, and strawberry. There was a sign saying that ice cream cakes were available for special order.

Bronka immediately loved the bakery aroma—the scrumptious and primal scent of challah baking, the luscious allure of an onion roll right out of the oven, the yummy call of all of the sweetest smells and tastes in the world—chocolate and sugar and sweetened fruit toppings and fillings. She saw her father in this new environment in his white apron, and he hugged her and JoJo. She thought he looked so fresh and clean in white. Bronka was filled with hope that this delicious place had given her a new father—one who was as sweet and delightful as the bakery.

Izzy whispered something to Aron.

"And what would my girls like to taste here?" Aron asked. "How about a cookie?"

"I want one with colored sprinkles," said JoJo.

"I want the one with chocolate chips," said Bronka.

He handed them the cookies with a smile.

As Bronka savored the delicious cookie, she imagined that her papa could be happy here in this place, which was pleasing to all the senses.

"Okay, we should be going now," said Faye. "Izzy and Papa have to work, and I want to show you May's Department Store two doors down, and then I need to stop at Morty's for the chicken. And we have to eat lunch and rest a bit before we go across the street. But let's pick out something to bring to Mindy this afternoon. What do you think we should bring?"

The girls compromised on a half-pound box of assorted cookies.

～

The Mandelsterns' brick bungalow was identical in construction to Faye and Izzy's house, except it had a large dormer on either side of the slanted roof. Jennie came to the door with Mindy in tow. Judy thought that Jennie could almost have passed for Mindy's mother. She was slim, with bright blue eyes and short brown hair and was dressed in a shirtwaist dress. She was a smiling, good-looking woman. She looked like she was in her late '40s, but Judy figured she was probably closer to Faye's age—in her '60s. Mindy clearly hadn't inherited her grandmother's good looks. She was rather colorless, with light brown hair twisted into two long braids secured with red ribbons. But she wore a beautiful outfit, a red sweater, white blouse, and a tartan plaid skirt. Judy noticed that although Jennie was warm and gracious, and Harry had an enveloping smile that crinkled his eyes and lit up his face, Mindy looked a little sad. Her heart immediately went out to the child.

As Jennie ushered them into the small living room, she chatted. "Mindy is going to be five in February. She'll be starting kindergarten next September. How old are the girls?"

"They'll turn four in July," Faye answered.

JoJo immediately spotted a large mahogany cabinet, with a ten-inch screen.

"*Vas iz das*?" she asked, pointing to the television.

"Don't you know what that is? That's a TV," said Mindy, incredulous that this little girl didn't recognize the television set.

"*Vas iz* TV?" JoJo asked.

"Mindy," said Jennie, "these girls just came from Europe. They've probably never seen one. Everyone in the world is not as blessed as we are here. Why, there are still children who are starving in Europe. You're older; you can teach them a lot of things. You can help them learn about America and you can help them with their English too."

"I watch *Howdy Doody* every day on the TV," Mindy offered. "Come, I'll show you my room."

Mindy's room was upstairs too. But while the girls' room in Faye's house had a slanted ceiling, Mindy had a large room, as did her mother, because of the extra space afforded by the second dormer.

On the door to Mindy's room was a map of Doodyville, which she explained was where Buffalo Bob and all of the people on the *Howdy Doody* show lived.

"This is a picture of Howdy Doody; my mother got it for me," said

Mindy as she pointed to the wall, where there was a framed black and white photo of a smiley puppet character wearing a plaid shirt and a red kerchief. It was signed in heavy black ink. "It says: 'Howdy Mindy! Your Pal, Buffalo Bob.'

"Maybe you can stay late and watch *Howdy Doody* with me tonight. It's the best show. My mother usually doesn't come home from work until it's over and I'm ready for bed or sometimes sleeping. You can keep me company. You'll love the show. There's a peanut gallery where kids sit and watch the show live.

"My mother said she's gonna get me a ticket to the show to watch from the peanut gallery. I'm gonna ask her to get you tickets too."

The twins had no idea what *Howdy Doody* or the peanut gallery were—and they barely understood much of Mindy's chatting, but they were happy to make a friend of an older girl who was taking them under her wing in America.

The centerpiece of Mindy's room was a handmade quilt, featuring patchwork girls wearing flowing dresses and matching bonnets. Each of the girls wore a different dress in hues of pink and red and turquoise and yellow and brown. Each held a tiny, whimsical bouquet in matching colors. The matching curtains featured petite flower arrangements in complementary colors.

And on the bed was an assortment of dolls and stuffed animals. Mindy gave them a tour. "This is my beautiful Ginny doll. Look at her velvet hat and coat and purse. This is Zippy, the chimp from the *Howdy Doody* Show. And this is Howdy Doody himself. And here's Princess Summerfall Winterspring."

She had the same hairstyle as Mindy, but her long thick braids were black.

"And this is Bridey." She pointed to a porcelain doll that had brown hair and eyes and wore a faded white gown, complete with a veil. "Don't touch her; we have to be very careful with her. She's very old; she was Bubbie's doll, and that's why she smells a little."

As Bronka was taking this all in, JoJo giggled.

"And *vas iz das*?" JoJo pointed to a baby doll in a pink and white dress.

"Oh, that's Tiny Tears; my mommy just got her for me last week. She cries real tears."

"But not real," insisted Bronka. "Dolls don't cry."

"She cries real tears, I'll show you. Let's go downstairs.

"Bubbie, we need you!" Mindy called out to Jennie.

Jennie and Faye and Judy were drinking tea at the kitchen table as the girls ran into the room. The box of bakery cookies was open, and Mindy grabbed one.

"Yes, Mindy. Are you having fun with your new friends?"

"Yes, Bubbie, we are having lots of fun. But Bronka doesn't believe that Tiny Tears cries real tears. Let's show her."

"Grandpa will do it; Faye and Judy and I are catching up. Harry, I need you in here," Jennie called out to her husband, who was reading the newspaper in the living room. "Can you come in here and help Mindy show the twins how Tiny Tears works?"

"I'm coming," he called back as he got up from his chair and walked into the kitchen where the women and girls were gathered. Harry was a very good-natured sort of man, and he liked nothing better than meeting the needs of his only grandchild.

With a big smile on his face, Harry took the doll from Mindy.

"You see girls, I'm going to show you how Tiny Tears can drink water from her bottle, wet her diaper, and cry real tears."

Jennie giggled. "He loves playing with the kids. He's just a big kid himself."

Judy looked totally bewildered. But she kept her mouth shut for fear it was her halting English that was making her think she had heard that a doll could cry.

Jennie picked up on her confusion.

"No, you heard right, Judy. If you look carefully, you'll see that there are two small holes located near the doll's eyes. When the doll is fed with water from her bottle, and her stomach pressed, she sheds 'tears.' You're probably wondering also why Mindy has every toy a girl her age could want. It's Lenore's boss, Al; he's constantly sending Mindy expensive presents. We couldn't afford all these things. But Lenore doesn't tell Mindy that the gifts are from him. So please don't mention that I told you."

"Who wants to feed Tiny Tears her bottle?" Harry asked.

"Me," called JoJo.

"Okay, JoJo," he said as he filled the bottle with water from the kitchen sink. "Now watch what I do," he said as cradled the doll in his arms and fed her the bottle.

"Now, it's your turn," he said to JoJo.

JoJo was beaming as she took the doll. Both adults and children gathered around the table to watch.

"Now, when you think she's had enough, you can press her tummy and she will cry."

"Now?"

"Yes, try it now."

JoJo pressed the doll's tummy, and sure enough, the holes next to her eyes filled with tears.

"Look and see, Bronka," said Mindy. "She does cry!"

Although Bronka was not swayed, she did not answer. Her English was not good enough, and she was tired.

"Bubbie, Grandpa, can Bronka and JoJo stay and watch *Howdy Doody* with me?"

Faye came to the rescue, calculating that this first visit had already lasted long enough for three preschoolers. Better to leave on a high note.

"It's getting late; we have had a very big day." she said. "But we will definitely do it another time soon."

That night, Bronka and JoJo once again snuggled together for what would become their nightly ritual. The bakery, Mindy's house, and Mindy's toys had bombarded their senses. But they continued to disagree about Tiny Tears. Bronka insisted that the doll was a fake and that dolls do not cry real tears. JoJo wanted one anyway.

~

Their second full day of life on 253rd Street in Bellerose dawned crisp and clear with a high of forty-two degrees Fahrenheit. It was a Friday, and that meant there would be preparation for Shabbos at home and in the bakery. Aron was raring to go. He had resolved that he could be successful in America by just trying to keep his head down, minding his own business, and being productive. But, of course, he needed God's assistance.

"Do you really need to go to the minyan again this morning?" Izzy asked Aron.

"Yes, I am going, and I should like you to come with me too."

"It's six fifteen already. We won't get out of shul until seven. It's Friday. We have to fill all the Shabbos orders. It's a really busy day for us. And I have to make an appearance at the Flushing bakery and do all this well before sundown."

Izzy was about to get angry, and then he stopped himself. He noticed that the elbows of Aron's jacket were threadbare. His cousin had spent only two nights in this strange new neighborhood, he thought. He needed to have more *rachmonos*, more compassion for this young refugee, his only remaining blood relative from the old country. Fine, he would humor him. Anyway, he didn't need him moping around all day when Fridays were so busy.

"Okay, I will go with you today, but if you must go every day, you are going to have to start going by yourself soon."

"I understand," Aron said in Yiddish, nodding his head.

As the two men left the house with their tallis and tefillin bags tucked under their arms, they were shocked to see that four black cars were parked on the street—two in front of the Mandelsterns' house and two in front of Izzy's.

Standing right in front of Jennie and Harry's house were six men in dark suits, wearing felt hats with wide brims.

"What the hell are those official-looking men doing in front of the Mandelsterns' house?" Izzy asked.

Aron started to sweat. This was the United States of America. What was going on?

Inside, two other men dressed identically to the ones outside were ordering Lenore around. Jennie and Harry had thrown robes over their nightclothes when the FBI agents had banged loudly on their front door at six o'clock. Lenore was in her nightgown. Thankfully, Mindy was still sleeping in her upstairs bedroom, unaware of the upheaval and upset downstairs.

"What are you doing here?" Jennie sobbed. "Surely this must be a mistake. You must be at the wrong house."

"What do you want?" Lenore cried out to the men.

"Lenore Mandelstern, you are under arrest."

All the color drained from Harry's face, as he stood there shocked, silent, frozen, and mortified.

"What for? I've done nothing wrong," she replied.

"You are being charged with conspiracy to obstruct justice. You will have to get dressed and come with us."

"I need a lawyer," Lenore screamed. "This must be a terrible mistake."

"You can get one later," one of the FBI agents told her. "Now get dressed."

"I don't want to wake my daughter," she said. "Just let me run upstairs, get my things, and I will get dressed down here."

"Okay, but we will have to come with you."

"Well, please be quiet. My daughter does not need to see this."

Two of the agents followed Lenore upstairs as she put her finger to her lips, motioning them to be quiet. She quickly grabbed her purse, brush, makeup, underwear, and a blue suit, matching high heel shoes, and nylon stockings.

"You're not going to the Waldorf, ma'am," one of the men chided her. "You're going to be questioned."

Lenore did not appreciate the joke. She believed looking good never hurt anyone's cause. Anyway, she wanted to look gorgeous when Al came later to get her out of this mess.

As Lenore hurried downstairs with the agents in tow, she knew she was racing against the clock. She wanted to get out of the house before Mindy or any of the neighbors awoke.

Two agents followed her to the downstairs bathroom and looked away as she dressed. She decided that in the interest of time, she would apply her makeup on the way.

Harry remained frozen with a look of horror on his face and his mouth wide open. Jennie threw her arms around Lenore.

"Don't worry, we'll get you a lawyer," she said, "We'll get this cleared up,"

"I'm sure Al will send over his attorney, Jerry Roginsky, as soon as he hears about this," said Lenore.

Just then, the doorbell rang. It was one of the agents, who had been waiting outside.

"What's taking so long? We need to get a move on."

"We're coming," the two inside chimed in unison.

Mindy suddenly materialized in the living room, still rubbing the sleep out of her eyes. The sight of the strange men milling around frightened her.

"What are these men doing here, Mommy?"

"They want to ask me some questions," said Lenore.

"Everything will be all right, sweetheart," added Jennie. "These men are taking Mommy downtown. They just want to ask her some questions about an important matter. She'll be home soon."

"Where are you going, Mommy?" Mindy sobbed as she threw her arms around Lenore. "I don't want the men to take you away."

Jennie scooped her frightened granddaughter into her arms and held her tight as Mindy's tears dampened Jennie's face.

Lenore scowled at her mother. Jennie had seen that scowl before. As much as Lenore needed and wanted her mother to raise Mindy, she resented the attachment that Mindy had to her. Lenore was spoiled and entitled, and when things didn't go her way, her mother was her punching bag. Jennie had learned to say nothing when Lenore displaced her anger on her. She knew that it would soon pass.

Outside, Aron and Izzy saw the agents escort Lenore to the car and drive away. Irv Rosen, whose nose for news was legendary on the block, had joined them. Izzy was not surprised. Irv's wife, Connie, often joked that he was so devoted to his work that if he heard fire engines he would get dressed in the middle of the night and follow them. But it wasn't a joke; Izzy had actually seen him doing just that. If he saw or heard something unusual, Irv would call the police to find out what was going on.

Both Izzy and Irv noticed that Aron was dumbstruck and shaking. "Is he all right?" Irv asked Izzy.

"You know, he just arrived from a DP camp this week. I can't even begin to fathom what he experienced in the war. But one thing I'm sure, it's worse than anything I can imagine."

Aron was speechless as thoughts so frightening swirled in his head that he dared not express them. He had never seen Lenore before, but there was something familiar about her. She could have been one of the Jewish girls he grew up with in Kielce.

How is this possible? Can this be happening in the United States? he contemplated in silent agony, *where strange men knock on your door and take you away? Are we in danger?*

"Aron, we're already late, can we skip the minyan today?"

Aron shook his head.

"Can you make it there yourself or do you want me to come with you?"

He raised his palms as if to say, "It's up to you."

Izzy was torn. It was Friday. He needed to be in the bakery early. He wanted to find out what was going on with Lenore. But he could see that his cousin was visibly shaken. He had read about Jews being taken by force from their homes by the Gestapo, and he knew how most of them had ended up. Who knew what Aron had seen and experienced and what Lenore's arrest was triggering in him? He hoped Aron did not think that history was repeating itself, but perhaps he did. He reconsidered his decision. Although the shul was only two blocks away, Aron was such a newcomer that he could get lost, especially in the state he was in.

"All right, Aron, let's go," Izzy said. "Irv, I'll check in with you a bit later."

"Okay, Izzy," said Irv. "I'll try to get to the bottom of this."

～

Once in the car, the agents tried to be cordial to Lenore, who was in the back seat. They offered her a cigarette, which she eagerly accepted. After she finished smoking, she brushed her hair and began to apply her makeup. Lenore was well aware that she was an attractive woman, but she also knew that she considerably enhanced her "wow" factor with eyebrow pencil, mascara, powder, rouge, and lipstick.

She heard the agent who was driving whisper to his partner sitting next to him, "Take a look at today's *Daily Mirror*; there's another story about Greenglass." A light bulb went off in Lenore's head as she finished applying the last of her lipstick.

Maybe looking beautiful got me into this whole mess to begin with, she speculated. After all, it was what had attracted Al, her boss, to her in the first place. And she had met David Greenglass and his wife, Ruth, through him. Greenglass was the brother of Ethel Rosenberg, who, along with her husband, was being tried for giving atomic secrets to the Russians. Lenore began to go over the chronology of her relationship with Al and his connection to Greenglass.

She had been twenty-two years old when she graduated from NYU with a degree in accounting in 1943. She immediately went to work for thirty-year-old Alvin Springer, who lived in Great Neck with his wife and two small children. Al, with his brilliant business sense and inventive mind—and his partner, Max Pearlstein with his scientific genius—were on the cutting edge when they founded the SpringPearl Company and began to manufacture and sell deodorant.

At the initial interview, Al told Lenore that he was looking for someone sharp, multi-talented, and hard working—someone who could work long and unusual hours. Al was involved in everything and wanted a person who could grow with the company.

Lenore eagerly accepted the challenge and soon became Al's right hand. She was totally and utterly devoted to him and to their work together. The company was on the cusp of developing and marketing a squeeze bottle for deodorant and also beginning to do research and development on a men's deodorant. "After all," Al said, "It's not just women; men can be convinced they smell bad, too."

They worked long hours side by side, often dining together in Manhattan at posh restaurants. While Lenore was a beauty, Al's looks were nothing special. He was neither too short nor too tall, too fat nor too thin. He had nondescript brown hair and eyes. To look at him, an objective person might have described him as bland. But when he opened his mouth, he was transformed from Average Al into a powerhouse, a force of nature.

Lenore had been captivated by Al's analytical mind, his knowledge of current affairs, his vision, his vociferously voiced opinions, and his incredible command of the English language. He had created a company that was in the forefront of a brand-new industry that would become essential to all Americans. By contrast, the boys her own age, who were now going off to war, were childlike and naïve. When Al touched her knee for emphasis, she was flattered. When he kissed her hand as a thank you, she melted at his chivalry. He hinted at the possibility of her one day owning a share in the company. He was unlike anyone else she had ever met. As their relationship progressed, Al spent less and less time with his family in Great Neck. And Lenore's world began to revolve around her affair with Al.

Toward the end of 1944, Al had been recruited as a scientist for the Manhattan Project and was sent to Los Alamos, New Mexico. Upon hearing the news, Lenore was devastated.

She had no idea what he would be doing, but she knew he had been chosen because of his scientific expertise. When he was gone, the day-to-day business operations would be left in Lenore's capable hands. Al insisted that she report to him on a regular basis. But reporting to him from afar did not take the place of daily physical contact. To the outside world, she was dedicated to her job, but what she really wanted was to be near Al.

Finally, after several months, he asked her to join him in New Mexico. In May, Lenore arrived at the Santa Fe Railroad Depot in Albuquerque, where Al met her.

For the first week, Lenore stayed at the Hacienda del Sol, an historic luxury hotel. But then Al asked her to move in with him, explaining that his wife was home in Great Neck with the two kids and had no plans to visit. Lenore tingled with excitement; she was twenty-four years old and infatuated with her boss. She assured herself that the safety of distance ensured that neither her parents nor anyone else would ever know.

Al was renting an apartment, which was located on North High Street. His neighbor was Ruth Greenglass. Her husband, David, was a serviceman stationed at Los Alamos as a machinist.

She remembered how Ruth Greenglass was so delighted when she first met Lenore. She told her she was thrilled to have a young Jewish woman, who was about her age, staying next door. And she promised that she would ask David to make a date with Al so the two New York Jewish couples could get together socially. And that's how the relationship began.

"Are you okay back there, ma'am? Do you want another cigarette?" one of the cops called from the front seat of the car, interrupting Lenore's recollections.

As Lenore lit the cigarette, it suddenly became clear. *David and Ruth Greenglass—that's why I've been arrested,* she thought. *It's because we were friendly back during the war. Their names had been all over the newspapers lately in connection with the Rosenberg trial. Hadn't Al been pulled in a year ago and questioned about his relationship with the Greenglasses? But they let him go! Why are they arresting me now?*

Lenore began to panic. She knew she had done nothing wrong, well maybe except for having an affair with a married man with two small children. She believed Al when he said he had never given David secrets from his work at Los Alamos. But she also knew he had lied to the grand jury, denying that he had ever been a member of the Communist Party. He admitted to her that he had joined when he was in college during the Depression, when so many people were suffering from economic hardship. But weren't the Russians our allies in defeating the Nazis in World War II? Why would that be a crime now?

She was no dummy—she knew the answer; there was hysteria about the Soviets.

She wondered if they had picked up Al too. She did not allow herself to weep; she was not going to ruin her makeup.

～

When Izzy and Aron arrived at the morning minyan, it was half over. But Aron, who prayed faster than anyone there had ever seen, quickly caught up. He remained pale and trembling while he prayed.

Izzy didn't even bother to put on his tefillin. He could not stop thinking about what he had just witnessed.

Following the service, Rabbi Herbert approached Izzy. He had been pleased—actually astonished—to see Izzy for the past two days, and delighted that he had brought his cousin, who was clearly a pious man.

"What's going on?"

"My neighbor's daughter was taken away this morning, I saw G-men parked right in front of our house."

"Do I know your neighbors?"

"Yes, the Mandelsterns are members here."

Consternation flooded the rabbi's face.

"Let me know how I can help. I'll try to connect with them as soon as possible."

"Thanks, Rabbi."

The rabbi then approached Aron, who appeared to still be in a daze.

"*Nu*, what's doing with you today young man?"

Aron dissolved into tears and answered the rabbi in Yiddish.

"I brought my family to America because we thought it was safe, safer than Israel. We believed Jews could have a new start here. We've only been here two days, and I see a young woman, the age of my wife, taken into custody by government officials, just like the Gestapo agents did in Kielce. Why? What did she do? Could it be for nothing, just like they did to the Jews of Poland?"

"We don't know yet why she was taken away, but I can assure you this is nothing like Nazi-occupied Poland," Rabbi Herbert answered in Yiddish. "And she wasn't arrested because she is Jewish. There may be anti-Semitism here, but it's not officially sanctioned.

"We Jews, like everyone else, have rights here. Look, even free countries experience nasty politics from time to time. This is such a time, but it too will pass. We have a strong country, based on a

Constitution that ensures the rights and freedoms of individuals. Please, don't think this is a Jewish thing.

"Everyone is fearful because of the Soviet Union and the nuclear arms race. But the pendulum will swing. It always does. Jews are safer here than they have been anywhere in the world at any time. If you want to be extra safe, follow my lead. Just tell the truth and don't discuss politics. I've learned that there are congregants on every side of every issue. Understand?"

Aron desperately wanted to believe the rabbi that his family was safe in America. But he had learned the hard way that most rabbis, no matter how much Torah they knew, could not predict the political winds. Hadn't his own grandfather failed to anticipate the escalating Nazi threat?

Rabbi Herbert shook Aron's hand vigorously and said, "Perhaps we'll see you in shul tomorrow, Aron?"

Aron looked surprised that the rabbi would even ask.

"Definitely," Aron replied.

The rabbi beamed. He knew he had just gotten himself another regular shul-goer. Not just a body, but a religious man—a swift davener who could lead the service.

"Gut Shabbos, Aron. See you tomorrow."

∽

The bakery was a busy hub, especially on Fridays. There were all the special occasion orders for the weekend, in addition to the synagogue's standing orders of challah and finger cakes for the Friday night *Oneg Shabbos* and Saturday services.

At hectic times like these, they had to give out numbers in the tiny narrow shop, which could just about accommodate a single-file line. Izzy had been looking forward to Aron's assistance behind the counter today, but he didn't want an unfriendly, brooding refugee just off the boat to greet his customers. He directed Aron to the back office, where he could help assemble the Sabbath orders.

"Make sure they put aside two challahs for us, as well as a *pareve* chocolate layer cake for tonight," Izzy said. "Faye is whipping up a delicious dinner for your family's first Shabbos in America. She's making matzo ball soup and roasted chicken and rice. If there's anything else you think your family would like, just add it to the bundle. And let's put together a little package for the Mandelsterns—maybe a challah and some brownies and a big black-and-white cookie for Mindy. I'll drop it off on the way home later."

When all the orders had been picked up, and the sun began to set, Izzy closed and locked the door to the bakery. He would make sure everything was in its place, and then he would take Aron home for a nice, traditional Shabbos dinner. Aron was still in the back, where he had been all day. Izzy had checked on him a few times, but it had been so busy, he really couldn't take Aron's emotional temperature every few minutes. They would have wine and Faye's wonderful home-cooked meal, and hopefully, that would calm him down. But just as he was about to go back and get him, there was a loud banging on the door.

"Izzy, Izzy, it's me, Irv, please open up."

Izzy opened the door and ushered Irv Rosen in.

Irv normally had a poker face, but now his face was flushed and he was agitated.

"I found out what went down this morning," he said.

"Please tell me."

"Lenore was arrested for conspiracy to obstruct justice. They first took her to Foley Square, FBI headquarters, fingerprinted her and asked her some questions. Now, she's sitting in the Women's House of Detention in Manhattan."

"*Oy, oy, oy*. When is she getting out?"

"Don't know; there's the matter of bail, and she needs a top-notch lawyer, not a court-appointed one, to get her out," said Irv. "I sure hope she has her own lawyer and is not relying on her boss to get her one."

"But she's his right arm, and I know they're friends," Izzy said. "Surely he'll help her."

"I doubt that he can be of much help to her now," Irv replied. "He was arrested this morning too—for conspiracy to commit espionage."

"I was just going to stop at the Mandelsterns' on my way home with some cake for them. Do you want to come with me?"

"Okay, sure."

"Let me give you something too for your family—brownies, cookies for the girls? Bread, challah, rye bread, rolls?"

"That's okay, Izzy, we're good."

"Let me just go in the back and get Aron. Here, please take some brownies and cookies," Izzy said as he quickly threw the items into a white paper bakery bag. "Here, I'm giving you a challah too; Connie can always use it over the weekend for French toast."

Irv laughed as Izzy thrust the bags in his arms. It would be rude not to accept.

Aron does not look well, Izzy thought as he went into the back office to fetch him. His cousin's elbows were on the small desk that was scattered with papers and his head was sunk in his hands. *How long has he been sitting like that?*

"Aron, it's time to go. Did you put aside the cake and challahs?"

Aron looked at Izzy, his shoulders slumping as he blinked back tears.

Izzy could see that Aron had forgotten his instructions. *No big deal about the challahs and cake,* Izzy thought. *There are more up front. But Aron's a wreck.*

"It's been a tough day for everyone," Izzy said. "Let's go home."

It was a particularly chilly January evening, but it was only a five-block walk home. When they got to their street, Izzy said, "Why don't you run ahead, Aron? You can change for Shabbos, and the women can light the candles. Here, take the challahs and cake. I'm making a stop with Irv. I won't be long."

The two men watched as Aron took giant strides as he hurried home; the sun was fading fast and it would soon be his first Sabbath in America—the day of rest.

"Should we ring the bell or knock?" Izzy asked Irv when they arrived at the Mandelstern residence.

"Definitely ring the bell," said Irv.

Jennie came to the door, still in her robe, looking like she had aged ten years. Harry was dressed, sitting in a chair, still in shock, staring into space. Mindy was also dressed, but her eyes were bloodshot and her face was red as she sobbed. When she saw the two men at the door, she dried her tears and said, "The takeaway men took Mommy away. When is she coming back?"

"Mindy, I'm so sorry about Mommy," Izzy said. "But I'm sure she'll be home very soon. I brought you a cookie."

"I don't want a cookie. I want Mommy. My daddy died when I was a baby, and now Mommy is gone too," she blurted out through her tears.

"What can we do for you, Jennie? Please tell us how we can help," Irv asked.

"Lenore called once at about eleven this morning," Jennie said. "She said she was only allowed two phone calls—one to her family and one to her attorney. She said she had already put in a call to Jerry Roginsky, Al's attorney, but she hadn't heard back from him yet. She asked me to call Al and ask him to go see her, along with Jerry. But I called the office and got Max. He said Al hadn't shown up at the office yet. He was beginning to get concerned."

"Sit down, Jennie," Irv said. "Al isn't going to be calling Lenore anytime soon. He was arrested this morning outside his home in Great Neck. I suspect Jerry is with Al. I strongly suggest that Lenore gets her own attorney and not rely on Al's."

"But who should we get? I know lawyers who do wills and real estate, but—"

"Jennie, Lenore needs a criminal attorney and she needs one now. I'll see what I can do. If you want, I'll go with you to visit her tomorrow."

"You mean she's not coming home tonight?" Mindy wailed.

"Maybe she will come home tomorrow," Jennie said.

~

Faye's small kitchen emitted the delicious smell of an Ashkenazic Shabbos dinner. On a cold January night, the onions, garlic, and chicken roasting in the oven, along with the chicken soup bubbling in a large pot on the stove, combined to fill the house with the warm aroma of the Sabbath. By the time Izzy returned home, the candles were lit, the table was set with a white tablecloth, and the two challahs were covered with an embroidered cloth. An open bottle of Manischewitz Concord Grape wine sat on the table, its fragrance adding to the festive feeling. The wine had been poured into the adults' glasses, while the girls got a drop of wine in their glass of seltzer.

Aron had changed into a white shirt, and as the family gathered around the table, he felt tears welling up. Hadn't his own family presented a similar picture of peace and contentment before the Nazis came and destroyed everything? Although he was grateful to be alive and in the United States at this moment, the pain and horror his own family had endured was never far from his mind. But he had already vowed to himself that he would not inflict his story on his children.

He and Judy had just had this conversation a week ago on the boat.

"But they have a right to know their family history when they are older," Judy reminded him.

"Do you really want them to know *all* of it?" he had sneered.

"It was not all bad. Good did come out of it for us. We found each other. And keeping it bottled up is not good for you," she said. "Perhaps one day when they are older, you'll change your mind."

But Aron was resolute that he would never reveal Judy's past to his children.

Izzy gave Aron the honor of reciting the Sabbath Kiddush, and Izzy recited the *Motzi* over the challah. He raised the two challahs together as he said the prayer, sprinkled them with salt, and ripped off pieces and distributed them to everyone.

"I like challah," said JoJo.

"I like chocolate cake," said Bronka, whose inquisitive eyes had already spotted the cake.

"How did you know the dessert is chocolate cake?" Izzy asked with a twinkle in his eye. "The best pareve chocolate layer cake in Queens."

As they finished dinner, Faye asked, "When was the last time you had a Shabbos meal like this?"

"Oh, we had Shabbos dinner at Warteplatz," Judy said. "But it was not as delicious as this one. You're such a good cook, Faye. I hope you will teach me your recipes."

"Of course, I'd love to," said Faye, beaming.

Aron, sensing that Faye was coming dangerously close to interrogating Judy, jumped in. "Aren't we going to *bench?*" Aron asked Izzy.

Both Faye and Izzy looked a bit surprised. They had dispensed with the custom of praying after dinner long ago. But they were accommodating hosts, as well as a bit guilty about their own lapses.

"Wow, Aron, it's such an honor to have such a religious person in our home," said Faye. "Did your family bench also, Judy?"

"No," Judy said.

Izzy, slightly annoyed that Faye was fishing already when it had been such a difficult day, said, "Go ahead, Aron, you lead."

As was Aron's style, the blessing after the meal was completed in record time.

"Great dinner, Faye," said Izzy.

"Yes, Faye, thank you very much," said Judy.

"I like Shabbos," said Bronka.

"I like Shabbos in Amewika," said JoJo.

No mention was made of the Mandelstern situation in front of the twins. Izzy had telephoned Faye and filled her in earlier in the day. And of course, Faye had shared the news with Judy.

~

Aron slept fitfully that night. He kept Judy awake with his crying and moaning. In his nightmares, he was transported back to April 1941 in Kielce, where his family had been eating a sumptuous Sabbath meal served by Judy, dressed in white. Suddenly, there were screeches, which reached a peak when he and his bride and his parents, grandparents, sisters, and brothers, along with his in-laws, were rounded up and herded into the ghetto.

At about six o'clock, while JoJo slept, Bronka was awakened by her father's screams. Frightened and upset, she grabbed her teddy bear and went into her parents' bedroom.

"Mama, Mama, why is Papa crying?"

"He had a bad dream."

"I brought him my teddy."

"Bronka, leave now!" Aron snapped at the child, suddenly awake and embarrassed that his little daughter had seen and heard him.

"But I brought you Teddy to make you feel better."

"Bronka, dear," Judy said. "Papa is very sad, and he needs to be alone now."

"But you are here with him. I just wanted to give him Teddy," she said as her eyes began to well up with tears.

"Bronka, *gay avek,*" he yelled in Yiddish.

She bolted out of the room, sobbing hysterically, and crawled into JoJo's bed, clutching her teddy bear. JoJo, who had been awakened by the yelling, put her arms around her twin.

"I don't like it when Papa yells at me and tells me to go away,"

Bronka sniffled. "I like it when he smiles and gives me a cookie in the bakery."

"I don't like it when you are sad, BonBon. That makes me sad too," said JoJo.

"I don't like it when Papa cries. It's scary," said Bronka.

"Mama is happy," said JoJo.

"Mama can make Papa feel better," said Bronka.

Bronka's tears soon turned into giggles as JoJo began tickling her.

It was on her second morning in Bellerose that Bronka decided that she would try harder to make her father happy. She would be like Mama.

~

On Saturday morning at nine o'clock, Irv parked his Chevy in front of the Mandelstern house. He rang the bell and Jennie answered, dressed and ready to go.

"Good morning, Irv," said Jennie. "Thanks so much for doing this."

"No problem," said Irv. "Is Harry coming too?"

"I don't know what's the right thing to do," Jennie said. "He's better today, but maybe he should stay here with Mindy. What do you think?"

Harry was in the kitchen with Mindy, assisting her with Tiny Tears.

"What's up, Harry?" said Irv as he entered the room. "Are you coming with us?"

"I'd like to, but I don't think we should bring Mindy."

"You should definitely not bring Mindy."

"I want to come. I want to come. I want to see Mommy."

"You'll see Mommy soon when she comes home, Mindy."

She started sobbing all over again.

"You know what, Harry," said Jennie. "Just stay here with her. If you need help, you can always ask Faye."

"Or Connie will help too."

"Okay," said Harry, "but I can handle it. Mindy and I are pals."

Mindy tugged at Jennie's dress.

"I want to see Mommy. I hate the takeaway men."

"We're going to check on Mommy now, and we will tell her you want her to come home soon."

Mindy cried, and Harry looked bewildered, but Jennie was on a mission.

"Let's go, Irv."

As they walked to the street, she noticed Irv's license plate for the first time.

"What does NYP stand for—New York Police?"

"No, it's New York Press; it makes it easier to park. There are specially designated parking spaces for the press in the city."

His answer made Jennie feel like they were on official business.

"You know, I think it's better we left Harry home," said Jennie. "Mindy could have stayed with one of the neighbors, but he and Mindy are joined at the hip; they just adore one another. He's really falling apart over Lenore. I think it's conjuring up a lot of other things for him."

"And you, Jennie?"

"I'm devastated, but I've gotten through worse," said Jennie. "And we'll get through this. Thank you so much for your help."

"Of course," said Irv. "I called around and got the names of a couple of prominent criminal defense lawyers."

When Jennie and Irv arrived at the Women's House of Detention at 10:15 that morning, they were shocked by Lenore's appearance. The normally glamorous, effervescent career woman looked pale and drawn. She wore no lipstick and had washed off her other makeup.

They sat in the visiting room at a small table, Jennie and Irv facing Lenore.

"I need a cigarette," she said to Jennie.

Always well prepared, Jennie pulled out a pack of cigarettes and a book of matches.

As Lenore took a long draw on the cigarette, she looked at Irv suspiciously.

"Forgive me for being rude, but aren't you with the press? I certainly hope you didn't come to take my picture and put it in the paper. They've already taken mug shots of me. Why are you here?"

"He's come to help, dear," Jennie said.

"And how can he help?"

"First of all, you've not been in the papers so far, Lenore," Irv said, "and I can give you some tips to try to avoid it. Second, I have the names of some top-flight criminal attorneys."

"I've already seen two attorneys."

"And who are they?" Jennie asked.

"First, the court-appointed attorney, some kid named Roger Something, looks to be about fourteen. He accompanied me yesterday when they set my bail at ten thousand dollars."

"Ten thousand dollars," Jennie gasped. "Our house is worth ten thousand dollars. How will we ever afford that?"

"Well, I guess I'll just spend the rest of my life in prison, and you can continue to raise Mindy. You're doing such a great job, I'm sure she didn't even notice I was missing."

"Of course, she did," said Jennie. "All she wants is Mommy. She wants to know why the takeaway men came for you and when you're coming back."

"I guess you can just tell her never."

"Oh, come on, Lenore, you're being overly dramatic. We're going to get you out of here as soon as possible. Mindy loves you and needs you."

"And who was the second lawyer?" Irv asked.

It was then that Lenore broke down, crying so hard that she was unable to speak for a few moments.

Jennie was used to being abused by Lenore and knew how to handle her.

"We're here to help you, dear. It was very kind of Irv to come with me on his day off. I'm sure he has better things to do. He drove me into the city. He's a well-connected man, very knowledgeable about these things. You want to get out? Irv is the man who can help you. Tell us who the second attorney was. Was it Jerry Roginsky, Al's attorney?"

Lenore's face flushed with embarrassment. If she wanted to get out, she had better play ball with her mother and Irv. She was beginning to realize they might be all she had.

"No, it wasn't Jerry," said Lenore. "Jerry never even returned my call. He sent over some kid, Lester Finch, a first-year associate in the firm. He said Jerry was very busy working on a defense for Al, who has been charged with conspiracy to commit espionage, a far worse charge than mine. He could end up like the Rosenbergs.

"According to Lester, Al is falling apart; he's sick with worry about his wife and kids. Lester said to let me know Jerry will get to me, probably by the middle of next week. He's looking for a way to defend both of us. But he wanted me to know that he's doing everything in his power to help Al beat this. In the meantime, Jerry said to use Lester as my attorney of record and drop the court-appointed lawyer."

Jennie was dumbfounded that Al had not taken more of an interest in Lenore's defense. Although it was never spoken of, she knew that her daughter was much more to Al than just an employee. Jennie was fully capable of putting together the pieces of the puzzle.

"Look, our time is almost up, and they're going to kick us out of here soon," said Irv. "Listen to me and listen well, Lenore. I'm your friend. I'm here to help you. You must know your mother and father always have your back. There are a few things that you'll have to do to get out of here.

"First, you'll have to trust us. Second, you must get your own attorney, one who is dedicated to defending you—just you. You can't share an attorney with someone who is going to let you sit here without doing anything for six more days. And you certainly don't want a novice when the stakes are this high. I'm out there every day, and I know a lot of people. I can give your parents the name of one of the best attorneys for this type of case.

"Third, if you agree, you have to promise to tell him the truth and the whole truth and nothing but the truth. Only the truth will save you—no half-truths, no lies, no embellishments, no omissions. Only the pure unadulterated truth will get you out of this. So think about it and let us know what you decide."

Lenore was sure that in her entire life she had never felt so insulted, so disrespected, so discarded, so bereft. But the love she felt for Al was an all-consuming force that had taken over her mind, her body, and her life. And she had been in the grip of his power for seven years. Every action, every thought, and every dream had its beginning and end in Al. She had hoped for a life with him. She had always put him first, above her friends, her family—even her daughter. And where did he put her? Lenore told herself it was time to face facts. *Irv was right. How could Al expect me to share his lawyer, who is willing to let me sit in jail for almost a week and not even have the time or the courtesy to speak to me?* She bristled when she remembered that she had not even gotten a "Jerry says Al is worried about you too" from Lester, the messenger. She wondered, was she really that dumb that it took a phony charge, imprisonment, unreasonable bail, and a newbie associate to see that Alvin Springer was a self-absorbed, narcissistic blowhard?

Through her wrenching sobs, she managed to extend her hand so she could shake Irv's.

"Thank you, Irv. Please give my parents the name of the attorney."

Jennie gave Lenore a hug, and they cried together.

"See you soon," said Jennie.

"Bring cigarettes and tissues," Lenore said through her tears.

∽

As Irv turned onto 253rd Street from Union Turnpike, Jennie spotted the Lubinski family walking up the street. Izzy looked out of place in his open topcoat, which revealed he was wearing a jacket and tie. It was a far cry from the white apron he wore in the bakery. Faye was all dolled up with her Persian lamb coat, matching hat, and scarf with the little mink heads.

Jennie could see that Faye was beaming with her newly acquired family in tow. Compared to Faye, the female members of the refugee family looked a bit raggedy, with coats that were faded and shabby. But their natural attractiveness helped compensate for their lack of style. Jennie guessed that Faye would soon supplement their wardrobe. She was an expert seamstress and would shortly be sewing up a storm, especially for her surrogate granddaughters. But it was Aron, in an oversized coat and baggy pants that must have belonged to Izzy, who had an unkempt, haunted, haggard appearance.

"I guess Faye and Izzy went to shul this morning to introduce their cousins to the community," Jennie said. "I wonder how long the shul-going will last for them?"

"Not very long if it's up to Izzy," Irv said. "Since those cousins came, I think Izzy has met his quota of services for the year."

As Irv pulled up to the Mandelsterns' home, Harry and Mindy came out of the house. The normally mellow Harry had an exasperated expression on his face.

"Bubbie, Bubbie," called Mindy as Irv opened the passenger door and helped Jennie get out of the car. "Did you bring Mommy home?"

"No, dear, but she will be coming home soon."

"I want Mommy," Mindy cried, clutching Tiny Tears. "Where did the takeaway men take her?"

"This has been going on all morning," said Harry to Faye. "We've been in the kitchen filling up Tiny Tears so she can cry for Mommy. When there's a lull, Mindy cries herself."

"Oh look, Mindy," said Jennie, attempting to distract her. "Here come the twins. Let's say hello."

She turned to Irv and gave him a peck on the cheek.

"You must have so much to do today. Thank you so much for taking me, and for handling Lenore so well. Please give Connie and Mrs. Mariani my regards."

"I'll be in touch," Irv said.

"Come on, Mindy, let's cross the street and see your new friends," said Jennie. "Harry, why don't you go inside and rest?"

When the Lubinski family saw their neighbors walking toward them, they stopped on the sidewalk under the maple tree in front of their house. No sooner did Mindy and Jennie cross the street than Mindy greeted Bronka and JoJo at the top of her lungs.

"Tiny Tears and I are very mad and very sad," she told them. "The takeaway men came and took Mommy somewhere. I don't know where or when she's coming back. I hope the takeaway men don't come to your house."

Then she started crying loudly.

JoJo looked at her curiously, but Bronka, who was standing in between her sister and her mother, started screaming hysterically as if Mindy's demeanor and remarks had tapped into some primal instinct. She grabbed tightly onto her mother's right leg and would not let go.

"I don't want the takeaway men to take you away, Mama," she sobbed. "Don't let the takeaway men take Papa away. I'm scared they will take JoJo and me away."

There was so much commotion that a couple of neighbors came out to see what was going on.

"Bronka's had a tough week," Faye, embarrassed by the scene, explained to the firefighter and his wife, who lived next door. "Can you imagine? This time last week she was on a boat heading to New York, and before that, she'd spent her entire life in a DP camp. I'm sure she's just exhausted and confused."

But Bronka was not confused. She had read Mindy correctly. And when she saw the look of horror on Papa's face, she knew that takeaway men were real, and they had taken away Mindy's mother.

Jennie took her cue from Faye and ushered a now hysterical Mindy across the street.

"Maybe we'll get the girls together tomorrow when everyone calms down," Jennie shouted over her shoulder.

Faye nodded. "Sure."

"Don't worry, BonBon. Mama and Papa will never let anyone take us away," JoJo said, as she put her arm around her twin.

"Of course, Bronka. JoJo is right," said Judy. "Mama and Papa are here to protect you. And you have Izzy and Faye to take care of you too. Izzy will not let the takeaway men come to our house. Right, Izzy?"

"Of course," said Izzy. "I'll beat them up if they ever come near anyone in our house—especially my girls."

JoJo smiled, feeling a bit more secure. Izzy was big and strong, and she took his words at face value. But Bronka was still frightened and continued sobbing, especially when she saw the look of anguish on her father's face.

One thing she knew. Mindy was telling the truth. The takeaway men were real. Papa was scared of them. And she was afraid of them too. She also knew that her tears and Mindy's were real. She did not need Tiny Tears to cry fake tears for her.

～

"Why do you think Bronka had such a fit?" Judy asked Aron in Polish when they were alone in their bedroom later that night. "Johanna didn't seem to be rattled at all."

"Are you blaming me?" Aron asked angrily, also in Polish. His mind began to race. *Is Judy implying that Bronka subconsciously knows something that she, herself, has not experienced? That on some level, she understands that the reason she has no immediate family is because the takeaway men—the SS—forced them from their homes and then starved, tortured, and murdered them? And is Judy insinuating that it is my fault because it happened to me and I have somehow transferred my memories to her? That's a preposterous theory.*

"No, I wasn't blaming you at all," Judy said. "It just breaks my heart to see her so gripped with fear and anxiety. She's not even four years old."

"I have no idea," Aron snapped. "They've never heard anything from me."

"One day, they will find out. It's better if they hear it from us."

Aron glared at her, stormed out of the bedroom, and slammed the bathroom door behind him. She could hear him sobbing.

This was only their fourth day in America, and already the demons were back. She couldn't even have a conversation with him without an explosion. For all of her kind-hearted attempts at healing him, Judy had to admit her husband was still a very troubled person. His memories of the terror, the suffering, and the loss were inescapable. Her experience, though it had taken place in the same time period, was quite different. She had not been a victim. So what did she know?

Sometimes Aron could go about his daily life, and the stabbing heartache took a back seat. He was most distracted when he was working and most at peace when he was praying. At times, he could muster enough joy to tease and tickle his daughters or even make love to his wife. But then, without warning, the darkness would return.

For close to a decade, Judy's life had been about saving and healing him. She was beginning to feel that, no matter how hard she tried, it would never be enough. And worst of all, her ultrasensitive, perceptive, precocious child was now showing that she was not only aware of, but vulnerable to her father's demons.

~

The first thing Monday morning, Ben Wagner, a prominent criminal defense attorney, paid a visit to Lenore at the Women's House of Detention. He was about six feet tall with green eyes and a sandy crew cut. A partner in a prestigious Manhattan law firm that also had offices in Philadelphia and Boston, he wore an expensive Brooks Brothers suit and tie, and his shirt cuffs were monogrammed with BW. His gold cufflinks also showcased his initials. Lenore judged he was about forty. He looked like a really elegant guy—except that he was chewing and snapping gum, and when he stopped chewing long enough to speak, he had a very thick Bronx accent. Ben sat across from Lenore at a table in the visiting room.

"So how do you know Irv Rosen?" he asked Lenore as he tossed her a pack of cigarettes and a box of tissues. "These are from Irv."

"He's my neighbor."

"Nice guy; fabulous photographer. Have you seen his photos of the Rosenberg kids? Very touching."

"No, I haven't," said Lenore. "Thank Irv for the goodies. It's impossible to get cigarettes or decent tissues here."

"Well, hopefully, we're gonna get you out of here soon."

Lenore liked the way he exuded confidence.

"Now, tell me what they asked you and what you told them," said Ben.

"They asked me about David and Ruth Greenglass. I told them that I met them in New Mexico. She was my boss's neighbor. And we socialized."

"Anything else?"

"I did say I wanted a lawyer."

"You know you're a small fish in this pond. You're just someone who happened to be in the wrong place at the wrong time. No one really cares about you. . . ."

"That is abundantly clear," Lenore interrupted.

"Nah, that's not what I meant. Your parents care about you, or they wouldn't have hired me. Irv cares about you or he wouldn't have contacted me. I mean you're not the one the government is after. If you give 'em what they want, you'll be outta here."

"And what do they want?"

"They want the dirt on Al so they can get more ammunition to press David Greenglass as hard as they can to continue ratting on his sister and brother-in-law. Greenglass is their star witness. They need to make sure he doesn't back out or walk back on his story that Julius was an atomic spy and Ethel was his accomplice."

"You don't think he's telling the truth?"

"Who knows? But that's not our concern. Our concern is you and getting you out of here. And the key to that is telling me everything you know about Al."

"Will Al go to jail?"

"I don't know, and I don't care—and neither should you," Ben said, cracking his gum for emphasis.

Lenore's face reddened as she thought about Al's lack of concern for her, and she nodded.

"I'm your attorney, and my only job is to help you. So let's start from the beginning. What was your relationship with Al?"

"He was my boss."

"And what were you doing in Albuquerque in May 1945?"

"I had been running the office for him for several months while he was at Los Alamos," said Lenore. "And I went there to report to him in person."

"Look at you," Ben scoffed. "Even now after three days in prison, I can see how beautiful you are. Do you really think a judge and jury would believe for a minute that you had a purely platonic relationship with Al?"

"But he was married and had two small kids."

"When did that ever stop a red-blooded man—especially a successful one?"

Lenore became uncomfortable, and her stomach began to turn. She didn't answer. Instead she opened the cigarette pack, pulled out a cigarette with her shaking hands, and put it in her mouth. Ben struck a match and lit it for her.

"Again, Lenore, I'm your attorney, and you gotta trust me. You must tell me the truth."

Lenore still said nothing as she inhaled deeply.

"Okay, Lenore, let's try this on for size. Fact: there's another single Jewish woman about your age, Elsa Epstein, who is currently sitting in prison. Just a few months ago, she was convicted of conspiracy to obstruct justice and she got a ten-thousand-dollar fine and a two-year prison sentence. Do you know why?"

Lenore remained silent but Ben continued.

"She refused to defend herself. She also lied about being a communist. She was so trusting that she used the same defense attorney as her lover, Ira Birnbaum. She didn't take the stand in her own defense, because she didn't want the affair exposed. She was afraid it would be plastered all over the papers and bring shame to her family and Ira's. Oh, by the way, he's in prison too. He didn't take the stand either, probably because he didn't want the world to know he was cheating on his wife and kids. In retrospect, do you think they're wondering whether it would have been better to just tell the truth? So we need to get this out of the way now.

"Oh and one more thing, the Feds most likely know everything you're trying to hide. So please tell me the truth."

"I love Al," Lenore said, weeping, but then quickly corrected herself. "I loved Al, but that's over now."

"Good girl," said Ben. "So tell me about your relationship with the Greenglasses."

"Well, Ruth was renting an apartment next door to where Al was living, so when I went down to New Mexico, she said she was so happy to have a member of the tribe—another Jewish woman from New York—there, and she started befriending me. She had me over for coffee several times. We'd go shopping and to the movies together, and also the four of us had dinner a few times."

"What did she discuss with you when you were alone with her?"

"Well, mostly her desire to have children. She told me she'd just had a miscarriage and hoped to get pregnant again. She had a burning desire to be a mother. I remember that because having kids was the furthest thing from my mind. And that was what she always wanted to talk about."

"Anything else?"

"She talked a lot about communism. She was a true believer. She thought that communism could solve all of the world's problems."

"Did you say anything about communism when you were alone with her?"

"No, I'm not political; I just listened."

"Good," he said. "And when the four of you were together, did David talk about communism?"

"No, not at all."

"What about Al?"

"I knew he had been a member of the Communist Party when he was in college, but I think he had mostly lost interest by the war. Al was very polite, so I think he humored Ruth since she was a good hostess. He would kind of smile and agree with her, but not get into anything too heavy."

"So Ruth and David knew he had been a communist? And do you know what Al told the grand jury when they asked him about his affiliations last year?"

"He told me he lied. He said he was never a member of the Communist Party."

"Bingo. Doesn't he know that you never lie under oath? Yes, that was bad judgment on Al's part, the same bad move that Elsa Epstein made," said Ben. "Now tell me more about David. When you were all together, did you ever hear or see anything unusual?"

"Like what?"

"Like did you ever hear David and Al exchanging information? Did they go off alone and appear to be discussing things furtively? Did you ever see them with anyone else that aroused your suspicion?"

"No, I never did."

"Did they discuss work at all?"

"Al knew what he was doing was top secret. He never talked about his work with me. And I certainly never heard him discuss it with the Greenglasses at dinner.

"The truth is, Al really couldn't stand David," Lenore added. "And he said no one else at Los Alamos liked him either. He was a very annoying, in-your-face kind of guy. But I guess Al was glad that Ruth was my friend—and you know, Jews have to stick together. So he tolerated David, both at work and socially."

"Did Al ever say what David was in-your-face about?"

"Not at the time."

"But later, when?"

"Actually, he just started talking with me about it in the last year or so—what with the Rosenberg trial and McCarthy and all that stuff in the news. And, of course, after they questioned him," Lenore said.

"What did he say?"

"Well, he recalled that David was very nosy—actually obnoxiously curious. Al said he was only a machinist—and a soldier at that—but he was forever asking Al and everyone else—the physicists, the engineers, the chemists—about their work. And many of the professionals, including Al, gave him information about what they were doing. It was all kind of casual. They didn't think anything of it. In fact, they weren't even sure he understood what they were talking about.

After all, they believed they were all part of the same team, and all had been sworn to secrecy. No one could have imagined anyone was a spy. People trusted that the government had vetted everyone very carefully. Al told me that, at the time, he thought it was just David being David, but lately he'd begun to think that David might very well have been a spy."

"Interesting," said Ben. "Oh, and one more thing. Who is the father of your daughter?"

All at once, Lenore's heart started beating so fast she thought it would burst from her body. At the same time, violent cramps roiled her stomach.

Ben took her soft, delicate, manicured hands and cupped them between both of his sturdy, rough ones. He looked into her eyes with kindness and compassion. "Lenore, If I were a betting man, I'd bet the Feds know everything about you already, and whatever they know they will use against you. I told you I am here to help you. I can help you only if you are completely honest with me."

"I think you know the answer to that," Lenore whispered. "I told Mindy that her father died when she was a baby. Now he's died a second time."

~

Ben convinced Lenore to cooperate completely with the authorities, including telling all she knew about Al's relationship with David Greenglass. In return, prosecutors dropped the charges and she was released. Lenore was home by Tuesday, a full day before the promised visit from Al's attorney, Jerry Roginsky. Lenore never knew for sure whether her honesty had helped or hurt Al. The charges against him of conspiracy to commit espionage were reduced to lying to a grand jury about being a communist. He spent six months in jail and paid a three-thousand-dollar fine. Ben tried to reassure Lenore that her willingness to tell the truth had probably helped Al more than it hurt him.

Ben said to her, "That's how much the prosecution needed David's testimony; they didn't charge his wife in order to get him to testify against his sister and brother-in-law. That's why Al was the last linchpin. They needed as much dirt as they could possibly get on Greenglass. Once they got what they needed from Al, they reduced the charges."

Lenore convinced herself that she simply didn't care about Al anymore. She was finished. She had seen his true colors and was done with him. All of the sycophants who surrounded him and did his bidding could have him.

It no longer mattered to Lenore that, despite his stint in prison, Al would become hugely successful. She still wanted no part of him. She didn't even have second thoughts when she read or saw on TV that the deodorant market had become a multi-million-dollar business. Yes, Al had been prescient—there were ads for male deodorant all over the place. Clever advertising had convinced American men that they needed to smell good too.

Lenore stayed with Al's firm until she got another job. Max, as Al instructed him, paid her lawyer's fees and gave her a glowing recommendation when she sought other employment. But Lenore was crestfallen after her brush with the law and her perceived humiliation and rejection by Al and his associates. She stubbornly refused to take Al's calls once he was out of prison, even though he had convinced Jennie that she should. He even came to her house once, and she instructed her mother to turn him away at the door. Jennie, always afraid of displeasing her daughter, complied. Without her association with Al, it made it easier for Lenore to perpetrate the lie she had told Mindy that her father was dead.

She felt that her personal and professional life was over. There was an enormous void in her life, and the intrepid photographer Irv Rosen saw his opening.

A few days after the ordeal, Irv stopped by the house, ostensibly to check with Jennie on Lenore. He brought a bouquet of yellow roses, which he said was for both of them.

"Just a little something to cheer up the strong and beautiful Mandelstern girls. And please give Lenore my regards," said Irv. "And if she needs anything, she knows where to find me."

"Well, actually," said Jennie. "If you have any thoughts about another job for Lenore, let us know. She can't continue working for Al."

"As a matter of fact, the new Jewish hospital on Lakeville Road, which recently opened, may be able to use her. I know the PR gal, and my friend, Leo Berkman, just started as head of personnel. I'll give Leo a call."

"That would be great," said Jennie.

The following week, Lenore had her interview with the personnel administrator. He noted her extensive experience and accounting acumen. He also complimented her on her professional appearance, while later saying to Irv, "You don't see too many glamorous career gals like that in Northeast Queens."

"Don't get any ideas, Leo," Irv said, all the while thinking that Lenore was someone he would like to know better.

The Jewish Hospital of Northeast Queens (JHNQ) was only two miles from her home, and the new position enabled Lenore's relationship with Mindy to improve, at least for the time being. But Lenore was a person who was drawn to successful and powerful men, and although she thought she had learned her lesson, she was still a young, beautiful, and lonely woman.

She took Mindy to the hospital and showed her the accounting office where she worked. Then she brought her to the hospital coffee shop, where Mindy had a black-and-white ice cream soda with whipped cream and a cherry on top. They both remembered the pleasantness of that day for a long time. But there was not enough sweetness in the world to erase the haunting memory of the takeaway men. Mindy would never forget it.

Neither would Bronka Lubinski. Only four days off the boat, the toddler had become collateral damage, not only in the Mandelstern calamity, but also in the tragedy of her father's unknowable and unspeakable legacy. The tale of the takeaway men would be not only a searing and scarring memory, but a metaphor. In many ways, it would define and organize Bronka's *weltanschauung*. As she grew, her worldview would continue to be shaped by these traumatic events.

1952

---◼◼◼◻ O ◻◼◼◼---

BELLEROSE, NEW YORK

B Y THE FOLLOWING YEAR, ARON and Judy had established a rhythm to
their lives in Bellerose. It was comfortable for them to live with
Izzy and Faye. The older couple took care of their basic needs and
helped them navigate their new environment. Aron appreciated Izzy's
guidance and support. He found Faye's bossiness a little hard to take,
but he was adept at ignoring her; retreating into his own world was
second nature to him.

Aron went to shul seven days a week—mostly without Izzy—and
to Rabbi Herbert's delight, he became a valued member of the congregation, where he often led the service and read Torah. When there
was a minyan in a house of shiva, Aron was always first there with
a cake or a box of cookies, offering to lead the service if there was
no one to do it. On the Sabbath, he insisted that Judy come with the
twins. His dutiful wife would arrive toward the end of the service and
sit in the last row with Bronka and Johanna. People were impressed at
how well behaved the little girls were and that a young mother would
attend so regularly.

Izzy was actually thrilled with Aron's work in the bakery. He was
a quick study and had a serious work ethic. He gradually took on

more and more responsibility, which allowed Izzy to devote more of his time to the original bakery in Flushing. Izzy even started thinking about eventually making Aron a partner.

Faye and Judy got along well. Judy just wanted to please and so, in a good-natured way, tolerated, if not always welcomed, Faye's instruction. And Faye was delighted to give it. Faye shared her cooking secrets, along with her mother and grandmother's favorite recipes. Together, they made chicken soup, matzo balls, chopped liver, pot roast, and many other traditional Ashkenazic dishes. Faye joked that if they didn't own two bakeries, they might bake—but what was the point? There was no cake or challah better than Luby's—Izzy said so himself, Faye reminded her.

Faye was a yenta, but not in a malicious way. She knew she was a busybody but prided herself on not being a *yachna;* Faye was not spiteful or mean. She was just nosy, excessively so. Once she became curious about something, she had to investigate and find out the answer. She knew Aron had spoken privately to Izzy about some of what he had experienced in Poland during the war, but Izzy had confided that Aron didn't like talking about it; it was much too raw and painful. And he was adamant that he never wanted it spoken about in front of the girls. Izzy had also mentioned to Faye that Aron told him that he had instructed Judy never to speak about the Shoah either. He did not want the girls to pick up on it.

It had not escaped Faye that Judy had the map of Poland on her face—and not Jewish Poland. There was nothing Jewish about her looks—either her features or her coloring. And the young woman barely spoke a word of Yiddish. Why, Lenore Mandelstern could understand Yiddish better than Judy. So could the twins. Faye knew full well that the Jews of Poland spoke Yiddish to one another.

Neither did Judy seem to know how to make any of the traditional Jewish dishes that Faye was now teaching her how to cook. *Okay, perhaps her family had been wealthy and had a housekeeper who cooked,*

Faye reasoned. *But she never spoke of her family either.* It was as if she was teaching Judy how to be a *balabosta* from scratch, making her an efficient Jewish homemaker.

On the other hand, Judy did light candles every Shabbos and on holidays, and she was kosher inside and out of the house. Faye thought it was very touching when she heard her reciting the *Modeh Ani* prayer with the girls when they woke up, and the *Shema* when she put them to sleep. It did not seem to Faye like she was just going through the motions. She chanted with enthusiasm. And although it was not then required for women to do so, Judy certainly attended synagogue services more frequently than Faye or most of the other women in the community. When she mentioned her uncertainties about Judy's origins to Izzy a couple of times, he had warned her to keep her mouth shut. Faye had controlled herself now for more than a year and a half.

With Rosh Hashanah fast approaching, Faye was going to make homemade gefilte fish with Judy. Izzy and Aron were at work, and the twins were playing with the Rosen girls at their house. So the two women were alone in the kitchen. The sun shone through the tiered apple orchard curtains, showcasing patterns of red, green, and yellow fruit on an antique white background. The tiny kitchen, painted lemon yellow, had little counter space. The Formica-and-chrome table, where they ate their meals, was the only place big enough to prepare food. As Faye brought her mother's grinder to the table from the basement, she thought, *What would it hurt if I ask her one little question? She's been living in my house for almost two years?*

She decided not to plunge in, but to start gradually.

"Have you ever seen a fish grinder like this, Judy? It was my mother's."

"No, I haven't. What are you going to do with it?"

"I'm going to grind the fish for the gefilte fish. I use whitefish and pike. My mother and grandmother made it with carp. In fact, they told me they used to keep the carp in the bathtub until they were ready to prepare the gefilte fish. But I never actually saw a fish in the bathtub. I'm not sure if it's true or just a *bubbe-meise*," Faye said with a giggle. "Did you ever see a carp in the bathtub when you were growing up?'

"No," Judy chuckled. "I never saw that either."

"Did your mother use carp?"

Judy said nothing but shrugged her shoulders.

"So first I grind the whitefish and pike, along with the onions," Faye said as she began explaining the preparation. "Notice we do not grind the head and bones. We're going to save them for the fish stock. I always ask David, my fish man, to take out the eyes. Some people leave them in, but I don't want the fish looking back at me," Faye laughed. "Do you want to try grinding?"

"Sure," said Judy. She really had no interest in grinding these smelly fish. It was bad enough that the grating of the onions was making her eyes tear. But Judy was a good sport, and she didn't want to offend Faye.

"Good job, Judy. Now, we're going to take the ground fish and combine it with matzo meal, egg, the grated onions, some salt, and also sugar. We don't want to skimp on the sugar because we want it a bit sweet. It's a nice contrast when we serve it with the beet horserad-ish. You'll notice I don't really measure ingredients. Like my mother and my grandmother before her, I *schit a rein*—throw things together by instinct—and it comes out great. Of course, you can't do that with baking. With baking you have to be exact. So that's another reason I don't bake. Do you know why it's called gefilte fish?"

"No," said Judy.

"Originally, the ground fish was stuffed back into the skin of the whole fish. *Gefilte* means stuffed in German. But now, most people take the easy way out. We just make it into balls and boil it in the fish stock."

Soon the smell of the fish cooking in the stock permeated the kitchen, and then filled the entire first floor of the small bungalow. Judy saw the door to the attic was ajar, and quickly went to close it so as to prevent the odor from wafting upstairs. The truth was that she thought she was going to gag, but she was terrified of insulting Faye. She had tasted gefilte fish at Warteplatz, and while she didn't love it, she could tolerate the taste. And Aron adored it. But the smell of it cooking was a different story.

"How about something to drink?" Faye said, noticing her discomfort.

"Good idea," said Judy. "Can we sit outside for a bit?"

"Sure, let's sit on the front porch, and I can check on the fish from time to time. How about some ginger ale? Go ahead, I'll just finish up in here and bring the drinks out."

Ginger ale was just what Judy needed. Relieved that she was away from the smell and taking deep breaths of the fresh air, she recovered quickly.

"It's such a beautiful day," said Judy as Faye came out, holding two glasses.

"Yes," said Faye. "It's much too beautiful to stay cooped up inside with the gefilte fish. From the smell of it cooking, you'd never guess that it actually is tasty. It's not my favorite food; I'm more of a chopped liver and eggs kind of gal, but it's a taste of tradition. I prepare it just like my mother and grandmother did. It makes me feel close to them when I do."

Judy took a sip of her ginger ale, not quite sure what she should say next, so she settled on, "That's lovely, Faye. You're keeping their traditions alive."

"And what about you, Judy, do you have any customs that conjure up family memories?" Faye continued.

"Well, we named Bronka after my mother and Johanna after Aron's sister and brother."

"Isn't Bronka a Polish name?"

"Yes, it is. My mother was Polish."

"And did your mother have any special recipes?"

"She was an expert at pierogies. That was my favorite comfort food growing up."

Faye knew she was onto something here and was close to the truth. Should she let it go? Judy's mother had been Polish. Her specialty dish was pierogies—not cholent or gefilte fish or brisket. Faye got the picture; she now understood why Judy didn't look the slightest bit Jewish and knew so little Yiddish. She wanted to hear her say she was not Jewish.

"So your mother was not Jewish?"

"No, she was Catholic."

"And when did you become Jewish?"

"Before I married Aron. I chose to, like Ruth in the Bible."

"Did a rabbi convert you?"

"No, Aron did. He taught me the Hebrew prayers."

"Did you go to the *mikveh?*"

"I don't know what that is."

"Did you immerse yourself in water?"

"No. Like a baptism?"

"No, not really."

So Judy had not been born Jewish. I wonder where Judy was during the war, Faye pondered. *How unusual for a Polish Christian woman to choose to become a Jew, especially in light of the slaughter and persecution of Jews throughout Europe. That must be quite a story.*

While Faye was not really surprised, she was shocked that Aron, who was such a pious man, had not followed the letter of the law in regard to conversion. She might discuss it with Izzy, but why bother? *He'd probably say Aron was evening the score with his son, Henry. Hadn't Henry adopted Christianity without a formal conversion?*

Faye's fact-finding mission was cut short when Bronka and

Johanna, along with Tina and Toni Rosen, suddenly appeared on the front lawn.

"*Tante* Faye," all of the girls called in unison. "We're hungry, can we have a snack?"

Faye quickly became distracted by the thrilling sound of her newly earned status. In a very short time, she had become "*Tante* Faye" not only to the twins, but also to the neighbors' children. She had also become a surrogate mother/mother-in-law/mentor to Judy. She vowed to herself that she would try harder to win Judy's trust.

"Let me check on the gefilte fish first," she said heading for the front door, "and then I'll bring out some milk and nice bakery cookies for everyone."

"Yay!" shouted the little girls in unison.

~

While Aron and Judy still had thick accents and struggled with English, Bronka and Johanna had become fluent English speakers—with just the slightest trace of an accent—by the time they entered kindergarten that fall. Children are much better language learners than adults, Faye explained to Judy, but she also insisted that purchasing a TV would help not only the girls, but their parents speak better English. Izzy didn't think they needed it. He said they could always go to the neighbors to watch *The Show of Shows*. But Faye maintained it would help the acculturation of the girls to watch the same programs as the other children—*Ding Dong School, Howdy Doody,* and *Kukla, Fran, and Ollie.*

Faye won out, and she told Judy that the girls would be entering school with a leg up, since several of their neighbors still didn't have a TV. But Faye was also quick to let her know that their elementary school building, PS 347, had not kept up with the times. To Judy and the girls, it looked like a typical old brick school building—three stories with narrow staircases. They had no basis of comparison. But Faye questioned the class size. She had read that the "baby boom" was straining existing classrooms, and many new schools would have to be built to accommodate the ever-increasing wave of children being born.

Right before school started, Tina Rosen showed the twins the new back-to-school outfits that her mother had bought for her from Mays Department Store. The twins were impressed. JoJo especially coveted the flowered dresses and pleated skirts and pretty blouses that hung in Tina's closet.

"Let's ask Mama if we can go shopping in Mays," JoJo said.

"Good idea," said Bronka

When the girls arrived home the same day, Judy and Faye both had big smiles on their faces.

"Faye has a surprise for you," said Judy.

"Come into my sewing room," said Faye. The sewing room was on the first floor, originally built to be a small bedroom. But Faye had transformed it with her sewing equipment and supplies. Hanging on the closet door were two new dresses for each of the girls.

JoJo noticed immediately that they looked a bit old fashioned, not at all like the clothing Tina's mother had just bought for her at Mays. But she didn't say anything, and Faye was oblivious, so pleased was she with herself. Bronka just smiled.

"Look, I'm constructing my own fashion industry," said Faye, beaming with pride. "I even took the subway into Manhattan and first checked out the children's department at Best & Company and Bonwit Teller, two of the fanciest department stores in the city. Then I chose chic patterns and beautiful material just for you.

"Look at this beautiful blue gingham," Faye said as she stroked one of the matching dark blue-and-white-checked cotton dresses. "I want you both to be the height of style."

"Now give Tante Faye a big hug and say thank you," Judy said. "She's put so much effort and care into your dresses."

The twins obediently thanked and hugged Faye, but they were not convinced that these dresses were fashionable at all. They were much too young to appreciate her efforts. And while they dutifully wore whatever they were given, once they noticed their other classmates had frocks like Tina's, they began to wish that they, too, had the same outfits as their peers. Johanna, in particular, really didn't want to wear these homemade clothes. She wanted to be like everyone else, but she saved her comments for her sister alone.

Along with thirty-three other kindergarteners, the twins and their neighbor, Christina Rosen, were squeezed into a classroom that had been built to accommodate twenty-five. While both girls went off to school for the first time without a peep, the two teachers, Mrs. Betts and Mrs. Allen, intimidated Bronka.

"They're strict, but not mean," JoJo told her mother the first day. "We play, hear stories, and have to follow the rules."

The twins were perfect pupils for their crowded classroom. They were well behaved and compliant and, as always, could cling to each other in this new situation. For the most part, they adjusted well to school the first week.

Except when Mrs. Betts, commanded "Take cover!" seemingly out of the blue. Bronka was gripped with fear, and her whole body started to shake.

"Don't worry, BonBon, the teacher said this is just a practice drill," Johanna whispered to her under the table as she grasped her sister's shaking hand.

Had the teacher said it was a practice drill? Bronka hadn't caught that, and it didn't feel like practice to her at all. There was no consoling her; she was terrified that a bomb would drop on their school, and they would all be smashed to smithereens.

After school that afternoon, they discussed it with Tori Rosen, Tina's seven-year-old sister, in the Rosen's backyard.

"I think Bronka didn't hear the teacher say it was just a practice drill," said JoJo.

"I did," said Tina.

"Yes," said Tori. "When you go to school, there are weekly bomb drills. We have to practice in case the Russians drop an atomic bomb on us."

"What's an atomic bomb?"

"It's a very scary weapon that can destroy the world."

"How does it destroy the world?"

"It lands with a very loud noise and sets off explosions that kill people."

"Who are the Russians?"

"My dad says they are very bad and mean, and they want to take over the world and take away our freedom."

"How do they drop a bomb?"

"They push a button."

"And if we hide under our desks, will we be safe?"

"I guess so," said Tori. "Why else would they make us do it?"

But Bronka simply didn't believe or understand Tori or her teachers. *If they needed to practice,* she reasoned to herself, *it meant it could happen for real.* Each time the teacher shouted, "Take cover!" she braced herself for an explosion.

Bronka's fears extended to the world outside school as well. When she heard sirens go off at any hour of the day or night, she was seized with dread. She could be playing with her friends on the street or lying in bed, and the wailing of the sirens would cause her to become short of breath. No matter how many times JoJo told her not to worry, or Mama said it was the firemen going to put out a fire, she was gripped with terror. The sirens tapped something deep and dark within her that she could not articulate. To her, sirens did not merely sound like there was a fire somewhere; they evoked a profound feeling of suffering and loss. Somehow, she associated them with the takeaway men and her father's haunted expression.

~

In kindergarten, the twins were also introduced to uplifting sounds—the sounds of music. Mrs. Allen played the piano, and the children marched around with chimes and triangles and cymbals. And they learned songs that were fun to sing together as a class, like "Twinkle, Twinkle, Little Star" and "The Itsy-Bitsy Spider."

As the Christmas season approached, the girls not only heard Christmas carols sung in their school but were required to sing them too.

The Christmas lights lit up the dark when Uncle Izzy took them for a walk right after sundown.

"Look at the lights," they marveled, but they didn't question why they didn't have them.

Now that they had turned five and were attending school, Christmas took on a whole different meaning with their required participation in the festivities.

"We are going to have a Christmas concert in December and the whole school will perform," said Mrs. Betts. "Mrs. Allen and I will teach our class two songs. How many of you know, 'Santa Claus Is Coming to Town?'" Most of the class raised their hands. "And what about 'Oh Come All Ye Faithful?'" About half of the pupils indicated that they were familiar with the classic Christmas carol.

"Good," she said. "I see many of you already have a head start. The rest of you will have to catch up."

Bronka panicked. What did the teacher mean by "catch up"? Did it mean she hadn't learned something that she should know? Did it mean the other students were better than she was? She began to worry and hoped that she would be able to learn the songs quickly so she would not be left behind. Every day when they rehearsed the songs in school, she became nervous. So she started practicing with Johanna at home. Her twin was not only the more relaxed of the two, but she had perfect pitch and a beautiful singing voice. Soon, both of them had mastered the Christmas carols.

One night, after they had recited the Shema with their mother, Johanna said, "Mama, do you want to hear the songs BonBon and I learned in school?"

"Of course, I would love to hear you both sing."

They began with a lively rendition of "Santa Claus Is Coming to Town." Their mother was charmed by how they seemed so happy singing together. But she also noticed the inescapable fact that Johanna was the more talented of the two; her perfect pitch barely compensating for Bronka's apparent tone deafness.

Judy clapped enthusiastically. "Very, very nice," she said.

"Tina and Toni Rosen say that Santa Claus comes to their house on Christmas Eve and brings them lots of fun presents, like dolls and toys. Why doesn't he come to our house?" Johanna suddenly asked.

"Is it because we have been bad?" Bronka added.

"Oh, no," said Judy. "This is a Jewish house and Santa doesn't come to Jewish homes."

The twins were not satisfied with this explanation. "Why not?" they asked in unison.

"Are Jewish children not nice enough?" Bronka added.

Judy realized she was entering dangerous territory; the girls were very well behaved. She didn't want them to think they were less deserving than their friends. Or especially that it was a negative thing to be Jewish.

"Well, actually, I will tell you a secret, but you must promise not to tell anyone. Don't tell the Rosen girls or any of your friends at school who believe in Santa Claus. You don't want to spoil Christmas for them. Promise?"

"We promise," they said in unison.

"There is no such thing as Santa Claus," she announced.

"Really, Mama?" They both looked at her with wide-eyed amazement.

"Really," she said. "Santa Claus is make-believe."

"Who leaves all the presents under the Christmas tree?" Johanna asked.

"The parents wait until the children are sleeping, and then they put the presents under the tree to surprise them when they wake up in the morning."

"So Santa Claus is not real?" said Bronka. "And it's a lie that he puts the presents under the tree?"

"Well, not exactly a lie," Judy said. "Maybe just a nice story that makes everyone happy."

"It would make me happy to have a tree with presents under it," said Johanna.

"But we have eight nights of Hanukkah, and you get one present for every night. The first night of Hanukkah is tomorrow, and we will light the first candle on the menorah. And you'll get your first present tomorrow night.

"Okay, now sing me the other song," Judy said.

Judy was even more shocked when the girls started to sing, "Oh Come All Ye Faithful."

They are going to public school, she thought. *I thought there was no official religion here. Should I tell Aron? No, I better not. He'd just get cranky and brood about it and take it out on me and the girls. Should I discuss it with Faye? No, she was likely to march into the school and tell them off. We don't want or need that kind of attention. Well, I guess this is what they do in America. At least, they're not persecuting Jews, like in Poland.*

Bronka picked up on her mother's troubled expression, and said, "Shira Yudenfreund told me that her mother went to school and complained to the principal about the song." Shira was the daughter of the part-time cantor at their synagogue.

"And what happened after Mrs. Yudenfreund complained?" Judy asked. "Did the teacher say the Jewish children don't have to sing the song at the concert? Or did the teacher choose another song?"

"No, we still have to sing it at the concert," Bronka said. "But Mrs. Betts said that if any of the Jewish children don't want to sing the 'Christ the Lord' part, they don't have to."

"Oh, really?" asked Judy.

"Yes," said JoJo. "Mrs. Allen said that if there are any Jewish children who don't want to sing 'Christ the Lord,' they can sing some other words instead."

"And what are the other words?" Judy asked.

"*Dominum*," both girls answered in unison.

"Christina Rosen said her mother told her that 'Dominum' means 'Christ the Lord' in Latin," Bronka added.

"Hmm, I see," Judy said. "Maybe it would be a good idea not to sing these two songs in this house. I think there are other songs that Papa and Faye and Izzy would like better."

The next night, as they lit the first Hanukkah candle, Judy made a mental note. She had to admit that even though Jesus and Christmas were part of her hidden past, Hanukkah paled next to it. *Hanukkah could never compete with Christmas. Christmas was compelling, all consuming.* It had always been a magical, special day, even in Poland, when she was a child. *Hanukkah was even frail as far as Jewish holidays were concerned,* she reasoned. *For example, Passover was far more powerful.* But still Judy thought she could see the value of Hanukkah, even though it was a weak counterbalance to the lights and the Christmas trees and Santa Claus and the colorfully wrapped presents. *Jewish kids needed their own winter holiday.*

Faye had knitted the girls pink angora hats with white trim. Aron gave them each a quarter for Hanukkah *gelt*. He had planned to give them a coin on the first and last night of the holiday. Tomorrow night, Faye had told Judy she would give them socks she had knitted. As she thought of the interaction from last night, she decided to discuss with Faye the possibility of going shopping and picking out a more exciting present for the eighth night. *It was easier to be a Jew in America than in Poland, but it still wasn't easy. Whatever anyone says, this is still a Christian country,* she thought. *And when you're a Jewish immigrant in Bellerose, you don't quite fit in, no matter how many Christmas carols you know.*

JUNE, 1953

―――――◦―――――

BELLEROSE, NEW YORK

IT HAD BEEN A BEAUTIFUL sunny afternoon as the girls played in the backyard of the Rosen home. The temperature had hit eighty, signaling that summer was just about here. There was only a week left of school, and then they could spend the rest of the summer having fun, engaging full time in their creative play. The enticing smell of Mrs. Mariani's meatballs wafted up from her basement kitchen.

The three Rosen girls were showing Johanna and Bronka their new Debbie Reynolds paper doll book. There was a cardboard cutout figure of the actress and then a host of beautiful outfits, including a bathing suit and a ball gown, which they could attach to the Debbie figure with paper tabs.

Tori, who was eight years old, was clearly in charge. She didn't always play with her younger siblings and their friends, but today she was there, her "big sister" presence clearly apparent. For starters, she told the younger girls that the movie star's real name was actually Mary Frances and Debbie was just her stage name.

Bronka thought that it would be great to have a stage name. She hated her own name, particularly because no one else shared it with her. She wished her name was Susan or Linda or Carol or Barbara—a name other girls had. Even her sister had a better name. Johanna easily morphed into JoJo, a cute and perky pet name. But as hard as she tried, Bronka just couldn't think of a suitable nickname that she could use with her friends. She would certainly not be "BonBon" to anyone but her twin.

"I'm going to be JoJo Luby," announced her sister, who always seemed to be more comfortable in her own skin.

"That's cute," said Tori approvingly. "I could be Victoria Rose or Tori Rose or Vicki Rose.

"My dad just took us to see Debbie's latest movie, *Singin' in the Rain,* with Gene Kelly," she added. "Have you seen it?"

"No," said JoJo. "I want to go. We've seen Debbie on TV. I love to hear her sing."

"You know," Tori said. "My dad met Debbie Reynolds. He said she's even more beautiful in person. He took pictures of her. They're hanging in the basement."

"Can we see?"

"Sure, let's go."

Tori led the girls down six concrete steps and opened the outside door that led to the finished basement. They entered the bright green kitchen, which had more counter space and a bigger refrigerator than the kitchen upstairs. The room smelled of tomato sauce. Mrs. Mariani, her curly pepper-and-salt hair covered by a hair net, was stirring a huge pot on the stove. She was plump in a soft and cuddly sort of way and wore a checkered apron over her black dress.

"We're going to see Daddy's photos of Debbie Reynolds," Tori announced.

"Do you girls want to taste the meatballs first?" She spoke with a musical Italian accent.

"*Si, Grazie, Nona,*" the Rosen girls answered together.

She began to put the meatballs in a bowl and started distributing them.

"Here Victoria, Christina, Antonia. And do your friends want to taste a meatball?"

"Yes," said JoJo.

"No thanks," said Bronka.

Bronka looked in amazement as her twin sister devoured the meatball. Faye had said Mrs. Mariani made her meatballs with pork. Didn't JoJo remember that she wasn't supposed to eat pork? But Bronka didn't say a word.

Perhaps Bronka would ask JoJo about the meatballs when they were alone, but for now she was glad the other girls had finished eating, and they could finally see the Debbie Reynolds pictures. Tori led them beyond the kitchen to a finished basement room with knotty pine walls, covered with black-and-white photographs. There was a light green kitchen table and chairs, a dark green couch, and a cabinet with a phonograph player and records. In the far corner was a tiny room, and next to it, a desk with more black-and-white pictures on it. Behind the desk hung a large bulletin board with so many magazine clippings that some overlapped.

"That's Daddy's darkroom," Tori said, pointing to the small room. "We're not allowed in there. That's where he develops and prints his pictures. Look at the wall. Here are some of his pictures. See if you recognize any of the famous people."

Not only were there pictures of Debbie Reynolds, Marilyn Monroe, Lucille Ball, Joe DiMaggio, and Frank Sinatra, but of presidents Truman and Eisenhower too. JoJo was in awe to think that her friends' father had come so close to all of these famous people. Maybe someday, Irv Rosen would take her picture for a magazine.

Tori led them to her father's desk. "Look at the bulletin board. If you look at the bottom of the photos, you'll see Daddy's name. In small letters, it says, 'photo by Irv Rosen.' That means he took the picture."

"Who are these boys?" Bronka asked as she pointed to a picture on the bulletin board. The photo was of two young boys who were standing with an older woman. The boys were both wearing baseball caps and white shirts and ties under their coats.

"Oh, those are the Rosenberg brothers—Michael and Robby," Tori said. "Their parents, Julius and Ethel, are gonna be executed today."

"What does executed mean?" Bronka asked.

"Killed."

"For what?"

"For being spies."

"What's a spy?"

"Someone who steals secrets. They say they gave the secret of the atomic bomb to the Russians."

Oh, yes, the Russians, Bronka remembered. When they started kindergarten, Tori had told them about how bad the Russians were. *That's why we have to crouch under our desks, because the Russians are going to drop an atomic bomb on us.*

"Their parents gave the Russians the secret of the bomb?" asked Bronka.

"That's what they say," said Tori.

"What are the boys doing in the picture?"

"They're with their grandmother, Sophie Rosenberg. They were outside the White House, where President Eisenhower lives. Daddy was there to take pictures. He said it was a protest. People held signs that said, 'Save the Rosenbergs' because they wanted the president to stop them from being killed. Many people stood outside the White House with Michael and Robby and their grandmother."

"Which one is Robby and which one is Michael?" asked Bronka.

"Robby is the younger one with the dark hair. Michael is the older one with the light hair."

Then Tori pointed to her father's desk.

"Oh and here's a new picture of the boys Daddy just developed."

They were dressed in T-shirts and held a newspaper that read, "Spies to Die This Week."

Bronka was immediately filled with sadness for the boys. Robby was six years old—the same age she would be in a couple of weeks. Like her, he must be in his last week of kindergarten. His dark eyes were filled with sorrow. Michael was ten, and he looked gloomy too. But Bronka imagined that he was trying to be strong for his younger brother.

What will happen to the boys if their parents are killed? Bronka wondered. *Who will take care of them? Why are they killing them if people are marching to save them? Don't they want to know the truth before they kill them?*

She wished the picture would come to life so she could give both boys a big hug and then tell them they could come home with her if anything happened to their parents.

"You didn't tell them how they are going to die," Tina reminded her sister.

"Do you want to know?" Tori said.

"Sure," the twins answered.

"They strap them to an electric chair and then send electric shocks through their bodies, and that kills them on the spot."

Bronka was speechless—and terrified. She had never heard anything so terrible, except perhaps the thought of the bomb raining down on her kindergarten desk and annihilating her and JoJo.

"How can they do that to someone's mother?" JoJo asked. "That's so mean."

"I don't know," said Tori. "I heard Daddy telling Mommy that he doesn't even think it's true that she's guilty. He thinks they just wanted to get Ethel to speak out against her husband. But she wouldn't."

"And now they are both going to hell," said Tina.

"What? What do you mean?" asked JoJo.

"If you're bad or if you're not Catholic, you go to hell after you die," Tina explained.

"*Everyone* who's not Catholic?" asked JoJo.

"Yes," she said matter-of-factly. "The Rosenbergs are Jewish so they're gonna go to hell."

"What's hell?" asked Bronka.

"It's the worst place to go after you die. There's fire there all the time, and it burns you and never stops," explained Tina.

"There are worms there too, and the worms torture you," added Tori. "But if you're Catholic and you believe in Jesus, you don't go."

"Can anyone who's not Catholic get out of going to hell?" JoJo asked.

"I don't think so," said Tori, "unless you become Catholic. My father used to be Jewish, but now he's Catholic. So he'll go to heaven, not to hell. The Rosenbergs are going to hell because they're not Catholic."

"But we're Jewish," said Bronka.

"Are we going to hell?" said JoJo.

"I guess so, if you're not Catholic," said Tina matter-of-factly.

This is very unfair, thought Bronka. *In fact, everything seemed unfair—the Rosenbergs, Robby and Michael, the electric chair, hell. Would JoJo get out of going to hell because she had eaten the meatball made with pork? It didn't sound like she would. She was still Jewish.*

Just then, Connie Rosen called downstairs for Bronka and JoJo. As they headed for the stairs, the Rosen girls followed them.

"Be sure to call for us again tomorrow," Tina said.

"Okay," they answered.

～

When they walked into their house, the Sabbath table was set, and they could smell Faye's chicken roasting in the oven. Papa and Izzy would soon be home.

"Let's take a quick bath before dinner, girls," said Judy, "and you can put on nice dresses for Shabbos. How about the pink ones that Faye just made you?"

They sat in the bathtub together in the tiny bathroom as Judy washed their hair, first one, then the other.

"Mama, are we going to hell?" Bronka asked. The soap was finally out of her hair and she figured her mother would be able to concentrate. "Tina and Tori say we're going to hell because we're not Catholic."

Judy had once believed in hell. It was a scary concept—especially for little children. But the truth was, she knew that the real hell could be on earth. She had seen enough in Poland during the war to know that it was man's inhumanity to man that led to more terrible things than the Rosen girls and all of the people on 253rd Street could ever imagine.

"No, we're not going to hell," she said confidently.

"Why not?"

"Because we're Jewish. Hell is for Catholics."

The girls looked relieved. They relied on their mother's word, and they trusted her. She knew more than all of their friends put together.

With worries of hell behind them, they were tucked into their beds after dinner.

"Do you really think they are going to kill Robby and Michael's parents in the electric chair?" asked Bronka.

"I don't know," said JoJo.

"I think we should ask Mama if we can adopt them if that happens," said Bronka. "Then it will be like Robby is our triplet and we will have Michael for an older brother."

"Where would they sleep? I don't think Izzy and Faye have enough room for them here."

"I don't know," said Bronka. "But I'm really worried about them. They look so sad. I wish I could make them happy."

"But you don't even know them," said JoJo.

"I feel like I do. They have sad eyes, like Papa."

"Let's not go to sleep feeling so sad," said JoJo. "Maybe Mama or Izzy or Faye will take us to the Hobby Shop and buy us a Debbie Reynold's paper doll set."

"Okay," said Bronka. "Good night, JoJo, I love you."

"Good night, BonBon, I love you too."

Before he went to synagogue the following morning, Aron saw a picture of the Rosenbergs in the morning paper Izzy was reading.

"What happened to them?" Aron asked.

"They were executed last night. The article says that while the execution had been originally scheduled for eleven at night, their lawyers had argued against it taking place on the Sabbath. So it was moved up three hours."

Dirty trick, Aron thought. *The attorneys' attempt to stall the execution backfired. And officials could still pretend that they were respecting the Jewish religion because they had moved the time up. Disgusting. I thought America was better than this.*

Izzy went on to tell Aron that he'd also learned from the article that Julius went first and died with the initial electric shock. But Ethel, who followed him to the electric chair, did not die instantly. She still was breathing after the standard three jolts. So the executioner had to give her two more to kill her. It took four and a half minutes for Ethel to die.

Aron could not get out of his head that they were Jewish, especially when Izzy told him that the Rosenbergs were the only two American civilians ever executed for Cold War espionage. Their sons were now orphans.

When the girls awoke the next morning, the haunted faraway look was back in their papa's eyes. He could barely say, "Gut Shabbos." When they went to call for the Rosen girls later that afternoon, they were greeted by the news of the day.

"The Rosenbergs are dead," said Tina.

Bronka bit back her tears. She knew her parents wouldn't adopt the Rosenberg brothers. Maybe someday when she was older, she could really help people. But what could an almost-six-year-old do?

She could pray for them, as she did for Papa every night. Please, God, make them smile again.

1956

―――――――◎―――――――

BELLEROSE, NEW YORK

JOJO WAS ESPECIALLY EMBARRASSED WHEN her father opened his mouth in public. He had a thick Polish/Yiddish accent and when he said words like bird, he would pronounce the "ir" sound as "oi" so bird sounded like "boid." His w's sounded like v's and his r's had a guttural roll to them. Judy still had an accent too, but she didn't find her mother's speech as offensive. She worked so hard to speak English well, taking night classes. She also spoke in soft tones.

"This is how Mama and Papa sound," Bronka told her sister. They had just gotten back from the bakery, where JoJo had complained Aron's voice echoed too loudly. "They're like Mrs. Mariani," Bronka said, referring to their neighbor's accent.

"Mrs. Mariani is a grandmother," JoJo replied. "She was already an old woman when she came here. Anyway, her Italian accent sounds more musical."

Along with her overall emphasis on appearances, JoJo was much more fashion conscious than Bronka. While Bronka tacitly accepted Faye's homemade dresses, her twin had lobbied for more and more outfits from Mays, so she could dress like her peers. Most of the girls in their circle already had poodle skirts. JoJo was particularly envious of Mindy's poodle skirt, which was a gray felt swing skirt featuring an appliqué of a pink fluffy poodle. She had begged for one for months, and both girls finally received the skirts as Hanukkah presents. Judy could not find a gray one like Mindy's but bought two matching pink felt skirts with black-and-white poodles, which the twins thought were even prettier.

While JoJo noticed that their mother now dressed like their friends' mothers—in simple, shirtwaist dresses—their father took no notice of his appearance. Sometimes, he forgot to shave and comb his hair. But what was even worse, he refused to buy new clothes for years. When he finally bought something new, it was the cheapest thing he could find. And then to compound matters, he would mismatch his clothes, putting checks with stripes and brown with black.

In fact, although Aron was no longer poor, he was very, very tight with his money. Judy had suggested to him on numerous occasions that they move out of Faye and Izzy's house and find a place of their own. She knew they could afford it. Aron had been socking away money for years, and Izzy had been more than generous. He had not only made Aron a partner, but he requested only a token amount for the family's room and board. It was a great deal.

"Why would we want to move?" he replied to Judy's appeals.

"It's not right; I feel like we're taking advantage of them," she would say.

Judy would have liked more privacy as well. Sometimes she didn't feel like talking to Faye and just wanted to be by herself. But the minute she suggested they were taking advantage, she knew it wasn't true. Faye and Izzy probably enjoyed having the young family there, even more than they wanted to be there. Judy did not challenge Faye; she was a dutiful assistant and good company.

That's why, when Faye received a postcard from Israel with a cryptic message just before Hanukkah, she started to worry. In a scrawling, barely legible handwriting, it read:

"*Chag sameach.* There is trouble here. I may have to leave. Love, Rebecca."

Faye had been content ever since Aron and his family had come to live with them. She loved them and she adored the new rhythm of her life.

Faye tended not to worry about her daughter because she was living on a kibbutz that provided for all of her needs. But after reading the letter, Faye started to wonder. After all, Rebecca was past thirty-five and had not mentioned a single marriage prospect since her father's death ten years earlier. After he died, she broke up with a longtime boyfriend, a doctor. Faye had thought the doctor would have been a very suitable husband for her daughter. But Rebecca said she didn't trust him; she had heard he was cheating on her.

Then, three years later—out of the blue—Rebecca informed her that she was going to Israel to live on a kibbutz that grew oranges. Faye didn't try to stop her, not that you could ever stop Rebecca when she got an idea in her head.

She showed the postcard to Izzy, and he winced. She quickly stashed it away in the drawer of her night table. She would not mention this to anyone else. *With Rebecca, you never knew. Had there been an incident in Israel? Was there danger of an attack on the kibbutz? Did something happen to the orange crop there? Had Rebecca had another breakup?* Faye told herself that it was entirely possible that by the time she had received Rebecca's postcard, it all could have been resolved.

～

The twins hadn't been in the same class since kindergarten. Still, they maintained a solid, loving relationship; they depended on one another and watched each other's backs. What they discussed stayed strictly between them.

Outside of their secret bedroom talks, however, things were

different. By the fourth grade, Bronka was about two inches taller and fourteen pounds heavier than her sister. JoJo was tiny and skinny with small feet and small hands, while Bronka's feet were almost as large as their mother's. JoJo still had blond curls, which matched her porcelain skin and azure blue eyes. She had a little turned-up nose, much like her mother's. Bronka was a pretty girl too, with a round face, intense and shining dark eyes, and wavy curls the color of chocolate. Even though she was attractive in her own right, she always felt big and gawky standing next to JoJo.

Although the girls on the block were their mutual friends, in their separate classes they began to make their own. JoJo was attracted to the popular girls—the prettiest, the most talented, and the best dressed. Bronka's friends were quieter, less popular, and more serious. She instinctively gravitated to those who were different, like the new Chinese girl or the girl who had braces on her legs from polio.

Every day after lunch, the students put on a talent show in the cafeteria. JoJo was always the first to perform. When Bronka was game, they would sing the popular song, "Sisters" together. But when Bronka didn't want to sing, JoJo would sing by herself or with one of her classmates. JoJo was the star of the lunchroom.

When JoJo heard a rumor in school that Walt Disney was coming to Queens to recruit new Mouseketeers for the *Mickey Mouse Club* show, she convinced her sister and the Rosen girls to watch out for his car.

"I think it will be a black Lincoln or Cadillac," she told them.

Then she enlisted them to perform on the front stoop with her—just in case Walt happened to drive by. She yearned to be like the talented Annette Funicello, who was five years older than the twins.

Meanwhile at school, the fourth grade began to study immigration. The introspective and intense Bronka was an excellent student, and when her teacher, Mrs. Feingold, asked each student to find an immigrant to interview, Bronka instantly thought of her father. *There was an advantage to having a father who spoke with an accent and had a different background than her classmates' parents.*

She was aware that her friends had many things that she did not have—grandparents, cousins, not to mention a host of material possessions. But the one thing she had that most didn't have was a father who was an immigrant. The rest of her classmates—with the exception of her Chinese friend—would have to hunt for relatives and neighbors and friends to find one. But she had one living in her house—right in the next bedroom.

She approached her father as soon as he returned from work, hoping that she would be able to interview him right after dinner. Bronka was shocked and crushed by her father's response, which was a loud and angry one. He delivered it with a red face, glaring eyes, and eyebrows knitted together.

"The noive—who does your teacher think she is?" he fumed. "Vat does she need to know my business? It's too poi-so-nal; I thought Americans were entitled to privacy."

"Papa, no, Mrs. Feingold isn't being nervy," Bronka replied. "She's a good teacher. She explained to us that we are a nation of immigrants. Every immigrant has a story. You don't have to say anything that's too personal. Please, please, Papa. I know it will be the best interview in the class. It's an assignment. Everyone has to do it. I don't want to get a zero."

"Feh! You can tell that buttinsky that this is America, and I have a right to my privacy. No yenta teacher has the right to pry into my life."

Bronka ran from the room crying and threw herself on her bed. She had thought this was the best assignment, and now she could see it was the worst. She hardly ever asked Papa for anything. Quite the opposite, she tried to please him, just like Mama did. And for this simple request, he said no. *He must hate me,* she thought. *Why can't he be like Jim Anderson in* Father Knows Best, *who cares about his*

children? My father doesn't even care if I get in trouble with the teacher.
And then he'll be disappointed when I don't get a perfect report card. I
should never have asked him.

Minutes later, Izzy stood at her bedroom door. He had overheard
the yelling.

"May I come in?" he asked. "I don't like to see my girl so sad."

Bronka's face was red, her eyes swollen, and she could not stop
herself from sobbing long enough to answer. Izzy stepped into the
room.

"Look, if you need someone to interview, you can ask me the questions. You know I'm an immigrant too. And you know I love to talk
about myself. We can do it after dinner."

His kindly smile lit up his entire face.

Bronka's essay about Izzy garnered her an A-plus. But it wasn't
enough to compensate for the rejection she'd experienced from her
father. She was beginning to think he did not love her at all. No
wonder, on Bronka's report cards, her teachers noted that she lacked
self-confidence.

~

Bronka found comfort and reassurance in prayer. Both Aron and
Judy encouraged their daughters to pray. By the time the girls were
nine years old, they knew a number of Hebrew prayers and were
encouraged to add their own words in English. Faye, with Judy's
assistance, made a Shabbos dinner every Friday night. They often
attended synagogue services on the Sabbath and on Jewish holidays.

Aron recognized that his wife had learned much from him and
was a dutiful spouse and a good mother. He knew that she did her
best to teach the girls about Judaism, but her knowledge and experience were limited.

JoJo was determined to become a genuine American girl. To her,
that meant dressing like everyone else, watching the same movies

and TV shows as her peers, eating what everyone else did, and pursuing her dreams of fame.

As she got older, JoJo grew more and more frustrated by the restrictions of keeping kosher. Most of the girls' Jewish friends came from families that were less observant and more assimilated than the Lubinskis.

On a cold February day, dressed in matching pink sweaters and gray skirts, the twins put on their hats and coats, and were about to leave for Mindy's birthday party across the street. Judy stood at the kitchen sink, washing her coffee cup. She planned to change and then head across the street to help Jennie and Lenore with the festivities. When she finished, she turned around to her daughters to give them a last-minute warning about the food at the party, one she believed Aron would want her to deliver.

"All the food isn't kosher. They're serving hamburgers and hot dogs; the hamburgers are *treyfe*, but the hot dogs are Hebrew National. So just eat the hot dogs. And the birthday cake they got from our bakery is pareve, so you can eat that. But if they serve ice cream with the birthday cake, don't eat it. You can eat the potato chips with the franks, but don't eat any candy, since it might be dairy. I don't want to embarrass you by telling you what to eat in front of your friends, so I'm telling you now."

JoJo wrinkled her nose and scowled.

"Why can't we just go to the party like everyone else and have fun and eat what we want? Why do we have to be different? Even Faye and Izzy only keep kosher at home, not when they go out."

"Because that's not what we do."

"And why do we have to be kosher anyway? I want to eat what everyone else eats."

At that moment, Aron walked into the kitchen, and stood behind Judy. He heard her say, "It's for sanitary reasons; it's healthier to keep kosher."

"No, it's not—you're wrong," he interrupted in a loud, angry voice. "You don't know what you're talking about."

Judy bit her lip to hold back the tears, but she couldn't stop them. She was speechless as she turned around to face him. She had tried so hard to learn everything about Judaism and to do everything right. She was just repeating what Faye had said: "In the old days it was healthier to keep kosher, but not necessary here in America, where everything is so sanitary."

And now she was just trying her best to keep the girls on the track Aron had mandated. She was trying hard, despite the influences of their Catholic friends and their Christian-friendly school and their assimilated American Jewish friends. He was snapping at her again. And all she was doing was trying to be a good Jew. She felt undermined and unappreciated. She slumped down onto a kitchen chair, put her face in her hands, and wept.

Bronka and Johanna didn't like this scene one bit, and they had seen it many times before. They glared at their father. Why was he always so quick to anger—not only with their mother, but with them too? They ran to Judy and threw their arms around her.

Gottenyu, he thought. *She's giving them wrong information. And now I'm the villain again. I know a lot of people think that it's about health, but it's not. It's about discipline. Every time I eat, I am reminded that I am part of a holy people. The dietary laws have kept the Jews together for thousands of years. It's about faith, not health.*

Aron decided he'd explain it to them another time. He understood that he would need more than his wife's teaching to ensure that his daughters would be the Jewish mothers he intended them to be. However sincere and spiritual his wife was, she did not have the background to teach the girls everything he wanted them to know. Judaism didn't come by osmosis in America; it required attention. He remembered the day the girls were born at Warteplatz DP

Camp. They were his answer to Hitler; that is what everybody said. And he now believed it. His entire family had perished, and he alone survived. Surely, his daughters had been born to repair the link the Nazis had tried so hard to break.

~

In 1956 in Bellerose, there were not many options—especially for girls—to get a Jewish education. Rabbi Herbert sent his four children—two girls and two boys—to the Queens Yeshiva Academy, which involved a long bus ride and substantial tuition. Aron was not about to pay for his daughters to attend a private school; he was much too frugal. In addition, Faye was very vocal in insisting that the girls should be Americanized, and public school was the way to do it. Judy agreed.

He sought advice from Cantor Yudenfreund, who worked as an insurance salesman during the week, and whose own daughter, Shira, was the same age as the twins. After the minyan, when everyone else had left the chapel, Aron approached the cantor to ask if he planned to send Shira to yeshiva like the rabbi's children.

"Would I like her out of that public school, where they're singing Christmas carols?" Cantor Yudenfreund asked. "Part of me would. But, on the other hand, going to yeshiva is too isolating and too extreme. The rabbi is Orthodox and has no choice but to send his children. On the other hand, my brother, who is not that strict, sends his son there too. My nephew Stevie is like a little cop. He's checking everything his parents do against what the school tells him. I'm not sure you want that."

"No, certainly not," said Aron. "Anyway, it's too expensive to pay for both girls at once, especially when the public schools here are good and the twins are doing so well. But I really want them to get some sort of formal Jewish education."

"Well, there's the Sunday School for girls, but that's not intensive," the cantor replied. "It's totally focused on imparting the skills a Jewish homemaker needs. I want Shira to be more knowledgeable."

"So do I," said Aron.

"There's the afternoon Hebrew School here," the cantor said with a sigh. "But I have to be honest with you. Most people think it's the boys who need the formal education, and not the girls. They figure the girls will learn from their mothers how to light candles and make a Jewish home. I don't see it that way. The women are the ones who are raising the children; they need to be able to impart their knowledge too."

"Exactly," Aron said.

"So here's the thing with the afternoon Hebrew School," the cantor continued. "It's four days a week, Monday to Thursday. It's a lot after a full day of school."

"My girls can handle it. They're both good students."

"I'm sure they can. Shira is a good student too. Look, I'm going to be honest with you. I've visited those Hebrew School classes and they mostly consist of boys—restless boys who don't want to be there."

"But do they learn anything?"

"Well, sure. They're able to perform by the time they reach *bar mitzvah*."

"Do they learn about *kashrus*?"

"Of course, they learn the dietary laws."

"Are there no girls there?"

"Almost none. Once in a while, there's a girl or two. They're allowed to go; they just don't. Most parents opt for the Sunday School for their daughters. And of those few girls who go to the regular Hebrew School, most of them drop out after a year or two. For girls, it's like the Wild West.

"In a way it's a shame," continued Cantor Yudenfreund. "I've heard that in other synagogues, not so much in Queens, but in Nassau County, girls go in larger numbers and they even have a ceremony called *bas mitzvah* on a Friday night. But Rabbi Herbert is very traditional. Although his own daughters are getting their yeshiva education, they're not going to have a bas mitzvah ceremony. And so far, there haven't been any here. I don't know if he would allow one in his shul. I doubt there's been anyone here who cares enough about it to make an issue. No one really wants to challenge the rabbi. He's such a fine person and a beloved rabbi."

"Bas mitzvah, I never hoid of such a thing."

"Look, I'm going to send Shira to Hebrew School, and I already spoke to Jakob Zilberman—from the minyan. You know he and his wife, Eva, are also from Poland. They came here about a year before you did. Their daughter, Esther, is the same age as our girls. They're going to enroll her too. So if you send the twins, there will be four girls in the class."

"Done," said Aron, relieved that his problem had been solved.

~

JoJo and Bronka were not particularly thrilled about going to Hebrew School four afternoons a week directly after public school. It meant that they couldn't play with their friends—or relax, or even do their homework until after supper. They couldn't go to Girl Scouts either, like their other friends. And it cut into *Mickey Mouse Club* TV time. But that wasn't the worst of it.

Since the synagogue was only a few blocks away, they walked there themselves. On their very first day of Hebrew School, when they reached the corner of Union Turnpike and turned right, two boys, Randy Lesser and Robert Moskowitz, were hiding in the thick green hedges in front of Dr. Pearlman's office. The boys were about a year older than the twins and big for their age. They suddenly came out of hiding, yelled, and jumped on the girls, knocking them to the ground. Bronka was terrified, not only by the shock, but by Randy's crushing weight as he pinned her down. He was the bigger, beefier, more aggressive of the two. She screamed in fright and then started crying.

JoJo extricated herself from Robert by scratching his face, and then she kicked Randy's right leg twice, as she screamed, "Get off her, you big oaf. I'm going to report you and you'll be in big trouble."

"And who are you going to tell?" said Randy as he released Bronka. "Your weird father, who looks like he belongs on the Bowery or in Creedmoor? What's he going to say when he finds out you scratched and kicked us?"

"What's he going to do? Throw some bagels at us? Report us to the police?" added Robert.

"Yeah," added Randy. "He probably couldn't find his way to the police station, and even if he did, the police would take one look at his clothes and think he was a bum. They wouldn't be able to understand him either. Once a refugee, always a refugee—he'll never belong here. You'd think he wouldn't still have that ugly accent."

Ever logical, Bronka stopped crying long enough to shout, "Policemen come into the bakery. They know my father."

"Your father is just a poor, schlumpy baker," said Randy as the boys began to walk away. "My father owns three dry cleaning stores and is friends with lots of policemen. They bring their uniforms into his shops, and he cleans them for free. They love him. Anyway, everyone knows who my father is. He's a genius and he's famous. He won forty-seven thousand dollars on the TV quiz show, *Man on the Street Genius*. But you probably didn't even see it; it's past your bedtime—you little babies."

Randy was right; they hadn't seen it, but they knew all about his celebrity father. Murray Lesser, the dry-cleaning king of Queens, had become a true star in their neighborhood. During the six weeks he was on the quiz show, people had followed his odyssey, rooting for him and marveling at the fortune he was amassing. Adults stopped him on the street to congratulate him and even asked for his autograph. The girls knew they had lost the argument, and the banter stopped abruptly.

As the boys scurried away, JoJo said to Bronka, "I think we better not report them. He's right. His father is rich and famous and friends with the police. And Robert will show his scratches."

"Okay," said Bronka. "But they might do it again. It scares me. I hate them."

"I hate them too. They're disgusting. Let's get some candy."

Stopping at Jonny's Candy Store was a pre-Hebrew School ritual that began on the very first day and continued throughout the school year. The students would crowd into the small shop with nickels from their parents and buy candy to sustain them through the class. That first day of school, Bronka bought Red Hots and JoJo got Necco chocolate wafer candies.

Once at school, the girls all sat huddled together in the left-hand corner of the small classroom, two rows back. It was the same room that doubled as the minyan chapel. The boys were already fidgety and naughty after six hours in public school, where they had been sitting and following orders.

The Hebrew School teacher, Mrs. Bergman, had a chirpy bird voice and a Polish accent. But it wasn't overpowering like their father's, and it had a different ring to it. She said she had lived in Israel. Her goal was to teach them how to read Hebrew so they could follow the prayer book and learn the prayers. Maybe, one day, they would visit Israel. They would also learn about Shabbos and the Jewish holidays. On the first day of school, she gave special recognition to the girls in the class.

"Welcome, *yeladim*. This is the most girls I have ever had in a Hebrew School class. I know why the boys are here. You boys will all become bar mitzvah on your thirteenth birthday and will be called to the Torah to recite your haftorah portion. Cantor Yudenfreund will teach you your portions starting the year before your bar mitzvah date. Girls, you will also technically become bas mitzvah on your twelfth birthday, but we don't have a ceremony for girls. But it's always good to learn. You will all be Jewish mothers, so you will instruct your children."

"My father wants me to have a bas mitzvah," Esther Zilberman called out.

"Esther, we don't call out in class," Mrs. Bergman said, letting Esther's comment slide without a response.

The teacher began to distribute blue, soft-covered notebooks to all the students.

"I am giving each of you a *machberes*. Where it says *shem*, you will write your Hebrew name once I teach you how to write the Hebrew letters. In the meantime, write your English name at the top of the notebook. Hebrew is read from right to left, not left to right like English. Before I teach you how to write the first letter of the alphabet, *aleph*, I am going to go around the room and ask you your Hebrew names. In this class, I will be calling you by those names, and not by your English names."

There were five boys named *Moshe*, three named *Daveed*, and three named *Yacov*.

A couple of boys didn't know their names, so the teacher named Elliot, *Eliyahu*, Harvey, *Hillel*, and Steven, *Shimshon*.

All four girls knew their Hebrew names.

"Shira, yours is the easiest," said Mrs. Bergman. "You have the same name in Hebrew and English."

"And Esther, is your Hebrew name *Hadassah*, like the women's organization?"

"Yes, Mrs. Bergman," said Esther.

"I want everyone to call me *Morah* Bergman in this class.

"And Johanna, what is your name in Hebrew?"

"Hannah Yosefa."

"And last, but not least, how about you, Bronka?"

"My Hebrew name is *Bracha Haya*, *Morah* Bergman."

"What a beautiful name," said the teacher. "Your parents must have given that name a lot of thought. Class, do you know that *Bracha Haya* means 'Blessed Life'?"

Bronka was embarrassed that she had been singled out. Moreover, she did not feel like her life was going all that well, especially after her encounter with Randy and Robert. Her feelings were confirmed as she began to be hit by a barrage of spitballs coming her way from the boys. And *Morah* Bergman didn't even notice.

1957

BELLEROSE, NEW YORK

ONE NIGHT TOWARD THE END of June, when the twins were already in bed, and the adults were watching *The Phil Silvers Show* in the living room, the phone rang. Faye went into the kitchen to pick up the phone, but when she spoke, no one answered.

"Hello, hello." There was still no answer, so Faye hung up.

A minute later, the phone rang again. Again, Faye kept saying hello but there was no response. She hung up again.

When the phone rang a third time, Izzy came into the kitchen to see what was going on and picked it up.

"Hello," he said in a loud, agitated voice.

"Is Faye there?"

"Faye, it's for you," he said with a look of disgust on his face. "I think it's Rebecca."

"Rebecca? Where is she calling from?"

"I have no idea; pick up the phone and find out before she hangs up again."

"Hello, Rebecca, is that you?"

"Is that you, Mother?"

"Of course," said Faye. "Don't you recognize my voice? Was that you who just called twice and hung up on me?"

"Yes," said Rebecca.

"Why did you do that?"

"I had to make sure it was you."

"Where are you?"

"I'm at the airport?"

"Which airport?"

"Idlewild."

"Idlewild? You mean you're in New York, in Queens?" Faye looked like she had seen a ghost.

"Yes, can you pick me up?"

"Sure," said Faye. "Which terminal are you at?"

"International Arrivals—I just came in from Paris."

"Let's go," said Faye to Izzy as she hung up the phone.

Izzy did not want to go out again. He had already changed into something comfortable, finished dinner, and was now watching his favorite show. Sgt. Bilko was trying to convince the gullible Sgt. Ritzik to play poker, despite the entreaties of Ritzik's wife. He resented being interrupted.

In addition, he hated driving to the airport; the Belt Parkway was always crowded, and the airport was a madhouse. Part of him wished that Rebecca had just taken a cab and turned up at the door. But that might have given him or Faye a stroke or a heart attack. Either way, he knew he was in for big trouble.

This is so typical of Rebecca, Izzy thought. *Leave it to her to just appear suddenly and make demands. It was all about her all of the time. And the hang-ups on her mother—what was that all about? What a wonderful respite it had been to have her in Israel. It was over now. Her presence could very well upset the nice little extended family we've created over the last six years. It's good for me. It's good for Faye. It's good for the cousins. It's even good for my business. Rebecca is capable of throwing a grenade into the situation and blowing it all up.*

Izzy grabbed the car keys, told Aron and Judy that they were going to get Faye's daughter at the airport, and motioned Faye into the car.

～

Izzy fumed all the way to the airport, but he didn't say a word to Faye. He knew his world was about to be upset by Rebecca. *She was a* meshuggene, he thought. *She couldn't even make herself sound normal on the phone.*

When he first spotted her at the airport terminal, with her one little beat-up tan suitcase, his worst fears were confirmed. She didn't look normal to him. *Women her age didn't walk around in public looking like that,* he thought. She wore a shabby, stained, tan raincoat and a paisley kerchief tied under her chin. *She looks like a refugee, right off the boat—only worse.* Her attire accentuated her pale complexion and the blank look in her hazel eyes.

"Rebecca, we're over here," Faye called out, dismayed that her daughter's appearance was so different from when she had first left for Israel. Then, she had been animated about her plans, radiant with excitement. Now, she looked like a lost waif. In addition, Faye was alarmed that as she walked toward them, there was barely a spark of recognition in her face.

Faye ran over to Rebecca and hugged her. But her daughter was stiff and wooden as her mother put her arms around her. Izzy took the suitcase, and the three of them walked to the parking lot together. Once they reached the car, he helped Rebecca into the back seat and he and Faye got in the front

Rebecca said little on the car ride home, only that she had left the kibbutz and gone to France. After a few weeks in Paris, she said she had headed to New York. But Faye insisted on knowing why she'd left Israel. After all, she had believed that everything was under control there for close to a decade. And now, remembering the cryptic post-card and observing her daughter's demeanor, she wanted to find out what had prompted her to leave.

"I may be in trouble," Rebecca said. "They're looking for me."

"Who, the Arabs?" Izzy asked.

"No, the Knesset is trying to find me," said Rebecca. "They've been talking about me."

"How do you know that?" Faye asked.

"I've heard my name has come up. They're spying on me; that's why I had to leave Israel."

Izzy rolled his eyes.

By the time they returned from the airport, it was almost eleven o'clock, and Judy and Aron had already retired for the night.

Izzy carried her one suitcase into the house. He headed for the back room, next to their bedroom. *Not only was she here*, thought Izzy, *but she's right next to us. God help us.* The nine-by-twelve-foot room housed Faye's Singer sewing machine, a cedar chest with her fabric and patterns, other sewing supplies, and a sofa bed.

"Where are you going?" asked Rebecca. "Aren't I going to stay upstairs? I thought you finished the attic so I could stay there when I came home."

"No," said Faye, "you're going to sleep in my sewing room. Didn't you read my letters? I told you Izzy's cousins were staying with us. They are refugees from Poland who suffered terribly in the war, and now we're helping them. Aron is managing the new bakery. And Judy, his wife, helps in the store and helps me at home too. They have the most adorable twin girls—you'll love them. The whole family is living upstairs."

"They're still here? Shouldn't they have a place of their own by now?"

Izzy thought, *Shouldn't you have a place of your own by now?*

"How do I know I can trust them?"

"They're family," said Faye.

"How are they related?"

"Izzy was a first cousin to Aron's father, Yosef, who died in a concentration camp. Izzy and Aron's father had the same grandparents."

"And the woman?"

"You mean Aron's wife? She's darling, we love her," said Faye.

"But who is she? What do you know about her? How do you know she's not spying on you or having your phones tapped?"

"Oh, Rebecca," said Faye, exasperated. "You're exhausted; you need some sleep. You'll feel better after you get a good night's sleep."

"Do you really think I'm going to get a good night's sleep on this old sofa bed?"

"I'm sure you don't plan on staying here indefinitely," Izzy said, hoping that if he said it aloud, that would make it true.

∼

The next day, Rebecca slept until two o'clock in the afternoon. By then, Faye had given everyone a heads-up that her daughter was there, that she was probably exhausted and maybe a bit disoriented from the trip. In other words, it wouldn't hurt if they tiptoed around her. At two o'clock, Faye brought a tray to her room.

"Good morning, Glory," she said in her most cheerful voice. "Well actually, it's good afternoon. It's two o'clock. That makes it eight p.m. in Paris. Time to get up. I didn't know whether to serve you breakfast or lunch, so I made a nice melted cheese sandwich for you with a cup of tea and a linzertorte from the bakery."

"I'm not hungry," snapped Rebecca.

"Come on, sweetheart, you have to regain your strength from all of your traveling. Have something to eat, and then get up, get washed, and get dressed. I want you to meet Judy. The girls will be back from school about three o'clock. Izzy and Aron will be home from work about five thirty, and we'll have dinner at six. You can't have dinner be your first meal of the day."

Rebecca sighed and rolled over.

About four o'clock, she finally emerged from her room. Faye, Judy, and the twins were in the kitchen when Rebecca made her entrance in a white sleeveless blouse, a tan skirt that was cinched at the waist, and sandals. She had reddish-brown, wavy, shoulder-length hair, and she made eye contact. Faye was relieved that she actually looked quite attractive and exhibited a warm, friendly attitude toward the immigrants.

"This is my daughter, Rebecca," said Faye. "Or do you want to be called by your Hebrew name, Rifka?"

"Everyone calls me Becky," she said.

"Okay, Becky," said Judy, eager to please both her and Faye. "And since you are Faye's daughter and the girls call her Tante Faye, would you mind if they call you Aunt Becky?"

"No, that would be wonderful," said Rebecca.

"Bronka and JoJo, meet your Aunt Becky."

The girls smiled.

"They're adorable," said Becky. "I notice they both twirl their hair; what does that mean."

"Oh, I don't think it means anything; just a habit," Judy said.

"I think it means something," said Becky.

"Okay," said Faye, becoming a little nervous. "When you figure out what it means, you can let us know."

"So the girls are having a birthday next week," said Judy. "They are going to be ten years old—their first double-digit birthday. And we're going to have a big party in the backyard. We hope you'll be here."

"What day is it?"

"It's going to be on Thursday, July the Fourth," said Faye. "We're going to barbecue hamburgers and hot dogs."

"Who's coming?"

"We've invited the girls' friends and their families," said Faye. "Some of the neighbors are coming; we've asked the Mandelsterns across the street. Lenore, Mindy's mother is a widow about your age, and her parents, Jennie and Harry. The Rosens, who live a few doors down, will be here with their three girls, and maybe the grandmother who lives with them.

"And then the Yudenfreunds and their daughter, Shira, and her brother will be joining us. Sol is the cantor of our shul, and he won't eat in many of the congregants' homes, but he'll eat here because he says, 'If it's kosher enough for Aron, it's kosher enough for me.' And then there is the Zilberman family. They have a daughter, Esther, who goes to Hebrew School with the girls, and also a three-year-old little boy."

"That's quite a crowd," said Becky, looking apprehensive. "I'll see if I can make it. But even if I can't, I want to get you—my beautiful new nieces—a special birthday gift. What would you like?"

That was easy; all of their friends already had one or more Ginny dolls, eight-inch, hard plastic fashion dolls with jointed walking legs and eyes that opened and closed. It seemed like ages that they had wanted one of those beautiful dolls with a blond or brunette wig in the hairstyles of the day. They were impressed with the dolls' dresses, made of high-quality fabrics like taffeta, organdy, velveteen, and brocade, some with lace trim. You could also buy accessories separately for them, including shoes, purses, eyeglasses, jewelry, and even a tiny dog.

"A Ginny doll!" the twins answered in unison.

"Well then, a Ginny doll for each of you," Becky said. "Where do we get them?"

"They have them in the Hobby Shop," said the girls.

"Okay and I'll tell you what," said Becky. "I want to make sure you love them, so I want you to pick them out yourselves. When can we go?"

"Can we go tomorrow, Mama?" said JoJo.

"Whatever is good for Becky," said Judy. "This is the last week of school and there are half-days for the rest of the week. So whatever works for you, Becky. Just not on Shabbos. You know we don't go shopping on the Sabbath."

"Why don't we go tomorrow?" said Becky.

Bronka could hardly contain herself. Just like that, there was a new relative in the house who was kind and nice and wanted to buy her and JoJo the coveted Ginny dolls. This was like a dream come true.

"Great, Becky," said Faye. "We'll all go, and I'll give you the Grand Tour of the neighborhood on the way to the Hobby Shop."

∽

"The Hobby Shop is right next to Dan's," Faye announced. She had already pointed out a number of the other landmarks in the neighborhood to her daughter. Becky had only visited the neighborhood a couple of times before she left for Israel, so she was unfamiliar with the area.

"Is this where you do your grocery shopping?" asked Becky.

"Yes, it has just about everything we need, except for the kosher meat, which we get at Morty's."

"I can do the grocery shopping for you," offered Becky.

"Whatever you want, Becky," said Faye.

By offering to do the shopping, Faye wondered if Becky intended to become a permanent fixture in her house. She feared the house was not big enough to contain Becky's quirks and issues along with the rest of the extended family. But she brushed that thought away. She was trying to live in the moment. She was grateful that Becky was behaving normally, and she was exulting in the sunshine and the excursion with her adopted family.

"I don't think we need anything right now."

"Sure, Mom. And what's that?" She pointed to Jonny's.

"Oh, it's a candy store with a soda fountain. There's a counter and a few tables."

"Why don't I take everyone for ice cream there when we're finished?"

"Yay!" shouted the twins.

The Hobby Shop was a small toy store. In the window were all the popular toys the twins recognized from TV ads. But their eyes were drawn to what was in the display. It was a Ginny doll trunk that was about ten-and-a-half inches high, almost six inches wide, and about six inches deep. It had a pink-and-white metal exterior with brass finish corners. A Ginny doll's head was painted in white on the pink trunk, and under the head "Ginny" was written in script. Two Ginny dolls—one a brunette and one a blonde—sat on top of the trunk.

"Let's go in," Becky said.

Inside, there were even more toys and games. But the twins were on a mission and quickly gravitated to the back where there was a display of Ginny dolls in a glass case. There were brunette ones in yellow, pink, and red dresses with matching bows. There were blonde ones in blue dotted swiss, green velvet, and lavender, trimmed with white lace; their outfits were topped with straw hats.

Mr. Shelton, who owned the store, saw the girls' enthusiasm for the dolls. Before they could even choose one, he told them he wanted to show them something else. He asked them to close their eyes.

He pointed to the same trunk they had observed in the window, but it was open. The inside of the trunk was lined with pink-and-white polka dot fabric. There were more outfits hung on a rack at the top of the trunk. The doll's accessories—hats and bows and tiny shoes and handbags and jewelry—were showcased in the drawers, which were lined with pink-and-white tissue paper. Pink ribbons secured the contents of the trunk.

"Oh, isn't that darling," said Becky.

JoJo and Bronka had never seen anything like that before. Not even Mindy or the Rosen sisters had one. They had not heard any of their friends mention it. But Judy started to get uneasy. This looked like a very expensive item; they had just met Becky yesterday. This was too much to ask.

"Let's pick out your dolls, girls," said Judy. "This is why we came here. Becky is so generous to get you each a Ginny doll for your birthday."

They returned to the doll case. The abundance of dolls was confusing. They looked at one and then another, seriously considering their choices. Finally, JoJo settled on a blonde doll that everyone said looked like her. She had a blue dotted swiss dress with a crinoline petticoat underneath, blue satin shoes, and white socks with lace. A matching blue bow was affixed to her hair. Bronka chose a brunette with a yellow taffeta dress, black patent leather shoes, white socks, and a straw hat with a yellow flower in it.

"Now what about the trunk?" said Mr. Shelton.

"Let's take another look at it," said Becky.

"The dolls are more than enough, Becky," said Judy. "You are so kind to get them such a wonderful birthday present. They don't need the trunk; it must be very expensive."

"I'm sure it is," said Faye. "I want to look too. Judy, you stay here with the girls."

Judy was happy to stay out of this discussion. She did not want Becky to be maneuvered into an uncomfortable situation. As it turned out, neither did Faye.

Off in a corner, where Judy and the girls could not hear, Mr. Shelton said, "This trunk will be all the rage this Christmas season; every little girl will want it."

Faye said, "First thing's first, how much are the dolls?"

"The dolls are six dollars each."

"That's a lot for a doll," said Faye.

"But look how beautiful they are, and the attention to detail."

"They are very lovely," said Faye. "The girls are very excited. So that's twelve dollars for the two dolls. How much is the trunk?"

"The trunk is $30," said Mr. Shelton.

"Thirty dollars—that's a fortune," said Faye. "You could rent an apartment for that." Although she knew they had given Aron a bargain, she considered that he paid about that much to Izzy and Faye for his family's monthly room and board. How could a child's toy cost that much?

"Not around here," said Mr. Shelton. "A four-room apartment in Glen Oaks is going for seventy-five dollars a month."

"So that makes a doll trunk worth almost half a month's rent?"

"Well, it depends on how much your granddaughters' happiness is worth to you."

Faye always loved when people assumed the twins were her granddaughters. It raised her spirits and made her feel validated and whole. But she was determined that Becky should not buy the trunk, even though she was afraid that her daughter would insist on it. It was ridiculously extravagant. She could buy the girls at least five pairs of shoes with thirty dollars. But Rebecca was not responsible with money. She was lucky her father had taken good care of her in his will. She was exulting in being Aunt Becky, and there was no guessing what she would do.

Although Becky never said a word during her mother's entire interaction with the storeowner, Faye was correct about her daughter's intentions. Initially, she had been determined to purchase the trunk for the twins. But the more Mr. Shelton and Faye spoke, the more Becky began to hear voices that told her not to buy it. The voices told her that the proprietor had gotten access to her bank account and knew how much money she had. She began to withdraw into her own mind, listening to the many ways the Hobby Shop owner was spying on her.

After a few minutes, Faye said, "I think we should just take the dolls. The trunk is just too expensive. Do you agree, Becky?"

At first Becky didn't answer; she was too deep into her own thoughts. Faye asked again, "Are you going to buy the trunk or only the dolls?"

"Definitely not the trunk," Becky said emphatically, looking at Mr. Shelton with a combination of fear and anger. "Just the dolls."

Bronka and JoJo were delighted with their new Ginny dolls. They said "thank you" over and over again and hugged and kissed Aunt Becky. Although the beautiful pink trunk would have been lovely, it wasn't as if they had wanted it for a long time. It was the first they had seen of it.

"I'm going to name my doll Joy," said JoJo. "What are you going to name your doll, Bronka?"

"Amy," she said.

Faye and Judy were thrilled to see the girls so happy. But Faye noticed that Becky had become withdrawn. She wasn't saying a word.

"Are we still going to get ice cream?" asked JoJo.

"Sure, let's go," said Faye.

They sat at the counter and ordered ice cream cones. Everyone but Becky, who just wanted a cup of coffee. Bronka could not help noticing the faraway look in her eyes as she stared at her cup of coffee and repetitively stirred it with a teaspoon. Bronka imagined that Aunt Becky had really wanted to give them the trunk, but that Tante Faye and her mother had deterred her. She really didn't care about the trunk that much, but she liked the thought that her new aunt had wanted to buy it. She loved her new doll, and she loved Aunt Becky too, who had given her and her sister such a special gift. She would do her best to make her happy.

∾

July 4, 1957 burst forth as a glorious day for a barbecue and a tenth birthday party. It was bright and clear and sunshiny with a high of eighty degrees. First thing in the morning, Faye was bustling around the house, tidying up.

"I'm so glad the weather is good," she announced to anyone within earshot. "I don't know where I would have put all those people in this house if it rained. But people may still come into the house to use the bathroom. We have to make sure everything is neat and clean."

The girls and Judy were grabbing a quick muffin, Becky was still sleeping, and Izzy and Aron had gone to the bakery for the morning. It would be a busy morning with customers buying their holiday cakes and desserts.

"How can I help?" Judy asked.

"I really don't want to wait until the boys come home from the bakery to set up. We're strong, right? Will you help me move some bridge tables and folding chairs outside? Then we can set everything up. Who knows when they'll return?"

"Of course," said Judy.

"Can we help too?" JoJo asked.

"Definitely, I would love your help, especially with the decorations." Faye had bought red, white, and blue crepe paper streamers and miniature American flags. She also planned to surprise the birthday girls with a cake for each of them. Each one would read *Happy Birthday* with their name inscribed in red icing. The cakes would also be decorated in red, white, and blue flowers, and there would be a miniature American flag on each one. Judy had insisted that one cake for the two of them was more than enough.

"We're in the bakery business; don't be silly," Faye had said. "If a child isn't a twin, she gets her own birthday cake every year. Of course, we'll order two. We can't have the baker's kids do with less than everyone else."

"I have the redwood picnic table and benches outside on the patio, and they seat about six," she said.

Faye continued her patter. "People are coming at three. I'll put out some *nosherai* so they can have something to drink and a nibble when they come. The deli platters are supposed to be delivered at four. I decided to make it easy. Izzy will barbecue hamburgers and hot dogs, and I ordered everything else from Brodsky's Kosher Deli—cold cuts, potato salad, pickles, and coleslaw."

If nothing else, Faye was organized, Judy thought.

Aron and Izzy arrived back at the house at two o'clock, and Faye had a fit when Izzy wanted to take a shower.

"I just finished cleaning the bathroom. Now I'll have to clean it all over again. Anyway, you're going to be standing at a hot grill. Do you really need to take a shower now?"

Izzy just rolled his eyes and headed into the bathroom.

The guests started arriving promptly at three. By then, Becky was awake and ready to socialize, and the girls were dressed in matching red-and-white party dresses, which Faye had made for them. They wore blue bows in their hair.

Jakob and Eva Zilberman, with their daughter, Esther, and their son, Jeffrey, were the first to arrive. They came bearing gifts—two large identical boxes covered with blue-and-white-striped wrapping paper and a big red bow on each. Eva also held a smaller box. The Zilbermans were a diminutive couple, but their warmth and friendliness made them seem larger. Judy thought it was not surprising that Jakob did so well as a jewelry salesman.

"Welcome," said Judy. "We're so glad you could join us."

"Thank you for including us," said Eva, who spoke with a thick Yiddish accent and was obviously thrilled to be there. "These are for the girls, and here's just a little box of candy for you."

"Thank you, that's so sweet of you, but it's unnecessary."

"We just wanted to thank you for including our whole family. We are so happy to celebrate a double simcha—the Fourth of July and the twins' birthday. No, it's a triple simcha—you have twins."

Everyone laughed.

"Why don't you make yourselves comfortable over there?" Faye said, as she pointed to the picnic table. "Oh, here's my daughter, Becky."

"Becky, these are the Zilbermans, why don't you get them something to drink?"

As more guests started to arrive with their birthday gifts, Jakob and Eva took a seat at the redwood table with their drinks, and Becky joined them. Esther and Jeffrey went to stand with the twins as they greeted the other kids.

Shortly the Mandelsterns, the Rosens, and the Yudenfreunds arrived at the party. Lenore, Irv, and Sol sat down at the table with the Zilbermans and Becky.

"As soon as the deli platters are delivered, we'll eat," Faye announced as she went from group to group. In the meantime, no one seemed to care as they munched on potato chips and pretzels and sipped their drinks. The children were preoccupied with pin the tail on the donkey, which Judy and Claire Yudenfreund were supervising, and some of the other adults were watching. This was followed by a spirited game of musical chairs. The rest of the adults were chatting in little conversational clusters.

At 4:10, the delicatessen order arrived, and Izzy began grilling the hamburgers and hot dogs. The deliveryman walked into the backyard with a huge cardboard box. Faye told him to set the box on the table and handed him a tip. As he began to arrange the platters, Jakob Zilberman suddenly took notice of him and all the color drained from his face.

"What's the matter?" Cantor Sol asked him. "Are you feeling all right?"

Jakob gasped and stared, his eyes wide open. He said nothing.

"Jakob, are you feeling all right? Do you want to go in and lie down? What's the matter?"

"No," he said. "It's just that I recognize him."

The man arranging the cold cut platters and bowls of pickles and salads on the table did not look particularly scary to anyone but Jakob. He was wearing a white apron over his clothes and a white cap. He had blond hair styled in a crew cut, and his eyes were light brown. He was about forty-five, and a bit overweight for his five-foot nine-inch frame. Jakob instantly knew his distinctive smirk; one he had seen countless times.

"Where do you know him from?"

"From the camp."

"Was he a prisoner or a guard?"

"He . . . he was a murderer," stammered Jakob.

Irv Rosen—always on the lookout for a newsworthy photograph, grabbed his camera, which he had brought to capture the birthday festivities. He walked right up to the table and brazenly snapped a picture of the man, who was putting the final touches on the food setup. With the click of the camera, the deli man scurried away. Irv went back to the table.

"I got a photo of him just in case," said Irv. "Do you really think the deli guy from Brodsky's is a murderer?"

"I'm almost positive," said Jakob. "I will never forget that smirk."

"So, tell us the story," Irv said.

"Oh, no," said Eva, she looked at her husband with pleading eyes, and spoke in a loud and anguished voice so everyone at the table could hear.

"This is a party," she continued. "It's not appropriate. We will never be invited back here if you have to recount your saga. I'm sure Judy and Aron have harrowing tales too. It's not a party game to show and tell what happened in the Shoah. You know I never talk about what happened to me to anyone but you."

She was wearing a white sleeveless blouse and held out her forearm to show a blue tattoo that read A-13852. "I got this memento from Auschwitz, so it's not that I can ever forget I was there; it's too upsetting to speak out loud. The memories come to me in nightmares, but I'd rather not share what happened—especially at a simcha. On the other hand, my husband just can't stop telling his story. Excuse me, I'm going to see how the kids are doing," she said, leaving the table in a huff.

Jakob Zilberman was a little man whose beaked nose made him look almost birdlike. But he had a big personality, and what was on his mind was often on his tongue.

"Don't mind Eva," Jakob said to the others at the picnic table. "She suffered in unimaginable ways. We just handle it differently. She prefers to keep everything to herself—bottled up with a cork that explodes from time to time. My therapy is to tell everyone I know."

No one at the table could think of another thing to say—even Irv had no more questions. There was dead silence. Jakob's mind went back to when his family first arrived at Auschwitz, and how he had been the only one not chosen for instant death. *That is because I was young and strong,* he thought, the guilt still tearing at him. No matter how many years went by, remorse was his constant companion. *Perhaps that's why I need to talk about it, as a way of doing penance. I wish Eva would understand. My parents, brothers, and sisters all died in the gas chamber, and I lived only because I assisted the Germans in their evil deeds.*

He shuddered, remembering the heinous work he was forced to perform. He, along with other strong, young Jewish men, had been ordered to open the doors of the crematorium after the Jews had been gassed, and then carry the bodies to the ovens. *The worst was when I recognized someone I knew, a friend or a neighbor or a cousin. Then it wasn't mechanical, and I knew in my heart and my mind what I was doing. The Germans forced us to crush the bones by pressing the bodies*

through a coarse sieve. When we were finished crushing someone's
wife, grandfather, mother, sister, daughter, or son, a car came to pick
up all of the ashes and pour them into the river so all traces would be
gone.

"So, yeah, Irv," Jakob finally said. "The deli man was in Auschwitz
too. He was an SS guard; he was the guy who stood there with a whip
and was in charge of the other SS guards—all with whips. He oversaw
the whole operation. I'll never forget that smirk of his. He told Jews
to hurry—that they were going to take a shower. Thousands of naked
people would come in at a time. The Germans tried to cram in as
many people as they could. The room would then be locked for about
seven minutes until the gas took effect and everyone was dead. My
job was to clean up after the Nazis and bring the bodies to the ovens.

"I was sure I would never survive to tell about it. They would kill
us because we knew too much; we knew what they were doing. We
knew the depth and breadth of their evil."

"Did you think about escaping?" Irv asked.

"I did, but I was sure I'd be caught. I also thought about suicide. I
could've easily done it, just by running into an electric fence or strik-
ing a guard."

"What stopped you?"

"It was an act of vengeance—to stay alive. I wanted revenge for
the deaths of my parents, my brothers and sisters, and all of the Jews
who were annihilated just because they were Jews. I wanted to live to
keep their memory alive. I wanted to carry on the legacy of the Jewish
people. I actually thought there were no Jews left in Europe, and I
wanted to tell all who would listen what the Nazis did."

"Did you lose your faith?"

"No, I grappled with it and argued with God. But in the end, I
still believe I survived for a reason. And that is to tell the story so
it will never happen again. I would prefer to tell you another story,
one in which I look brave and fearless. I would prefer a story where

I was a hero and saved people. But that wasn't possible in those circumstances, and I wouldn't be honest if I embellished what really happened to make myself look better. If you wanted to live, you did as you were told. And then most people still didn't survive. Someone needed to survive to tell what happened. I did, and I'm telling you the God's honest truth."

The group at the table sat in stunned silence. Irv knew he had asked enough questions; anything more would be superfluous. Lenore had tears in her eyes. Cantor Yudenfreund looked ashen. Becky had a glazed expression on her face.

After a minute or two, Jakob spoke. "Let's get something to eat before the food is all gone."

"Okay," said Irv, judging from the faces of the other guests at the table that they had heard enough. But for Irv, it was never enough. He always wanted more detail. He was in the news business. He particularly wanted to know more about the man who delivered the delicatessen, the man whose photo he had snapped.

As they walked to the food table, Irv put his arm around Jakob.

"I think you're very brave, Jakob. You not only survived that horror, but you're courageous to speak about it honestly. Most people in your circumstances wouldn't say a word, or they would invent another story. If you like, I'll develop the photo of the deliveryman, and if you think he's the murderer from Auschwitz, I'll try to help you do something about it. I'm not sure if anything can be done, but I'll give it my best."

"Thanks," said Jakob, as he began to pile his plate with food.

~

For Bronka and JoJo, the birthday party was a big success. For Eva and Jakob Zilberman, it unleashed their profound differences and gave them a reason to continue their ongoing argument.

"I don't know why you have to talk about Auschwitz to everyone you meet," Eva said to her husband as they walked the few blocks home from the party. "I don't tell the whole world about what happened to me."

Eva had been the subject of one of Mengele's experiments, and although she survived, she had almost died from typhus later. In addition, she had also lost her entire family.

"It's my private hell," she told Jakob.

"That's your choice. I need to talk about it."

"Other people would hide the fact that they were *Sonderkommandos*. It's hardly something to be proud of. Why do you have to tell complete strangers?"

"It's not any more shameful than having Mengele experiment on you. What choice did anyone have? If you wanted a chance to survive, you went along with it. And what of those who didn't? Sure, a handful escaped, but wasn't there a woman who shot a guard? The word was that she was stripped naked and about to be gassed, and she pulled a gun from a vicious guard, and shot and killed him. So, she made a point, but where is she now? They killed her instantly, and she doesn't even have a grave on which to put a stone. She went up in smoke like everyone else."

Esther, who was walking a few feet in front of her parents, holding her little brother's hand, was starting to put two and two together.

"Are Faye and Izzy the twins' grandparents?"

"No, they're relatives, but they're not their real grandparents. I suspect, like you, they have no grandparents," said Eva.

"Why don't I have any grandparents?"

"They were killed by the Nazis."

"Why did they kill my grandparents?"

"Because they were Jewish."

"What's wrong with being Jewish?"

"Nothing, dear," said Eva.

~

Ever since the day her daughter arrived, Faye hoped she could foster a friendship between Becky and Lenore Mandelstern. Since her scrape with the law, Lenore had lost some of her airs and was friendlier. With her new job, she stayed closer to home. Lenore was about Becky's age, and she had a social life, as was evidenced by the young men who occasionally parked their cars in the Mandelsterns' driveway. Faye had no idea that these dates provided a subterfuge for Lenore's ongoing relationship with Irv Rosen. She reasoned that Lenore might agree to bring Becky to a dance or go on a double date with her. She worked in a hospital; perhaps she could even introduce her to a nice young doctor. She told herself that a boyfriend or a husband would provide Becky with the stability she needed. As progressive as she was, part of her agreed with Izzy when he said, "The most important degree a woman needs is an MRS."

As they were cleaning up from the party, Faye said to Becky, "How was Lenore? Did you like her?"

"She was okay."

"Did she discuss her social life?"

"Not really; she just said that she plays the field."

"Anything else?"

Faye was now hanging on her every word.

"Yes, she mentioned that she would work on finding someone for me, so we can double date."

"That's great," said Faye, feigning surprise, pretending the thought had never occurred to her. "How was the food at the party? What did you eat?"

"I just had some turkey," Becky said.

"That's all?"

"I had a piece of cake."

"I know you love hamburgers. Didn't you have one?

"No, I was afraid to."

"Why? We got the chopped meat fresh from Morty's this morning. People told me they were delicious. Izzy grilled them just perfectly."

"I heard that Hitler poisoned the hamburgers."

"Hitler?"

"Yes, and I also heard that he's looking for Aron. He's going to come after him."

"That's ridiculous, Becky. Hitler has been dead since 1945."

"I know what I heard," Becky insisted.

Faye had been living six thousand miles away from her daughter for years, and the respite from Becky while she was off in Israel had dimmed her concerns. Now she found herself shocked by these kinds of comments, which had become increasingly frequent over the last few days. She scoured her memory to see if Becky had behaved like this before Israel. She recalled now that Becky had been troublesome as a teenager, with mood swings and angry outbursts. After a particularly nasty breakup in college, she'd lost thirty pounds, been hospitalized, and even had to drop out of school for a semester. But she was able to return to school, do her work, and graduate. So she'd convinced herself that her daughter had recovered. Faye did not think she remembered these types of bizarre comments, which had no basis in reality. Although she recalled that when Becky broke up with her boyfriend right before she moved to Israel, she told Faye that she had heard on authority that he was cheating on her. Faye had never questioned it at the time, but now she wondered. Had it been as true as Hitler poisoning the hamburgers or being hunted by the Knesset?

Izzy was not a subtle man, and he had never concealed his dislike for Faye's daughter. This bothered and hurt his wife, especially because Faye was so accepting of his son, Henry, and his family. Now that Becky was living in their home, he would roll his eyes and make disparaging remarks about her. This made Faye even more defensive.

She continued to rationalize her daughter's behavior. *She is a smart girl and a good-looking one too, especially when she fixes herself up. Look how loving and generous she is with the twins. She was social at the birthday party. The strange behavior isn't consistent. Some days, she is as normal as apple pie.*

So, instead of accepting that there was a problem with Becky and addressing it, Faye did nothing.

~

"Can you imagine Jakob Zilberman holding court at the party about his time at Auschwitz? Most *Sonderkommandos* wouldn't even admit it," Aron said to his wife when they were finally alone in their room.

"It wasn't his fault. He had no choice. He did what he could to survive," she said. "You know the girls are getting older," she added. "They're in Hebrew School, they talk to the Rosen girls, who know everything, and now they're friends with Esther Zilberman, who must be very well aware of the Shoah. It's only a matter of time until they figure out that we have a story too."

Aron's face became sullen and he did not answer her.

"You are so ashamed of our story? You are so ashamed of our love? You should be proud of it!" Judy cried. "I am."

"You are proud of your father, of your people, of your country?" He turned red as he said it, and he knew as the words shot from his mouth that he should not have said this.

"I forsake them for you and your religion, like Ruth in the Bible. Isn't that enough for you? I love you so much I gave up everything for you. And you are ashamed of me. I don't think you love me anymore. In fact, I wonder whether you ever loved me."

Aron could not say a word. He didn't know the answer. Had he ever loved her, or had he gone with her because he was bereft and at the end of his rope? Had it just been an easy fix? But those were feelings that were best unuttered. She did not deserve those thoughts.

She had done everything for him; he doubted that he could live without her. She was his guardian angel; of course, he must love her.

He understood that she had loved him from the moment she'd first seen him as a young boy. He knew that she continued to love him, even though he was not available to her. It was an unspoken, pure, hidden love, but he could see it in her eyes and in her actions. At the peril of her own safety, she had protected him when Jews were endangered. The punishment in Poland for hiding Jews was death. But she helped him over and over again. With the agility of a cheetah and the cunning of a fox, she had hidden him and moved him from place to place—always at her own peril.

After the war, when he returned to Kielce and experienced yet another catastrophic persecution, she'd lifted him up again. He'd been numb and had not wanted to go on. But it was she who gave him hope and comfort and provided him with a roadmap to move forward. For him, she renounced her family, her religion, and her country. She declared herself a Jew and said she would go with him. She had even quoted Ruth. "For whither thou goest, I will go; and where thou lodgest, I will lodge. Thy people shall be my people, and thy God my God."

Why couldn't he make her a Jew? He had pondered this question and prayed on it. *How many Christians had Hitler made Jews in order to torture and eliminate them? How many of the baptized—who had never thought nor uttered a Jewish thought or prayer—ended up in the ovens of the crematoria because the Nazis had determined that they were Jews. Hitler's definition of a Jew included tens of thousands of people who did not think of themselves as Jews. Even if they had converted to Christianity from Judaism, they were nonetheless considered Jews by the Nazi regime. Even if their parents or grandparents had converted, they were still Jewish in the eyes of the Nuremburg Laws. Why couldn't the reverse be true? Why couldn't a Christian woman—who wanted to be one—become a Jew?*

After the Kielce pogrom in 1946, like many other displaced persons, Dyta and Aron had headed to the American sector in Germany. They were both done with Poland—forever. Poland was a graveyard filled with people who still wanted all the Jews gone.

On the way to Germany, he continued to pray. He prayed for the souls of his entire family. He prayed for understanding of why he alone—of all of his loved ones—had been the one to survive. Surely God who made the heavens and the earth would provide him with an answer.

Dyta begged him to teach her about his religion, and she absorbed his lessons like a sponge. He began to teach her how to pray—the Shema, Modeh Ani, Shehechiyanu. Prayer came to her naturally; she had been a devout Catholic. Although prayer was also intrinsic to Aron's being, he now questioned his faith. He sometimes wondered why he was still praying. He had lost his entire family—not only his immediate family, but also his extended one. The vast majority of his friends and acquaintances were gone too. But he was still alive. It must be for a reason. God was infinite; God knew why. He was praying for the answer to his existence, to his survival. Then it came to him in a flash—a message from *HaShem*—even before they reached Germany. God wanted him to marry Dyta and raise a Jewish family. By the time they reached Warteplatz, they were a couple, ready to be married in one of the many group weddings.

"Why don't you just leave me now?" she cried, interrupting his reverie, and bringing him back to the present. "Marry a nice Orthodox wife with yichus from a family of rabbis. A divorce—that's what you really want; isn't it? I renounced my religion, my family, my country. I have taught our daughters to pray the Jewish prayers. I pray with them. And it is not just lip service; I pray with my whole heart. I am kosher and have taught them to be kosher. I go to synagogue. I observe all the holidays. I have stood in the kitchen with Faye for six years. I have absorbed everything she knows about Jewish living.

What more do I need to do to be Jewish in your eyes? No matter what I do, you still think of me as a *shiksa*."

Aron knew he would never leave her. And even if he wanted to, how could he? She had saved his life—he owed her—and she was the mother of his children. He now felt ashamed. He knew that he had committed a sin. She was innocent; he had made her complicit in his scheme. He should have told her at the outset that only a rabbi could convert her. But then, in his grief and his pain and in the chaos of anti-Semitic Poland, he could not have imagined finding a rabbi who would officially transform her into a Jew. Weren't most of the rabbis dead anyway?

Who was to say what was true and what was false in the shadow of the Shoah? What did right and wrong mean in the crucible of World War II and its aftermath? What was real and what was fake? Wasn't everything relative?

He had made her a Jew as best he could. She had given birth to their two children, who were being raised as observant Jews. She had done everything he had wanted her to do—and more. And she had done it all without guile, with sincere *kavannah* and a good heart.

He cradled her in his arms as she sobbed.

"I would never leave you; you are my life," he said. "And I would die if you ever left me. I cannot live without you. You are right; we cannot keep so many secrets. When the girls ask, we will tell them about what they need to know about the Shoah, and that it was you who saved my life in a terrible time. We will tell them that you chose to become a Jew and now you are a model Jewish mother."

~

It was a rainy summer Sunday, and the girls were reenacting a scene from *Little Women* by Louisa May Alcott. Mindy had joined them since her mother and Becky had gone to Manhattan to see a Broadway matinee, *Brigadoon*. Lenore had gotten Becky a blind date, a friend of a man she occasionally dated. While Lenore carried on an intense long-term affair with Irv Rosen, she casually dated others, so as not to arouse suspicion. Bringing Becky along provided even more cover.

All three of the girls were in the process of reading *Little Women*, which chronicles the life of the fictional March sisters who lived in New England during the Civil War. The girls were busy setting up the living room of the March family's home on their bedroom floor and assigning roles of characters in the book to their dolls. Mindy had brought along her Ginny doll.

The game had been triggered by their interest in reading, which Aunt Becky had started to assiduously encourage since she came to live with them. Becky, unlike most women of her age, was a college graduate. She had a degree in English Literature from Smith College. Lenore's BA was from NYU, so the two of them quickly bonded because they both considered themselves intellectually superior to the vast majority of their peers.

"I love reading," Becky had told the twins a few days after their birthday party. "And I want you to love reading too. I want you to keep a list of every book you read this summer."

The twins readily agreed. Then she gave each of them a pink leatherette book with lined pages. On the cover was a girl with a ponytail, wearing an oversized button-down shirt with dungarees rolled up at the cuffs, bobby sox, and saddle shoes.

"Oh, I love the book. It's so pretty," said JoJo.

"Thank you, Aunt Becky," said Bronka, thinking that Aunt Becky must be the kindest, smartest, most generous person in the world. She was so thrilled to have a youthful aunt, who instinctively knew what she wanted.

"I want you to put the name of each book you read in this notebook and the date when you finish it. Look at my notebook. I've kept it for years."

They thumbed through Becky's black marble notebook; it was

the type they used in school, not like the trendy, pretty ones she had gotten for them. They saw pages and pages of lists in her practically illegible handwriting. She pointed out that she had recorded the names of the books and the dates she had read them.

"I started this when I was in high school, and I continued it even when I was in Israel. That's why some of the writing is in Hebrew. And I'm still adding to it."

When Lenore and Becky returned from the city at about seven o'clock, Faye had already given the three girls dinner.

"The show was great," said Lenore. "The music and dancing were incredible."

"Yes, it was wonderful," said Becky. "We really should take the girls to a Broadway show some time."

Faye was delighted that Becky now not only had a girlfriend, but one who was willing to set her up with a date. She knew it meant that she was probably not going to move out anytime soon, but as long as she was stable and happy, Faye would make the situation work.

"Okay, Mindy, it's time to go. Say good-bye to Bronka and JoJo, and thank Faye and Judy for giving you dinner.

"Oh, and tomorrow when I go back to work," Lenore added. "I'm going to check with personnel to see if there's a job for you at the hospital, Becky."

"That would be great, thank you, Lenore."

"Do you want something to eat?" Faye asked her daughter.

"No thanks, we had a big brunch, and then we grabbed a bite after the theater. I think I'm just going to get into bed and read."

The rest of the family gathered in the living room at eight o'clock to watch *The Ed Sullivan Show*. When it was just about over, Judy said, "Girls, it's time for bed; it's almost nine. Let's go upstairs." As Judy escorted the twins upstairs right before *The Dinah Shore Show* began, Faye decided to check on Becky.

She knocked on the door to her room and entered. Becky's face had an expressionless look, which alarmed Faye. She had seen that look before, but she'd always interpreted it as loneliness. In the past, Faye rationalized that Becky was just a high-strung, moody girl. Sometimes she chalked it up to her menstrual cycle. It was true that Becky had experienced a nervous breakdown in college, but Faye told herself that if there were really a problem, Rebecca wouldn't have been able to finish college, and get a job—or be settled on the kibbutz for years. *Didn't that make her normal?* Yet a still, small voice in her head knew better. There was something not quite right with her daughter.

"So how was your big day in the city? Did you like your blind date?"

Becky did not answer; neither did she make eye contact with Faye.

"I thought you had a nice day with Lenore; at least that's the impression I got when you both came back."

Becky still did not answer. She lay in bed and had now turned her head and body toward the wall, away from Faye.

"Don't you want to take a shower?" said Faye. "It must have been hot and sticky in the city."

"I don't remember what the weather was today," said Becky.

"Did you like the young man? Will you see him again?"

"I don't think so. He might be a secret agent. I understand they hide out in Bellerose. I'm hearing that Judy is working with the Russians. Don't be fooled by her."

"That's ridiculous. Where did you get such an idea?"

"I have connections. She's not to be trusted. Watch out for her."

"Becky, that's pure nonsense. Judy has been living here for six years, and she is the sweetest, kindest person I know. What are you talking about?

"I know what I know. I hear what I hear. I have it on good authority that she is not what she seems. She's spying on all of us."

Exasperated and exhausted from the conversation, Faye saw no point in continuing the dialogue.

"Dinah Shore is on. Do you want to come out and watch it with us?

"What day is today?" asked Becky.

"Today is Sunday, all day. You knew it was Sunday because Lenore was off work, and she got you a date for the matinee. I told you we always watch *Ed Sullivan* and *Dinah Shore* on Sunday night. You said to let you know when *Dinah Shore* was on."

"Did I say that? I don't remember."

Then Becky pulled the pillow around her head and over her ears to block out her mother's voice.

Faye walked out of the room. Dejected, she went back into the living room. How long could she continue to ignore Becky's outlandish comments and behavior? *I really don't think she's just saying these things to push my buttons. It sounds like she believes them.*

"You know Dinah's Jewish?" she heard Izzy say.

Faye sat down on the sofa and decided that she would not mention Becky's behavior to anyone. She hadn't uttered a word about Becky's suggestion that Hitler had poisoned the hamburgers at the party. Maybe her daughter was just suffering from exhaustion or stress. Perhaps if she ignored it, it would go away. Perhaps if she just gave her as much love and care as she could, she would be able to heal her.

Why annoy Izzy even more? He didn't like having Becky around anyway. He thought she was spoiled and lazy and an intellectual snob. Why alarm Judy and Aron? They might decide to move out of the house if they were fully aware of Becky's erratic conduct. Why rock the boat? The girls seemed to like Becky, and she seemed to be a good influence on them. They were reading up a storm.

If she opened her mouth now to the family, she could jinx everything. But in her heart of hearts, she knew that this had little to do with jinxing. Her intuition told her that this was only the start of trouble. Actually, if she were honest with herself, it probably wasn't really the beginning either. The trouble might have begun with

Becky's original postcard from Israel or her surprise telephone call from the airport. Or maybe it had started when Becky ran off to Israel—or perhaps even before that.

As the show ended, Dinah Shore sang:

"See the USA in your Chevrolet,

America's asking you to call.

Drive your Chevrolet through the USA.

America's the greatest land of all."

At that moment, Faye felt like getting into that Chevrolet Dinah was singing about and driving it as far away as she could. If only she knew how to drive!

~

By the time school started in September, the twins had read eleven books, including *Charlotte's Web, One Hundred and One Dalmatians*, and *Cinderella*. They also enjoyed the popular series of the day, including *Henry Huggins* and *Beezus and Ramona* by Beverly Cleary. In addition, they developed a taste for female sleuths *Nancy Drew* and *Trixie Belden*. They recorded everything they read in their pink ponytail notebooks, and when she was up to it, discussed the books with Aunt Becky. She encouraged them to try and write their own stories too. Bronka took to the task with great enthusiasm, while JoJo was more interested in practicing her singing. Lenore had gotten a job interview for Becky in the public relations department of the hospital. It was a part-time job, three days a week from one to five.

"They're looking for someone who is a good writer," Lenore had told Becky. "Your job is to draft press releases. The head of the public relations department is Helen First. She's very vivacious and dynamic and handles all the interfacing with the public. She was a PR person in the army. She needs someone to just help with the writing. That's the only job they have now; if you're interested, I can arrange an interview. But look, the hospital is growing, and it might develop into something bigger. If you think it's not up your alley, I understand."

Faye pushed her fears out of her head when Lenore mentioned the job. Becky had now been living with them since the end of June, and Faye had witnessed her daughter's cyclical bouts of depression, memory loss, and lack of concentration. She constantly overslept— often until two or three in the afternoon. And once awake, she sometimes failed to comb her hair or brush her teeth. There were days when she sat down for dinner in her nightgown. She was suspicious of the mailman, saying his uniform was meant to hide the fact that he was actually a spy. She was convinced that the cashier at Dan's Supreme was a thief, out to steal her money. Her observations were becoming more and more outrageous. The adults in the house had begun to notice. Faye suspected the girls too were also becoming aware of Becky's unusual behavior. But it came and went.

Of course, Faye knew that she had covered up the worst of it— and who knew what was to come? But maybe a part-time job was the answer. At least, she would be forced to get out of bed to be there by one o'clock. She would have a place to go and would feel productive. Maybe it would even lead to her getting her own place. Maybe the structure would be a good thing.

The day of Becky's interview, she showered, applied a bit of rouge, mascara, and lipstick, and dressed in a blue suit and high heels, which made her look professional. When she headed for the bus stop, Faye was pleased that she appeared lucid and alert.

A few hours after the scheduled interview, Helen popped into Lenore's office.

"Lenore, your friend never showed up for the interview. She didn't call to cancel either; do you know what happened?"

"Don't have a clue," Lenore said. But, of course, Lenore had more than a suspicion.

"I'm sorry," Helen said. "She sounded like quite a find—a Smith graduate, with a degree in English Lit."

"I'll find out."

But Lenore had no intention of asking. Some things were too good to be true. Helen did PR for a living; she should know that.

∽

By fifth grade, the girls no longer had bus service to school. New York City regulations permitted students who lived one mile or more from school to have transportation. But 253rd Street was nine-tenths of a mile from the school, so all the children on their street had to either walk or be driven by their parents.

Izzy had a car, which he seldom drove, and Faye did not drive at all. Since he was out of the house by six-thirty, he was generally not available to chauffeur the girls to school. Neither Aron nor Judy had learned how to drive; they had decided it was unnecessary because they could walk or use public transportation to go to the few places they needed to go.

So JoJo and Bronka either had to walk to and from school, or be driven by the neighbors. Most mornings, Irv Rosen would drive his daughters and JoJo and Bronka to school before work. When the weather permitted, they all walked home together. They generally got a ride in inclement weather.

"You know your friend Esther's father was at our house over the weekend," said Tina to the twins who were in the back seat with her and her sister.

"Yes," said Toni, who was a year younger than her sister. "He and dad were in the darkroom together."

"Girls," said Irv sternly. "I told you not to mention that to anyone. And here you are right out of the gate, yapping about it."

It had taken Jakob Zilberman the entire summer to muster the courage to contact Irv Rosen about the photo Irv had snapped at the twins' birthday party of the presumed Nazi murderer. Jakob did not want anyone to know he had come to see Irv, especially because he had not told his wife. He also knew that the Lubinskis never discussed their wartime experiences with anyone. He would not be surprised if the twins knew nothing.

"Sorry, Dad," said Tina. "We won't say another word."

"You better not say another word, or you'll be in big trouble."

The following Saturday afternoon after the twins had gone to synagogue services with their parents, they went to call for the Rosen girls.

Tori came to the door.

"We're on our way to confession. If you want, you can walk with us to Our Lady of the Blessed Angels. You can't confess because you're not Catholic, but you can wait outside while we go in, and then we'll all walk back to the house and you can play with Tina and Toni."

The girls nodded their heads in acquiescence to the plan.

"You know," said Tori to her younger sisters as the five girls began the six-block walk. "You have to confess that you disobeyed Dad by mentioning his meeting with Mr. Zilberman. It was supposed to be a secret, and you know how upset Mom was with you."

Irv had told Connie about the incident that evening when he returned from work, and she had given the girls a tongue-lashing, explaining that what they heard at home stayed at home. Tori had overheard the yelling and had thought the punishment of not watching TV for one day was too lenient.

"Yeah, I guess so," said Tina. "But I don't know why Dad got so angry or why it's such a big secret that he took a picture of a murderer. He takes pictures of criminals all the time. And he doesn't hide them from us."

"I think it's because it had something to do with Hitler and the Nazis," said Toni.

"Who's Hitler? Who are the Nazis?" Bronka wanted to know.

"They were in power in Germany during the war and they tried to take over Europe and kill all the Jews," Tori explained.

"Why?" asked JoJo.

"Because he was a madman, and he hated the Jews."

"The Zilbermans were in a concentration camp," said Tori with the superiority of a knowledgeable seventh grader. "Don't you know about this? How do you not know about this? Aren't your parents refugees from Europe?"

"Sure," said JoJo. "Can't you tell my father wasn't born in America? That's why he has such a funny accent and doesn't know how to dress. I've told him a million times that checks and stripes don't go together, but he doesn't listen."

Tina and Toni laughed, but Bronka didn't like her father being the butt of jokes.

"Dressing has nothing to do with it," said Tori, the older fashion maven. "Your mother dresses like a normal person."

"The Zilbermans have tattoos on their arms," said Toni. "Do your parents have tattoos?"

"We've never seen any," said JoJo.

The girls reached the church, and the Rosen sisters went inside, leaving JoJo and Bronka sitting on the brick steps in front of the door with the crucifix.

"Why do you think Mama and Papa never mentioned Hitler or the Nazis to us?" Bronka asked JoJo.

"I don't know," said JoJo. "I think either they didn't want us to know about it or it's not true."

"Why would the sisters make up a story like that?" Bronka asked. "The things they tell us are usually true. And Tori talked about it too. Their father is in the news business, and they find out a lot of stuff from him."

"Well Santa Claus isn't true, and hell isn't true," JoJo said.

"Santa Claus and hell are true for Catholics, but not for us," Bronka said, parroting her mother. But as the words came out of her mouth, she felt confused. How could there be different truths for different people? Wasn't there just one truth?

"That doesn't make sense," said JoJo. "Should we ask Mama or Papa about Hitler and the Nazis?"

"I don't know," said Bronka. "I don't know why, but I have a feeling like maybe we shouldn't. I'm almost positive they don't have tattoos. But let's check their arms again and then ask Esther Zilberman what she knows."

Ten minutes later, the three Rosen sisters rejoined them outside the church after completing their confessions.

Bronka was curious about confession. She was thinking that her friends would not purposely lie because then they would have to confess their lies.

"What happens at confession?" she asked.

"Well first, the priest welcomes you. Then you make the sign of the cross, like this," Toni said as she crossed herself. "Then you have to say, "Forgive me, Father, for I have sinned. And tell him when your last confession was."

"Who's Father?"

"Father is the priest," said Tina, "like my uncle, Father Tony, not like a regular father. Then you list all your sins, like if you missed Mass twice or if you lied, or if you disobeyed your parents."

"So Toni and I had to confess for disobeying our father because we told about his meeting with Esther's father."

"So, what happened after you confessed?"

"I had to say three Hail Marys."

Now Bronka wasn't sure. That seemed to be an easy fix for lying. You could just confess, say some prayers, and it was off your conscience. She really didn't want to think her friends were lying. She would check with Esther about Hitler and the Nazis.

Izzy joked to Aron that every year people would say that the High Holidays were either early or late—they were never on time. In 1957, they were late. The first two days of Rosh Hashanah occurred on September 26 and 27, and Yom Kippur did not take place until October 5.

For Aron, who attended shul just about every day of his life, the holidays were especially poignant, particularly Yom Kippur. The holy day evoked powerful memories. Aron dressed in white, as did the clergy, because he had important responsibilities during the service. It was his job to blow the *shofar* during Rosh Hashanah services and at the end of the final Yom Kippur service. White signified purity as those assembled came before God to petition for forgiveness. The words and the cadence of the prayers, which Cantor Yudenfreund intoned, transported him back to Kielce before the war. Before Hitler destroyed what had been Poland's living, breathing, vibrant Jewish community of three million people.

Perhaps that was why his comfort level was so great within the walls of the synagogue. If he closed his eyes, he was suspended in a timeless cocoon that could be anywhere. He could be in Queens, or he could be in Kielce. It barely made any difference to Aron that services were being held for the first time in a newly renovated sanctuary that accommodated three hundred worshippers. Wooden pews with cushioned seats had been permanently installed to replace the folding chairs. Sunlight crept through stained glass windows, each one depicting a scene from the Ten Commandments. The permanent ark, which contained the Torahs, was covered in a brand-new embroidered curtain of white and gold. The red eternal light hung over the ark, impossible to miss. Other congregants applauded the renovations, but what touched Aron's heart was the liturgy. And the gold words, carved in Hebrew letters above the ark, which translated into English, read: *Know Before Whom You Stand.*

He was deeply stirred by the identical prayers and the familiar

melodies. As he and his fellow congregants recited the group confessional aloud, he beat his chest as his father and grandfather had
done. But it was only during the Yizkor service that he broke down,
sobbing. He wept for all his family and friends who had been slaugh-
tered by the Nazis.

While High Holy Day services were open only to dues-paying
members of the congregation, the synagogue welcomed the entire
community for the Yizkor service. To accommodate the influx,
congregants who did not have family members to memorialize, left
the sanctuary. Most of them gathered on the sidewalk outside the
building. Children were also asked to leave and to attend junior
congregation.

At junior congregation in the basement, Bronka and JoJo found
seats with Mindy Mandelstern, who was reserving half a row. Soon
Esther Zilberman and Shira Yudenfreund joined them.

"Oh, I love your shoes, Mindy," said JoJo. "I wish I had a pair of
flats like that. They match your dress perfectly."

Indeed, Mindy's red patent leather ballet flats complemented her
red-and-white polka dot dress and red belt.

"And look, I got my ears pierced," Mindy said, as she showed JoJo
her newest acquisition—small gold hoop earrings.

"Are those real gold?" JoJo asked.

"Yes, my mother said she would only let me wear real gold in my
ears."

Sharona Herbert, the rabbi's eldest daughter, was distributing the
prayer books and asking everyone to settle down. She said that *Moreh*
Steinberg, one of the Hebrew School teachers, was about to start the
service.

While the other girls continued whispering, Bronka started
thumbing through the prayer book.

"She thinks she's hot stuff," Randy Lesser, the feared bully, said
in a stage whisper, "just because she's the rabbi's daughter. She's just

a creepy girl. My father could buy and sell her father and still have a bundle of cash left over."

He was seated in the row behind the girls with a group of his friends, including Robert Moskowitz, the other boy who had terrorized the twins on their way to Hebrew School.

Bronka turned her head and saw that Randy had grown over the summer; it made his appearance all the more menacing. He curled his lip and snarled at her.

She did not know what gave her the courage to speak. Perhaps it was because her friends surrounded her, or maybe because it was Yom Kippur and she was in God's sanctuary, but Bronka looked him straight in the eye and said, "Randy, you were told to be quiet because the service is about to start. We are about to pray for forgiveness."

"Who are you telling what to do—you little creep? Why don't you tell your father to buy a new suit and to learn English?" He pronounced learn the way her father did, "loin."

Bronka girded herself and summoned all of her strength to refrain from answering him. It was the Day of Atonement, and she did not want to commit a new sin.

However, Shira Yudenfreund turned around and said, "Knock it off, Randy; you're a big bully."

The girls giggled and opened their prayer books as Moreh Steinberg began the service. The Hebrew teacher was a very young man—about twenty-one—and he couldn't control the persistent whispering.

And Randy wasn't finished.

"I can't wait to get out of this crummy neighborhood," said Randy to Robert, but he said it loud enough so the girls could hear. "Too many low-class people here. We're like the richest people in Bellerose now. Well actually, we were pretty rich before, but now that my father won the quiz show money, we're going to get out of this shithole. After my bar mitzvah, we're moving to Roslyn, where the girls are prettier and the people are classier."

None of the girls said anything, but they were all happy to hear that Randy would be leaving town. JoJo was insulted that he didn't think she was pretty enough. Bronka was horrified that he had cursed in the synagogue on Yom Kippur. She decided that it would be all right to add his speedy removal from the neighborhood to her prayers.

~

The public confessional mesmerized Bronka. She had been intrigued with the idea of confessing ever since the Rosen sisters had explained the Catholic ritual to her. She thought about her friends going into the booth with the priest and individually confessing their sins to him. Here, it was done aloud—only once a year on Yom Kippur— with everyone together. Tina and Toni Rosen said they had confessed their one sin to the priest. But here—in black and white—there were forty-four sins listed in the prayer book for which everyone in the congregation must atone.

She doubted that she had committed all—or even most—of the forty-four sins. Her Hebrew School teacher, *Morah* Cohen, had said the whole congregation had to say the prayer together because everyone must take responsibility for the community's sins. Bronka wanted to stay on this page forever; she was so fascinated by the listing of the sins.

As she read, she evaluated.

"For the sin we committed before Thee by hardening our hearts."

No, she did not believe she had a hard heart. In fact, she knew she had a soft heart. People told her she was kind and caring. She worried about others constantly, especially Papa and Aunt Becky.

"For the sin we committed before Thee by disrespecting parents and teachers."

No, she had tried her best to respect her parents and teachers. She behaved in class and followed instructions. She always tried to do exactly what Mama and Papa told her to do. Well, honestly, she did cover up for JoJo when necessary. Did that count? She decided it was better not to be a tattletale, especially since both girls trusted that what they confided in each other was never shared with anyone else.

"For the sin we committed before Thee with vulgar speech."

No, that one must have been especially put there for Randy Lesser, a boy who would curse on Yom Kippur in the synagogue.

"For the sin we committed before Thee by running to do evil."

That was another sin tailor made for Randy Lesser, the bully.

"For the sin we committed before Thee through idle gossip."

Yes, she had to admit that was the one that really hit a chord. She pleaded guilty. She loved gossiping—or "yenta-ing," as Faye called it. She yearned to find out what was going on behind every door of every house on the block. She wanted to know what the lives of her classmates were like. And she truly enjoyed eavesdropping on Faye and Izzy, both of whom seemed to be oblivious to her listening to their *lashon hara*. On the other hand, her parents did a great job of not committing this sin, as far as she knew. She never heard them say one bad word about anyone. Not even Hitler. She would have to remember to ask Esther about him.

"For the sin we committed before Thee in eating and drinking."

No. She had tried to be kosher inside and outside of the house, unlike JoJo. Her twin ate all kinds of *treif* when Mama and Papa weren't with them. But Bronka never snitched on her sister, even if it meant concealing a sin.

"For the sin we committed before Thee through jealousy."

Yes, definitely. Jealousy was a big one—for her and for her sister. They had both sinned by being jealous. It was obvious that JoJo was envious of everyone who had nice things, and she wanted them for herself. Even on Yom Kippur, hadn't her twin just eyed and envied Mindy's earrings and Mindy's shoes? From the time she was very little, JoJo was desirous of Mindy's toys, and all the beautiful presents under the Rosens' Christmas tree. And her sister preferred to be friends with the popular, pretty girls in her class who had all the nice things. She enjoyed going to their homes and seeing their pretty rooms and the clothes and jewelry that she and Bronka didn't have. She liked that their parents spoke without foreign accents, wore beautiful clothes, and drove fancy cars. That's why JoJo wanted to be a rich and famous singer, so she could be a real American with lots of material possessions.

But if she were honest with herself, Bronka knew that she too had committed the sin of jealousy many times—she was just not as obvious as her sister.

Although she never expressed it, Bronka was envious of her seemingly carefree, self-assured, and accomplished twin. She had enjoyed the spotlight they'd shared as young children—adorable little girls with curls and matching outfits. But now they barely even looked like sisters, with very distinguishable facial features. In addition, she towered over JoJo, and her petite twin was constantly showing off her singing and acting talent.

Bronka was jealous because JoJo was the star of the lunchroom, the block, and every school play. She was envious that her twin sister could make friends so easily and did not have the fears and anxieties she had. JoJo had the ability to just let things roll off her back. Bronka hated herself for being jealous of her sister. She sometimes thought that if it were not for JoJo, she would never have been able to leave the house. Her sister gave her cover and courage, enhanced her, and made her complete. She could not imagine life without her sister, but she was still jealous of her. She envied in her sister all of the attributes she desperately wanted—self-confidence, fearlessness, friendliness, and focus.

But she was ten years old, and people tended to see her as a shy, sweet, compliant girl. How was she going to heal the world if she was afraid to volunteer in class? She had received an "N" for "Needs

Improvement" in class participation on her report card. She wanted so much to raise her hand when the teacher asked for volunteers. She knew she had something to say, and she wanted to contribute. But she was simply terrified to do it.

She would not only atone, she told herself, but she would try hard not to commit these sins again in the New Year. Bronka prayed with all her heart:

"For all of these, God of forgiveness, forgive us, pardon us, grant us atonement."

∼

When Yizkor let out, those who were not synagogue members left the sanctuary. So did many of the regular congregants. It was going to be a long day of praying and fasting that would not end until nightfall. Some left because they were going home to take a nap, and others just wanted a breath of fresh air. In addition, there were an unknown number of men and boys who wanted to hurry home to stealthily catch the beginning of the World Series on radio or TV. It was the third game between the New York Yankees and the Milwaukee Braves, played at County Stadium in Milwaukee, Wisconsin.

Junior congregation had been timed to let out a half hour after Yizkor was over so the children could reunite with their parents.

There was a huge crowd milling around the sidewalks in front of and on either side of the synagogue. Young mothers pushing baby carriages, men carrying prayer shawls, and women sporting a variety of hats greeted one another and stood chatting. The Jewish community was out in force, and this gratified Jakob Zilberman. Hitler had failed.

As he left the building, he was shocked to see Irv Rosen on the street. He had understood that Irv had become a Catholic; what was he doing in front of the shul on Yom Kippur? They had not been in touch since their meeting in Irv's darkroom a month before. Jakob had concluded that if the photographer had something to tell him, he would call. Jakob was ambivalent about pursuing the Nazi guard, especially because Eva was so opposed to dredging up the unspeakable past.

He saw that Irv was engaged in conversation with a very large man. Compared to diminutive Jakob, Irv's companion was tall and beefy. He appeared to be uncomfortable in his suit, like a teenager who was forced to wear one for a special occasion. And the top button of his shirt was open, making his tie not lie quite straight. What he lacked in grooming, he made up for with energy. He could not stay in one spot, and he spoke as much with his hands as his mouth, gesturing constantly.

Jakob was curious. He especially wanted to know what Irv Rosen was doing here. And the timing was perfect for him to find out. He had left his wife engaged in an animated conversation with some women at the door of the sanctuary. He'd told her he would meet her outside in about a half hour when Esther was finished.

"I guess you're wondering what I'm doing here," Irv said as Jakob approached.

"I would never be so rude as to ask," replied Jakob. "It's none of my business."

"Even though I go to mass with Connie and the kids, I feel I want to honor my father's memory by going to Yizkor on Yom Kippur," Irv explained. "He lived and died as a Jew, and I'm his only son. There is no one else to say Kaddish for him. I feel I have an obligation to do it."

Jakob couldn't think of a thing to say in response. He was too busy wondering—was the man he was speaking with Catholic, or was he Jewish, or was he both? He extended his hand and introduced himself to the stranger.

"Hi, I'm Jakob Zilberman."

"Nice to meet you. I'm Morris Solomon. People call me Moe."

"Actually, we were just talking about you," said Irv. "What a coincidence that you should show up just at this moment."

"Talking about me?" Jakob said incredulously.

He couldn't imagine what Irv could tell this huge, unkempt, threatening character that would be of any interest to him. He felt like a Lilliputian next to him. The big guy could probably stomp him out like an ant if he tried.

"Moe is being modest. He is Detective Sergeant Morris Solomon of the Third Precinct in Queens," said Irv.

"I didn't know there were Jewish policemen," said Jakob.

"There are actually quite a few nowadays," said Moe.

"Anyway, I just filled him in on the Nazi you recognized at the Fourth of July party, and he has a few questions for you."

"Go ahead," said Jakob.

"First, do you know his name?"

"Rudolf Schmidt."

"And what did he do at Auschwitz?"

"He stood at the entrance of the gas chamber with a whip. I think he was in charge of all the other guards who herded the men, women, and children to their deaths. When people cried and asked where they were going, he lied and said they were going to take a shower. He explained that the showers would rid them of lice. He lied."

"Do you think it would have been better if he'd told the truth? Wouldn't that have increased the panic?"

Jakob shrugged. "He stood there day after day, lying, telling people they were going to come out on the other end—free of lice."

"And what did you do there that you saw him every day?"

"I was part of a group of young Jewish prisoners who were forced to dispose of the bodies after they were gassed."

"Hmm," said Moe, thinking. "Unless he's here illegally, there's not much we can do. The NYPD has no jurisdiction over residency anyway. The sad truth is that America wants to move on. The US is busy courting West Germany because we need it as an ally against the Soviets. Communism is considered the big threat now. I have heard that there are actually former Nazis here who are helping the US government track down Russian spies. And even former Nazi scientists who are working on nuclear defense and rocket development for the space program."

"*Oy vey iz mir,*" groaned Jakob.

"I'm sorry to tell you that there's currently no taste for revenge on the Nazi bastards—here or anywhere else in the Western world. The dirty little secret is that hardly anyone has been punished for the greatest crime in history. Sure, the big brass were tried at Nuremburg. But can you believe that only twenty-four individuals were convicted and punished for their heinous crimes against humanity? It's kind of ridiculous to say that only twenty-four people killed six million Jews."

"So I guess I should just forget I ever saw him?"

"No, not necessarily," said Moe. "Remember that I have the power of the NYPD behind me, not to mention my own considerable strength."

He winked.

"What can you do if there's no mechanism for justice?" Irv asked.

"Well, I would like to get my hands on that vile anti-Semitic son-of-a-bitch, though not literally, of course. I want to keep my job. But let's say that Detective Sergeant Moe Solomon goes to Brodsky's and pays a visit to our Nazi murderer. I could turn the siren on in the police car and park in front of the shop; that would set off an alarm. Dressed in my police uniform with my gun in plain sight, I could just ask him a few questions and see how he reacts. I can't guarantee if I'll find anything for which to bring him into the precinct for questioning, but we'll see. I bet Sid Brodsky won't be too happy to find out that his deli man is a Nazi."

"I could come and take a picture of the encounter," offered Irv.

"Would you do anything with the photo?" asked Jakob.

"It all depends on what he says," said Irv.

Moe added, "It's your call, Jakob. Do you want revenge or not?"

Jakob wrinkled his brow. He would have to think about this. Did he want to open this can of worms? Eva would be hysterical. And what would he gain if the Nazi was not going to face punishment?

1958

---◄○►---

BELLEROSE, NEW YORK

THREE MONTHS LATER, THE LUBINSKI family ushered in the secular New Year by gathering around the TV to watch the ball drop in Times Square. Bronka and JoJo were delighted to stay up until midnight and to participate in the festivities. Izzy poured them each a glass of cherry soda to accompany the potato chips and onion dip they were devouring. Faye had also put out M&Ms to munch on, and later that was topped off with a "Happy 1958" cake from the bakery. "Sweets for a sweet New Year," Faye had declared. Before the ball dropped, the girls watched grown-ups in tuxedos and gowns with funny hats dancing to the strains of Guy Lombardo and the Royal Canadians.

On a piece of paper, Bronka kept writing December 31, 1957; she knew this would be her last opportunity to write this date in real time. The girls were so happy to be part of this adult party. It was way past their bedtime, and chips and soda and candy were doled out only on special occasions.

As much as Faye had tried to create a memorable party experience, there were two party poopers in the crowd.

"This debauchery is disgusting," said Aron in Yiddish. "Look at these people drinking and making fools of themselves."

"They're just unwinding, having a little fun," said Izzy.

"I bet it's a pretty penny to go and celebrate with Guy Lombardo at the Waldorf Astoria Hotel," said Aron.

"Sure, it's probably a small fortune," said Izzy.

"I'm glad we decided not to go to the Rosens' New Year's Eve party," said Aron. "There wouldn't have been anything for us to eat."

"It might have been fun," said Judy wistfully. "I'm sure we could have found something to eat. But you never want to go anywhere."

"Who sends out an invitation and asks for ten dollars a couple?" Faye piped in. "I never heard of such a thing."

"I guess that was to cover the cost of the liquor," Izzy said. "I'm sure Mrs. Mariani made all the food, but liquor is expensive."

"But we don't drink, so why pay for everyone else's drinking?" Aron asked. "Anyway, I believe the Jewish way of ushering in the New Year is the proper way—with prayer and reflection."

"Oh, Papa," said JoJo, "you just don't know how to have fun. This is the United States. Everyone celebrates New Year's Eve. The Rosens are having their own party. And Mindy's mother went to a party too."

"Oh, Papa would never spend money on such frivolity," Judy said.

"Aron doesn't like to spend money on anything," Faye said with a chuckle, but everyone knew she wasn't joking.

As Guy Lombardo led the Royal Canadians in "Auld Lang Syne," the ball dropped with 1958 emblazoned in shining lights. Everyone kissed and shouted, "Happy New Year."

Suddenly, there was a blast of icy cold air that caught everyone by surprise. It didn't take long to realize that it had come from the dinette, where Becky was sitting all alone with her elbows on the table, her head cradled in her hands.

"What's going on, Becky?" Izzy shouted. "It's freezing outside; why did you open the window?"

As she sat there motionless and expressionless, Faye's happy party face turned into a scowl.

"Girls, time to go to bed; let's get upstairs now."

"First, I have to wish Aunt Becky a Happy New Year," said Bronka.

Bronka put her arms around Becky's back, snuggling her face into the softness of the inert woman's flannel nightgown. She gave her a long hug, but Becky remained unmoving.

"Come on Bronka, upstairs now," said Aron.

Her eyes filled with tears; it was hard to let go. But she was an obedient child, so she followed her parents and sister upstairs.

Faye's New Year's resolution had been to decide what to do about Becky. Bronka also contemplated what she could do to make Aunt Becky feel better. JoJo decided that she would ask her mother if they could move to a different house. She couldn't continue to bring her friends home with Becky's bizarre and unpredictable behavior.

∽

Back in Hebrew School after the winter break, Morah Cohen made an announcement:

"Does anyone know why 1958 is a special year?"

"Because it's when we get our bar mitzvah dates," called out Michael Abramowitz.

"Well, that is correct, *Mikhayel*," said the teacher in her high-pitched Hungarian accent. "You boys will get your dates two years before your bar mitzvah. But that's not the answer I was looking for. Can anyone tell me what else is going to happen this year?"

Not a hand was raised.

"Okay, I'm going to give you a clue. Look at the map on the wall. You are all going to turn eleven this year, and what country is going to celebrate its tenth birthday?"

"Israel," Shira Yudenfreund called out.

"Good, Shira. The State of Israel was founded the year after you were born. Didn't anyone else know that?"

Again, silence.

"So look at the map, yeladim. You can see what a tiny, narrow country Israel is, and it is surrounded by hostile neighbors. Egypt, Jordan, and Syria all want to drive Israel into the sea.

"You know after the war when I left Europe, I lived in Israel for a few years, and I served in the army. Israelis have a hard life, but they are very proud and strong. Do you know that both girls and boys join the army when they graduate from high school? They serve willingly because they are determined to make sure that Israel survives.

"It has survived for ten years, and so on May 14, we are going to have a big celebration in honor of Israel's birthday. In the meantime, I'm going to give you each a blue box to take home—a *pushka*. Put coins in it—whenever you want—but especially before your mothers light candles on Friday night. It is a mitzvah to give *tzedakah*. Then, we will collect all of the coins and with our money, trees will be planted in *Eretz Yisrael* in honor of our class."

Bronka pictured a row of trees with a sign on each one saying The Bet Class of Northeast Queens Jewish Center. She noticed that there was a Star of David and the same skinny map of Israel on the blue tin boxes. It said: JNF and below that, *Keren Kayemet L'Yisrael*, in Hebrew and in English.

"JNF and Keren Kayemet stand for Jewish National Fund," said Mrs. Cohen. "Any questions?"

"Why do girls serve in the army but can't have a bar mitzvah?" asked Shira.

"First of all, we say 'bas,' not 'bar.' The country is Orthodox, and only boys have a ceremony on their thirteenth birthday. Girls don't have it in our synagogue either. But that's an issue for the rabbis, not one we should be discussing here."

Eager to move on, the teacher asked, "Any other questions about the State of Israel and its tenth birthday?"

"Why did you go to Israel after the war?" David Gladstein asked.

"That was one of the places Hitler's refugees were being sent. Not many Jews stayed in Europe, and I wanted to help build the Jewish State."

"Why didn't you stay there?" another boy asked.

"I met an American who had come to Israel to serve in the War of Independence. He wanted to get married and go back home. So I left. It's not like I had any family in Israel. They were all dead. He had family here. Okay, enough of the personal questions, anything else?"

Bronka was too shy to raise her hand, but she knew that if you asked Mrs. Cohen a question, she would answer truthfully. She loved that about her.

She whispered to JoJo, "Ask her about Hitler; she mentioned him."

JoJo's hand shot up.

"Hannah Yosefa, do you have a question?"

"Yes," said JoJo. "Who was Hitler?"

"Hitler was an evil dictator who was head of Germany and wanted to take over the world. He did conquer much of Europe before he was finally defeated. He believed Jews were inferior, and he tried to get rid of all of us, first by making laws that discriminated against us, and later by starving, torturing, and killing. This was called The Final Solution."

The students began to shout out questions, while a number of the boys hooted out epithets and made crude gestures with their fingers.

"Yeladim, yeladim, *sheket b'vakasha*."

Just then, Mr. Levinson, the Hebrew School principal walked into the room.

"What is going on in here? Let's pipe down."

With the appearance of the principal, the children stopped yelling.

"Mrs. Cohen, please see me when class is over."

When Hebrew School ended an hour later, as the children left the classroom, Bronka and JoJo made a beeline for Esther Zilberman. They walked up the stairs together from the basement classroom and when they were out of the building, JoJo said, "We need to have a private conversation with you, Esther."

"Okay," said Esther. The girls huddled under a tree.

"Do you know what Mrs. Cohen was talking about?"

"A little," she said. "I've heard my father talking about it, and it's true that Hitler wanted to kill the Jews. It was called The Final Solution. He put them in concentration camps."

"What's a concentration camp?"

"It was a terrible place where they starved people and worked them to death and killed them by putting them in gas chambers. My mother has nightmares and cries out at night," said Esther.

"So does Papa," said Bronka, the right side of her forehead pounding with a throbbing pain, as she remembered her father's screams.

"I feel nauseous," said Bronka, as her mouth filled with saliva and she felt a strong urge to vomit. She remembered the expression on Papa's face when Mindy talked about the takeaway men. She thought about his screams in the middle of the night and how he had shooed her away, because only Mama understood and could comfort him.

"Okay, let's go," said JoJo. "Just one more thing—were your parents in a concentration camp?"

"Yes," said Esther. "They have tattoos on their arms to prove it. And I don't have any grandparents because the Nazis killed them there."

"I really need to go home," said Bronka. "I don't feel well." She began to cough.

"I think we better go, Esther," said JoJo. "How do we find out more about Hitler?"

"I'm reading *The Diary of Anne Frank*. I'll lend it to you when I'm finished."

"Thanks, Esther. See you tomorrow."

As the twins started walking in the direction of home, Bronka stopped at one of the large maple trees that lined the sidewalk. She could feel it coming; she was going to throw up. She started gagging and then vomited. She put her hands on the tree trunk and tears came to her eyes. She didn't know if they were for Papa and the concentration camps and gas chambers, or for the embarrassment and humiliation of throwing up right on Union Turnpike.

~

Mrs. Cohen stuck her head into Mr. Levinson's office once all of the students were gone.

"You wanted to see me?"

"Yes, come back tomorrow at 2:45 before class starts. We have to discuss your classroom management skills."

By the time of their meeting the next afternoon, Mr. Levinson had a bigger issue than discipline to discuss with Mrs. Cohen. He had been fielding phone calls and visits from parents for much of the day.

"Have a seat, Mrs. Cohen," said Mr. Levinson as he pointed to a chair opposite his desk. He looked stern and displeased.

"I wasn't aware, Mrs. Cohen," he said in a sarcastic tone, "that Hitler and his virulent anti-Semitism, which resulted in starvation, torture, and the killing of six million of our people, was in our curriculum for our Bet class. The children are ten-year-olds. In fact, to my knowledge, it's not even taught to our bar mitzvah students."

"Don't you think it should be? There would have been no State of Israel without the Nazi horror."

"That is your opinion, Mrs. Cohen. But in any case, it was not your place to tell these impressionable children about it. They are much too young. They don't even teach it in the high schools. I'm not even sure about college. Why, some of the parents of our students are victims themselves. Don't you think it's the decision of the parents to tell their child at a time and place of their choosing? And if they choose not to, if they want to try to pick up their lives and never mention it, isn't that their right."

"I am a survivor myself," said the teacher. "You can't live your life fully and honestly by never dealing with it."

"Well, I am truly sorry that you suffered. But the fact that you want to talk about it does not make you judge and jury on this issue. You will find it nowhere in our curriculum. It is a very sensitive topic. Our enrollment has been increasing, and we don't want parents to take their children out of Hebrew School en masse because we are usurping their prerogative. They don't like your remarks, and they also don't like the utter lack of discipline and decorum in your classroom. And neither do I. I could not believe what I saw and heard— cursing and obscene gestures. Is that par for the course?"

Mrs. Cohen knew that every teacher in the Hebrew School had a discipline problem. The children were tired after sitting a whole day in public school—and many were bored. At least, she tried to make it interesting for them. She actually wanted to say, if anyone deserved to be cursed at, it was the Nazi dictator. But she decided not to go there.

"No sir, they became agitated when I mentioned Hitler and The Final Solution."

"As indeed most people still do. It's not even been fifteen years. It was a traumatic event for our people, and everyone reacts differently, so it's best not to bring it up."

Although she had a feisty personality and was stubborn and tough, Deborah Cohen began to cry. She had survived the Shoah, immigrated to Israel, and then learned yet another language and adapted to life in the States. She was not going to let this wretched man push her around. *What did he know? When had he ever put his life on the line? What had he done to help? He seemed too old to even have been a World War II veteran.*

She had what he wanted, and she knew it. It was not easy to find a fluent Hebrew speaker in Northeast Queens, let alone one who was conversant with Jewish history and tradition. She would not let him get away with this tongue-lashing, which was assaulting her soul and dredging up her worst memories.

"I lost my whole family, and *you* are lecturing *me* about the proper way to handle such a massive and immeasurable loss?"

"I'm truly sorry, but you can't inflict your losses on your students and their families."

"I look at it that I am teaching them history—the history of the Jewish people—both the good and the bad. I am a living part of that history. Unlike the six million, I was fortunate enough to survive. The students are a link in that history, and they should know it."

"Mrs. Cohen, you are being insubordinate. If you want to work here, you have to follow the curriculum and the rules. I am going to put you on probation, and it's highly likely that I may not ask you to return next fall."

She had known when she started this interaction with Mr. Levinson that she might have to make the ultimate move. She was now prepared to do it and suffer the consequences. It never ceased to amaze her that once you were paid for a job, you were open to the worst criticism. And most people just endured it, but she would not. She was a survivor, and the principal had hit below the belt.

"Mr. Levinson, with all due respect, you are assuming that I still want to work here. Why would I want to continue to teach in a place that hides the truth and then punishes someone for telling it?"

"So, you are going to leave at the end of the school year?"

"No, I am going to leave right now."

And that's how the fifth graders got a new Hebrew School teacher in the middle of the year. But the departure of Mrs. Cohen did not solve Mr. Levinson's problem. She had let the cat out of the bag. Mrs. Cohen had spoken the truth. And it was left to the principal, teachers, and parents to pick up the pieces.

～

When the twins returned from Hebrew School, both Judy and Faye were alarmed at Bronka's appearance. She was crying, her face was white, and remnants of orange-and-white vomit clung to her blue dress. Judy gagged as the girls walked in the door.

"Bronka said she didn't feel well, and then she got sick when we were about a block away from Hebrew School," JoJo reported. "She grabbed onto a tree and threw up."

"Are you sick, sweetheart?"

"I don't know. I suddenly felt very nauseous and then I just couldn't help it and threw up on the way home from Hebrew School.

"None of the other kids saw it," added Bronka, relaying her main concern.

"Well, let's get that dress off you," said Faye. "Give it to me and I'll wash it."

"And I'm going to take your temperature," said Judy.

Once she ascertained that Bronka's temperature was normal, Judy drew a bath for her. She never ceased to marvel at how very different her two daughters were. It was good they had each other.

The twins had agreed to keep the classroom discussion and the follow up with Esther just between them—for the time being. Neither of them had enough nerve to broach the subject with their parents.

Bronka had sensed from the time she was three and a half years old that there was some tragic mystery surrounding her father. As she grew older, the feeling became more pronounced. She felt it when she looked into his gloomy and faraway eyes, when he yelled at her or JoJo erratically, and when she heard him screaming in the middle of the night. She had first noticed the look the day Mindy told them about the takeaway men, and it never went away.

She began to feel unworthy and unloved because he rarely smiled or expressed affection, as she saw other fathers do. She sensed his smoldering anger when Faye said something that displeased him. And he often yelled at her mother for trivial matters. She was not eager to cause another explosion, just to satisfy her curiosity. She wanted affection from him, and he just didn't know how to give it. She wanted him to take her in his arms and tell her he loved her. It didn't seem to her ten-year-old mind that asking him about a forbidden topic was going to win that affection.

JoJo didn't want to rile her father either. She was well aware that her mother tiptoed around him, catering to his every need. Often she felt that it was at the expense of her and Bronka. She especially bristled when he snapped at her mother for what appeared to her to be no reason at all. And now, with Aunt Becky's increasingly bizarre behavior, the adults trod lightly around her too. It was becoming a stifling atmosphere, one where she did not feel free to express herself. She spent more and more time at her friends' homes, not wanting to expose them to either Becky or her father.

On the other hand, she did not take her father's behavior to heart in the same way her twin sister did. And as she grew older, she simply found him more and more annoying. She was embarrassed by the way he spoke and dressed. She hated his stinginess. Every time she asked for something that all her other friends had, his first response was no. And it did not escape her that her mother rarely bought anything for herself.

He was not generous, either with material things or with emotion. He could be animated and friendly at work or at shul, but at home, he brooded most of the time. He was only generous when it came to giving away bread and rolls to the neighbors at the end of the day. But JoJo knew that he couldn't sell day-old bread. He never went anywhere other than the synagogue or the bakery, and he never took the sisters to the movies or a museum or the beach like her friends' fathers did. She tried to steer clear of his outbursts. She didn't want to get caught in the crossfire of the consequences of his anger. She had somehow figured out a way of doing what she wanted to do when she wanted to do it, and she liked it that way.

~

When Esther Zilberman came home from school and told her parents about Mrs. Cohen's comments, they were of two reactions.

"It's about time the truth has come out," said Jakob.

But Eva was distraught. Did that mean she would now have to discuss Mengele's experiments with her ten-year-old daughter? *No way,* she thought. That was not going to happen if she had anything to do with it. Of course, Esther, unlike the Lubinski twins, was already somewhat inoculated. She had heard the basics already, so she was not particularly shocked about what her Hebrew School teacher had told the class.

"Bronka and JoJo asked me if what the teacher said was true," said Esther to her parents, "and I told them it was."

"That's okay, dear," said Jakob.

"And I told them about the concentration camps and offered to lend them my copy of *The Diary of Anne Frank* when I'm finished with it."

Eva said nothing in response to her daughter's report of her interaction with the twins. What was done was done. But she decided she should alert Judy Lubinski about the conversation the twins had had with Esther regarding Mrs. Cohen's remarks. *It was the right thing to do; what if the girls didn't mention it? Their mother needed to know what was going on.*

Actually, she had an additional agenda. Although she had reciprocated by inviting the family to their home once after the birthday party, she really wanted to nurture a relationship with Judy. She seemed like a genuine, hard-working person.

Eva often felt she had nothing in common with her neighbors. The vast majority had been born in America and had very different backgrounds and experiences than hers. They might have lived through the Depression, but that was very different than coming of age in

Nazi-occupied Poland. Many claimed they had not even known what Hitler was doing to the Jews. She found that difficult to believe, but she wasn't sure.

She did not like the way the women—most of whom were housewives and did not work outside the home—spent their days. Once their children were in school, all they did was shop, play Mah-jongg, go to the beauty parlor, and gossip with one another. They showed off their new cars, fur coats, and jewelry. Every year, a few of the neighbors would pack their things and move to the greener, more spacious and affluent suburbs—Manhasset Hills, Roslyn, or Jericho.

Judy was different than the rest of them, Eva thought. *She was certainly not living a frivolous life and did not seem to be materialistic. She was a fellow Pole, although she did not speak Yiddish, but her daughters comprised half of the girls in Esther's Hebrew School class.* Her daughters were lovely, and Eva was happy they were Esther's friends.

She decided that instead of calling and risking that Faye or someone else might answer the phone, she would pay Judy a visit in the bakery. Judy had mentioned to her that she usually got to the bakery at about ten o'clock, so Eva decided to stop by the next morning.

As usual, Judy was behind the counter when Eva walked in.

"Hi, Judy," said Eva with a smile.

"What can I do for you today?"

"I'd like two onion rolls, two plain, a prune Danish, and a cheese Danish."

"And how are you today, Eva?" Judy asked as she put the items in a white bakery bag.

"I'm okay," said Eva. "Where's Aron?"

"He's in the back. Do you want me to get him?"

"Oh no, I just want to talk with you about something important—woman to woman. Can you meet me later—just the two of us?"

"I guess so," said Judy, with a look of alarm on her face. "But you're making me nervous. Is something wrong? You have to give me a clue."

"It's about something that happened in Hebrew School yesterday?"

"Are the girls in trouble?"

"God forbid, no. Just something the teacher said that you should know about. What's your schedule for the rest of the day?"

"I'm finished with work about two o'clock. Do you want to meet then?"

"Okay," said Eva. "Let's grab a late lunch at Brodsky's."

"See you then," said Judy as Eva left with the bag of rolls and pastries.

∼

Throughout the day, Judy pondered her forthcoming date with Eva. She decided that she wouldn't tell anyone about it—not even Aron. While she was friendly and cordial to her neighbors, the people in the synagogue, and the customers in the bakery, she had no real friends. Long ago, she'd had girlfriends in Poland and a sister too. But since she had lived in America, she'd kept her innermost thoughts to herself, always on guard, and never daring to confide in anyone, except perhaps a bit to Faye.

She sometimes even felt left out of her daughters' lives. While she tried to be interested in what they were doing, working and ministering to Aron's needs was a full-time job. In addition, the twins had each other. Although they were developing into two distinct personalities, she began to sense that they were beginning to rely more on one another than on her.

Yes, she would like to have a friend. Eva was Polish and had clearly been scarred by her time in the concentration camp. Judy could see that she had a difficult husband too. She remembered how people had told her that Eva had chastised her husband for bringing up Auschwitz at the twins' birthday party. Judy had gone into the house shortly after the incident to bring out some more soda, and she'd spotted Eva coming out of the bathroom with a tear-stained face and swollen eyes. Yes, maybe they could support each other. She could use a friend, and she bet Eva could as well.

Throughout the day, she imagined what it would be like to unburden herself to Eva. In the seven years she had lived with Faye, she was the only person in whom she confided. Surprisingly, Faye, the yenta, was satisfied with the lack of detail; Judy had given her all of the information she craved. She had merely wanted to solve the mystery of Judy's heritage. She knew she did not look or act Jewish. She was not interested in hearing about suffering during the war. She was suffering in the present. In Becky, Faye had her own albatross.

Judy was certain that Eva had a terrible story to tell. But Eva had always been a Jew, not like herself, who had waited until the war was over to embrace the religion that Hitler had tried to extinguish. She knew that Eva's suffering was far worse than anything she'd experienced. She had seen and heard enough to know that. So how could she complain to Eva that her own mother had died when she was eighteen—a loss that had transformed her life for the worse?

Should she tell Eva what she did during the war? Despite all she had endured, perhaps Eva would look at her with disdain because of her Polish Christian heritage. Auschwitz was, after all, located in Poland.

At five minutes to two, Judy stuck her head into the back room and called to Aron that she would be leaving for the day. Aron barely looked up from his paperwork as she said goodbye. She thought to herself that she could run off while he was at work, and he would never notice. He would only realize she was gone later when he was at home and needed something—food, a clean shirt, a pair of socks, someone to snap at. She was proud of herself that she had not told him about her lunch with Eva at Brodsky's. She might never tell him about it.

～

As Judy sat down at Eva's table at Brodsky's, she said, "Thanks so much for inviting me, Eva. I've never eaten here. Of course, Faye takes out deli from here and ordered the food for the party, but I've never sat down and been served. I feel like a princess already."

"Well, then I'm glad we decided to meet here."

Eva ordered a corned beef sandwich, and Judy asked for a turkey sandwich with Russian dressing.

"How about sharing some French fries," Eva asked. "And let's get something to drink. I'm going to have a Dr. Brown's Cel-Ray soda."

"Sure, why not? I'll have a cherry soda."

"So," began Eva. "How were the girls yesterday after Hebrew School? Did they say anything or did you notice any change in their behavior?"

"Well, as a matter of fact, Bronka threw up on the way home yesterday. She seemed upset, but I thought it was because she wasn't feeling well. Although, you know, she's very sensitive and sometimes does get physical symptoms. And then I took her temperature and she didn't have fever. She went to school today, and I haven't heard from the nurse that she's sick or anything."

"Well, let me tell you what happened yesterday in Mrs. Cohen's class. It might have something to do with her vomiting."

Eva proceeded to repeat the class discussion about Hitler and the Nazis as Judy looked somber.

"I guess it was only a matter of time that they should hear something. I told Aron we should have told them."

"It's a *bissel* ironic," said Eva. "Your husband doesn't want to say a word, and mine can't stop talking about it.

"But that's not all," she continued. "Your girls asked Esther what she knew, and she told them about the concentration camps and the gas chambers. I'm sorry they heard it from her, but you know how the *kinder* are; what's on their minds is on their tongues."

"That's all right," said Judy. "I don't blame Esther or Mrs. Cohen.

We can't keep pretending it didn't happen. We have to talk about it if we don't want it to happen again. I'm just not sure what age is appropriate. But I guess the time has come. Do you have any ideas about how to handle it?"

"Well, you can tell them you know Mrs. Cohen mentioned it in class. I don't know if I'd tell them that we met and you know about their talk with Esther, but that's up to you. Esther is reading *The Diary of Anne Frank*, which is about a young girl hiding with her family from the Nazis in Amsterdam during the war. You might want to broach the subject, give them the book, and then ask if they have any questions."

"Hmm, that's interesting."

"Oh, and one more thing. Mrs. Cohen is no longer their teacher. I don't know if she got fired or quit, but Jakob told me the talk at minyan was that she was gone. They seem to think it had something to do with what she said."

"Oh, no," said Judy. "That will really upset Bronka. I know she likes her a lot. I think it's because she can see that she's a very earnest person, just like she is."

Suddenly, a siren began to wail outside, followed by the sound of a car coming to an abrupt, screeching halt in front of the restaurant.

Both women froze in silence.

Judy was facing the door, so she saw the policeman enter first. He was big and tall and walked with a swagger. She noticed his gun was showing.

Eva saw the look on Judy's face and cried out, "What, what's going on?"

"Turn around," said Judy.

And then to the two women's amazement, Irv Rosen with his large flash camera around his neck and tiny Jakob Zilberman followed the cop into the deli. To Judy, the threesome looked so absurd that she put her hand over her mouth. She didn't know if she wanted to laugh or cry. But then she remembered that she had planned not to tell Aron about her rendezvous with Eva. Now she would be forced to share this very odd situation with him. How could she not tell him? It figured—the one time she wanted to do something just for herself and keep it secret, and she's exposed. But she had to admit, whatever this scenario was, it was much too interesting not to report to him.

But poor Eva was in shock. Her fear of men in uniforms had not dissipated much since the war. *And what the hell was Jakob doing with a cop and a newsman in Brodsky's Delicatessen?*

"Should we go over and say hello?"

"Absolutely not," said Eva. "Let's just sit here and see if they notice us. Maybe we can find out what they're up to."

"Is Sid Brodsky here?" The police officer barked at the cashier in a loud voice.

"No, he'll be back at four o'clock."

"Do you have someone named Rudolf Schmidt working here?"

"No, no one by that name works here."

"We're looking for a blond man with a crew cut. He makes deliveries for Brodsky's"

"Perhaps, you mean Roy Smith. He's in the back."

"Maybe. Please ask him to come out. We want to ask him some questions."

"I'll get him for you."

The frightened cashier went to the back room of the store, where Roy was assembling Eva's corned beef sandwich.

"There's a cop and two other guys who want to ask you some questions. I think it has to do with a delivery you made. Sid isn't here, so they asked for you."

"What happened? Are they accusing us of shortchanging them on the cold cuts?" The deli man, who spoke with a German accent, was smirking.

"I don't know," said the cashier, "but you better go out. Luckily, it's quiet now, so go out and get it over with. I have to go back to the register."

The cashier led Roy to the front of the store, where Detective Sergeant Moe Solomon, Irv Rosen, and Jakob Zilberman were waiting to pounce on him.

The deli man looked at the three men and thought of the Three Stooges. *They were obviously Jews, here to complain about an order. But did they really need to bring a cop with them?*

Moe said, "I have a few questions for you. Can we sit down somewhere where we can talk?"

"Why don't you sit at the first table over here?" said the cashier.

The four walked to the table and sat down.

"So what's the difficulty?" the deli man said with a smirk. Jakob would never forget that smirk or the sound of his voice. "Problem with a delivery order?"

"No, not at all," said Moe. "This man," he pointed to Jakob, "has an issue with you that we would like to resolve."

"And it's not about corned beef or pastrami?" The deli man said, smirking again.

Jakob had his back to Eva and had not noticed her. He began grinding his teeth as he felt his heart beating rapidly in his chest and his palms sweating. Irv had told him to sit next to the accused, so if he wanted to snap a picture, he could capture both of them together. Irv and Moe were on the other side of the table.

"Let's get straight to the point," said Moe, "We don't have a lot of time. Are you not Rudolf Schmidt, who worked at Auschwitz Birkenau ordering naked men, women, and children into the gas chamber?"

"Of course not, I am Roy Smith."

"And where were you born—the Bronx, Alabama, or London— with that accent? Don't tell me you're not a German."

"Well, of course I was born in Germany, but I knew nothing about what was going on."

"When did you come here? You better tell the truth because I can check," said the cop.

"I came in 1949."

"And when did you change your name?"

"When I entered the country."

"Who did you come with?"

"I came by myself."

"Who do you live with now?"

"My wife and my two children."

"What is your wife's name and your children's names and ages?"

"My wife is Margaret and my children are Brian who is eight, and Doreen is five."

"Is your wife German too?"

"No, she was born here."

"What is her heritage?"

"Her parents are Irish."

"What does your wife know about your time in Germany?"

"I told her that I was a soldier in the German Army, that I had nothing to do with the extermination of Jews. In fact, I had no idea what was going on at the time. I only found out when the war was over, and then I left the country as fast as I could. Who would want to stay in a country that committed such atrocities?"

"And does your wife believe you?"

"Why not, of course she does."

"Because you're not telling the truth," said Moe. "I know you're lying."

"How do you know I'm lying?"

"Because I have proof. Proof that will cause you to lose your job. Proof that can land you in jail. Proof that can get you deported. Proof that will make your wife want to divorce you—if not kill you—and you will never see your children again. So you better tell the truth. If you tell us the truth, I may even let you go. But we must have the truth from you, and then we will see what I will do with you."

Moe was lying; he had absolutely no proof. But the deli man didn't know that. He was frightened. He had been living a lie for close to ten years. He had built a family on that lie. He liked his life here. Margaret was a nurse who worked the four-to-midnight shift at JHNQ—and with her earnings and his salary and tips, they lived quite comfortably in Queens. While his wife was at work, he watched the children, gave them dinner, and put them to sleep each night. What's more, Margaret was a devout Catholic, and she would never tolerate the wanton killing of human beings. She would leave him in an instant. And then where would he be—back in Germany?

To sweeten the pot, Irv Rosen joined in. "Look, I'm a news photographer, and I brought along my camera to take a picture of you and Mr. Zilberman for my magazine. The story would be about a former concentration camp prisoner confronting a Nazi guard. If you tell us the truth, I will forget about it. I will tell my editors the story did not pan out."

"Just tell us your SS member number, and we will be done," Moe chimed in.

And with that, the former Nazi caved.

"It was six, six, six, seven, nine, one." The number rolled off his tongue reflexively. But then, at the thought of losing his family, his home, and his livelihood, Roy/Rudolf broke down.

"Correct," said the police officer. "Thank you for being honest. Do you have anything else you want to say to us?"

"It's true; I was there, but I was only following orders. What choice did I have? But I never directly killed anyone myself."

"What do you mean you never killed anyone yourself? Didn't you mislead tens of thousands of innocent people into the gas chamber by telling them they were going to take a shower? Didn't you usher men, women, and children to their deaths?" Moe was relentless.

"But that wasn't like pulling the switch or putting the noose around someone's neck or shooting someone in cold blood."

"I'm not so sure," said Irv. "It had the same effect; in fact, it was just more efficient."

Jakob Zilberman, who had been silently grinding his teeth and wiping his sweaty palms on a paper napkin, finally broke his silence.

"I saw you; you enjoyed it. You felt powerful as you led people into the gas chamber. I will remember your smirk forever."

"And what were you doing at Birkenau that you survived to know what I did there? If I directed you to the gas chamber, why is it that you are still alive?"

"I was a Jewish prisoner, see." He thrust out his arm to show his tattoo. "I was forced to clean up the dirty work of the Nazis. I disposed of the bodies after you and your ilk murdered my people."

"Ah," said the Nazi guard turned deli man, whose smirk had returned. "You were a *Sonderkommando*, so you are complicit too. Why didn't you refuse to do the job? I think it is because you wanted to live. Nothing wrong with that, I say. But if I'm guilty, you must be guilty too."

At that moment, Jakob wanted to lunge at the German. How dare he compare a Jewish prisoner to a Nazi killer? After all this, the Nazi had gotten under his skin again. He wanted to scream at the top of his lungs, *You son-of-a-bitch Nazi bastard!* He wanted to grab Moe's gun and shoot him. He wanted to take Irv's camera and hit him over the head with it. But that's not who Jakob Zilberman was. He'd had his confrontation, and surprisingly, he now felt worse than before.

"Okay," said Moe. "I have to get back to policing the streets of Queens. And I'm sure these other gentlemen have to leave too. And you must have work to do."

"So, you're not going to turn me in?"

"No, you told us the truth," said Moe. "A deal is a deal. But you'd better be on your best behavior from now on. Your secret is safe for the time being. Just no more anti-Semitic remarks or innuendos, or I will be back. And then I will crush you."

At that moment, Roy remembered the unfinished sandwiches in the back. He ran back to Eva and Judy, who forgot they had ordered them; they had been so engrossed in eavesdropping on the conversation. He apologized profusely. The two women said they didn't want them anymore because they had to leave. Roy said the food was on the house, and he'd bring it to them to go.

While Judy and Eva waited for their take-out bags, they saw Jakob and the two men leave the deli. Jakob had been so absorbed in the interrogation that he'd never noticed his wife. But his wife had noticed him, and she knew she had to think long and hard about how to handle it.

Judy, on the other hand, knew what she had to do. She could not wait a day longer to discuss the Shoah with the twins.

As he walked outside, Jakob was now so agitated that he felt he needed to get away immediately. He thanked Moe and Irv and told them he was going to walk home by himself. He needed to clear his head.

As Irv walked Moe to the police car, he said, "You really didn't have any proof, did you?"

Moe laughed. "Of course not. Look, we put the screws to the Nazi. I really had no authority to do what I did. And what about your scoop?"

"The truth is that the editors weren't interested in the story. They said no one cares about Nazis anymore. If it was about Commies, that would be a different thing. It's all about Communists now."

∽

The minute Eva walked out of the deli, she sadly came to the conclusion that she would not be socializing with Judy. She could not bear the embarrassment of ever discussing the incident with her again. She was mortified that the Nazi had said in public that Jakob was no different than he was—that they had both done what they needed to do to survive. It was so much more complicated than that. *Of course, everyone knows that the Nazis were cruel and vicious and hateful.* But still, she was afraid that Judy would now think less of her and Jakob. She didn't want to discuss this further with her. She was concerned that Judy would surely think of it every time she got together with her. Eva just wanted to push it to the back of her mind with all the other bad memories. She could only hope that Judy had enough discretion not to tell the whole world about it.

By the time Eva arrived home, she had also decided that she would not mention the incident at Brodsky's unless Jakob brought it up. She was sure that the accusations of the guard would unleash a new round of soul-searching and self-recrimination for him.

There was no comparison between the healthy, well-fed, strong Nazis, who ate and slept and bathed in comfortable homes with their wives and families, and their Jewish prisoners, who were starved and beaten, and who slept in rows of crowded barracks, stacked one on top of another, she thought. *The Jews lived with terror and typhoid; the Jewish prisoners served at the mercy of the SS.*

Most of the *Sonderkommandos* had been shot after six months on the job. Jakob Zilberman was an exception. He bore witness to the heinous crimes he had observed first-hand. He was more courageous than she, his wife had to admit. He was not afraid of sharing his truth. Eva faced her demons alone—in her mind and in her heart—both in nightmares and in sleepless nights.

~

On the way home from Brodsky's, Judy stopped at the library to take out a copy of *The Diary of Anne Frank*. But the librarian informed her that all of the copies had already been borrowed. She told her that she could reserve the book, and she would contact her as soon as a copy was returned.

"I must have a copy now," she said. "It's very important."

"Well, I can call the Jamaica Library, but I doubt they'll have it either. It's become especially popular, ever since the Broadway play. Perhaps they have it at Barry's Stationery Store across the street. It's in paperback now, so it shouldn't be too expensive."

Judy made a beeline for Barry's, now intent on this mission as if her life depended on it. Inside the store it was on prominent display, so she snatched it up and then realized that she was holding the last copy.

She returned home, and as soon as the girls entered the house from Hebrew School, she sat them down and showed them the book. After what she had witnessed in the deli, she knew she had to give her daughters a version of her own story that she found palatable. She would not wait for her husband. She could not trust what he would or would not say.

"I heard what Mrs. Cohen said in Hebrew School, and I want to tell you our own family history and answer any questions you may have. Papa lost his whole family in Europe—his parents and grandparents, sisters and brothers, aunts and uncles, and cousins. It's true that Hitler wanted to get rid of all of the Jews and he killed about six million."

With that, Bronka blurted out, "Esther's parents were in a concentration camp and have tattoos. Why don't you and Papa have them?"

"We weren't in a concentration camp."

"Did you lose family in the war, Mama?" Bronka asked.

"My mother died right before the war broke out."

"So how did you and Papa survive?"

"By hiding," she said.

"Where did you hide?"

"First I found a hiding place in an attic, and later in the forest."

"Wasn't it cold in the forest?"

"Yes, it was. I brought blankets, and we built a dugout and covered it with a tarp."

Judy made a snap decision. It wouldn't be exactly a lie, she told herself—just an edited version of the truth. Some people embellished the truth, like Faye, to make it more entertaining or palatable—or to portray themselves as important. Others edited it, like Irv Rosen. He told you only what he wanted you to know. But Judy reasoned that JoJo and Bronka were ten years old. She had the right to tell them what she thought they could handle. Besides, Aron would be angry that she had broached the subject at all—especially without first consulting him. She did not want to risk another scene. She realized that in leaving out her true origins, the obstacles she had overcome, and her good deeds, she forfeited painting herself to her daughters as the hero she truly was. But she reasoned that she could always deal with that in the future.

"The Zilbermans were in a concentration camp, but we weren't. There were many concentration camps, and a death camp like Auschwitz, where they were, was the worst place to be. Other Jews who weren't captured, hid—in Christian homes, in barns, in the forest," she explained. "There were people who weren't Jewish, who defied the government and helped the Jews. But most of the Jews in Poland died. Not just those in the camps, but those who hid as well. Just in our hometown, Kielce—there had been more than twenty thousand Jews living there before the war, and afterward there were only two hundred."

Judy felt relieved, as if a weight had been lifted from her. She had given the girls just enough, not too much. The information was sufficient for their age. They would not think she was withholding a secret. As they got older, they could find out more.

"And I got a book for the two of you to read. The library was all out of it, so I bought the last copy at Barry's," she said as she showed them *The Diary of Anne Frank*. "You can take turns reading it, and then I'll answer any questions you have."

JoJo was satisfied. Mama had answered the twins' questions. The stories she had heard were true. The Nazis had wiped out most of the Jews of Europe. She would read the book and find out more. She would discuss it with her sister and maybe ask her mother some questions.

But for Bronka, it was not enough. When she became obsessed with something, she had to know every last detail. Moreover, ever since she was a little girl, she had been fixated on the truth—what was real and what wasn't. Tiny Tears' fake tears had not fooled her. Neither had Mindy. Despite all of her material possessions, Mindy was a sad girl. *Was it because her father was dead? Was it because her mother was rarely present?*

And while Bronka was glad that her mother had finally brought up Hitler and the Nazis, she wondered why the subject had not been mentioned before. Esther Zilberman knew about it, and so did the Rosen girls. Mrs. Cohen had discussed it in Hebrew School. Everyone was reading *The Diary of Anne Frank*. The library was out of it, and Mama had bought the last copy at Barry's. Why were she and JoJo the last to find out about something that had affected her parents so deeply? Something about the way her mother told the story made her curious.

Bronka resolved that she would get to the bottom of this. She would find out the truth. She would read *The Diary of Anne Frank* and ask questions. She would have her antennae up for clues. Mama had not given them the whole story—and she was determined to discover the secret, no matter how long it took.

"So at least we know the truth, now," JoJo said once they were in their beds, the lights off, the dark like a protective blanket in which the girls could talk without seeing each other. Bronka often felt it was easier this way.

"Do we?" Bronka asked.

"Mama told us. We can read the book and find out more."

"It's not going to tell us the truth about our family, JoJo. Mama told us what she wanted us to know. I bet there's more to the story."

~

Judy Lubinski was hardly the only one in the neighborhood who harbored a secret. But in her case, she didn't believe she was lying, just not sharing the whole truth with her daughters. Across the street, Lenore had actually perpetuated a boldfaced lie to Mindy about the existence of her father. And then there was Irv Rosen, who was an enigma wrapped in a puzzle. Was he Catholic or Jewish? Was he a celebrity or just a blowhard?

Irv Rosen enjoyed his work very much. He could feel the adrenalin rushing when a good lead was about to break. In the morning, he read every newspaper he could get his hands on, and each evening he did the same. His photographs—especially those of the Rosenbergs—had won him prestigious awards. Those who were smitten with the rich and famous wanted to be in his presence.

Irv Rosen would hold court, mesmerizing his listeners with tales of what Dick Nixon had said to him or how Marilyn Monroe had blown him a kiss. His position got him free tickets to ball games and the theater, as well as access to exclusive cocktail parties. Actually, he liked nothing better than to get a few drinks in a bar after work, sharing experiences with his fellow newsmen.

While Irv generally drove the girls to school in the morning, his wife Connie didn't really know where he was for the rest of the day and evening. He was rarely in the office, and his assignments were far flung. He would call in from time to time, and when he returned home, he would tell her where he'd been and whom he had met. She would listen and ask questions. She liked following current events; she had developed a taste for breaking news during World War II when she worked on *The Belvoir Castle*. And her daughters could not get enough of their father's exploits. She had warned them not to repeat what they heard in the house, but she knew it was a losing battle. So breaking news became a unifying force in the Rosen household.

On the other hand, Connie wasn't all that impressed with the famous people her husband often bragged about meeting and socializing with. She figured they were just like anyone else, except perhaps for their talent, wealth, luck, or connections. From what she read about their personal foibles, she wasn't envious either. Neither was she interested in accompanying Irv to encounter them at swank events in Manhattan.

Connie's family was her life, and she wanted to have more children. She was one of eleven, and she liked being part of a large Catholic family, one that she was attempting to build for herself in Bellerose. But after three miscarriages, she had almost given up on her desire to have more children, specifically a son.

Over the fourteen years of their marriage, Irv had used his freedom to full advantage. He came and went as he pleased. He could accompany Jennie Mandelstern to the Women's House of Detention to visit her daughter, confront a former Nazi in the middle of the day at Brodsky's delicatessen, or sneak into services on Yom Kippur. He also used his flexible schedule to carry on clandestine affairs with women who were the very opposite of his wife.

He had started out slow with Lenore—bringing roses for her and her mother that first week after her release. Then he helped her get a job at JHNQ, and had a plant delivered to her on her first day at work. He was very cautious at the beginning, stopping at the hospital perhaps once a month to check in on her. He knew she was fragile, and he was gentle with her. They would sit in the hospital coffee shop for a half hour or so, and she would confide in him. After all, he had seen her shame and humiliation; he was one of the few people with whom she felt comfortable. She did not need to hide anything; he needed no explanations.

But after a year of being Lenore's friend, they became lovers. Five years after Lenore's arrest, the mutual attraction continued to deepen, and Irv was juggling a double life.

~

In Becky's case, her double life was in her head, but it was beginning to manifest itself in ways that affected those around her more and more.

It was a crisp fall Saturday, and after they returned from services and had lunch, the twins headed upstairs to their bedroom to play with their dolls. With Thanksgiving a week away, Bronka had an idea.

"Let's build a boat out of blocks and then act out the dolls coming to America, just like the Pilgrims and like us."

"Good idea," said JoJo.

As always, Judy had neatly lined up their growing collection of dolls on their beds, but their Ginny dolls were missing.

"What happened to Amy and Joy?" Bronka asked, as she got down on the floor and looked under the bed.

Johanna opened the drawers of their chest and looked in the closet. "They're not here; do you think a robber came in and stole them?"

"Aunt Becky was the only one in the house while we were gone," said Bronka "Let's go down and ask her."

The door to Becky's room was ajar, so they walked in. The sofa bed was open, and Becky was lying on her side with one doll in each hand, mumbling unintelligibly. Even though it was two o'clock, she was still in her green flannel nightgown, which was bunched up, exposing a light brown birthmark on her leg. Her hair was greasy and her breath was stale.

"Aunt Becky, what are you doing with our dolls?" JoJo asked.

At first, Becky said nothing. She had a vacant look on her face.

"Are you playing with them?" Bronka asked her.

Becky bent her index finger, motioning that the girls should come closer as she spoke in a barely audible whisper.

"No, girls, this is no game. This is serious business. The dolls have been warning me about serious trouble here. They know things that we don't know. Now, don't tell anyone because this is top secret. I may have to take you away from here. We are all in danger. Maybe I will take you back to Israel with me. Go and pack your things so we will be ready to go at a moment's notice."

"Aunt Becky," said JoJo. "We don't want to go; we want to stay here with Mama and Papa."

"That could present a problem," said Becky.

"Why?"

"Your mother's being hunted; she is a spy. And your father and Izzy and Faye are in danger for hiding her here. They're all in trouble. We need to get out of here soon, so we don't get caught up in it. Go pack your things. The dolls say time is of the essence. They know what they're talking about."

Bronka loved Aunt Becky, but even the suggestible and anxious sister knew this made no sense at all.

"Dolls can't talk, any more than they can cry or eat or drink," said Bronka.

"Bronka," Becky snapped at her. "I know what I heard. These dolls talk to me, and they are warning us. Go pack your things."

Johanna had lost her patience, and she wanted her doll returned to her.

"Okay, but give us our dolls back,"

"I can't do that," said Becky. "They want to consult with me more. This is for your own good."

Johanna bolted out of the room, but Bronka stayed behind to give

Becky a hug. There was something wrong with her aunt; she better tell Mama. Mama would know what to do. Maybe if they could just make Becky happy, she wouldn't need to have imaginary conversations with the Ginny dolls.

~

How do you solve a problem called Rebecca? Faye had struggled with that challenge every day since her daughter had returned from Israel. Other than her friendship with Lenore and the occasional dates she got for her, Becky had no social life.

Becky could be caring and giving, as she had demonstrated with the twins. But more and more, she was receding into her own world. Faye did not know where to turn. She was afraid that if she brought her to a psychiatrist, people would find out. She also suspected that if Becky became dependent on a local doctor, she would never move out of the house. But things were definitely getting worse; she could no longer pretend there was nothing wrong.

Faye was spooked by Becky's bizarre comments, the voices she said she heard, and her erratic behavior. Above all, Faye wanted *shalom bayis,* a peaceful home. As a second wife, she especially wanted to keep Izzy happy. She also wanted to make sure that the younger Lubinskis would remain in her home, and she was deathly afraid that they would move out if Becky continued to deteriorate.

Aron had told Izzy that they were planning to go house hunting in the spring. This was not his doing, he explained to him. He was content to continue with their arrangement. Why wouldn't he be? He had few expenses and saved his money. Having hid from the Nazis in the most challenging physical and psychological environments, he could tolerate Becky's presence by simply blocking it out. He had a roof over his head, running water, and three meals a day. That was enough for him. But while Judy was sympathetic to Becky as a human being, she was increasingly concerned that this was not a wholesome environment for her children. And she did not appreciate Becky's wariness and hostility toward her, which was becoming increasingly evident—especially since the Ginny doll episode.

From the time of Becky's surprise arrival at Idlewild, Faye had not intended for her to stay with them more than a few weeks. Originally, she thought it would be a stopgap measure. She had suggested time and again that Becky move out and get a place of her own, but Faye's entreaties were met by frozen silence and even hunger strikes.

Bronka sat with Becky, stroking her hair and talking to her, bringing her cookies and milk, and telling her she loved her. Judy's young daughter's caring and compassion moved her. But she also knew that Bronka's kindness would not cure Becky.

Johanna was a different matter. Judy was troubled that Becky's situation had engendered the first major war between the sisters. In no uncertain terms, JoJo wanted her out of the house, or she wanted the family to move. She had made her feelings abundantly clear. The happy, outgoing, popular twin stopped bringing her friends home. It was enough that her father's speech and dress were an embarrassment to her; now she was afraid that her friends would see Becky's bizarre behavior as a reflection on her. She lobbied and cajoled Bronka to support her position, but Bronka believed that if everyone gave Becky enough love, she would be fine.

Judy had endured enough to make her an acute observer of human nature. In addition, as her mother's nursing assistant, she had seen the whole panoply of physical illnesses and mental disorders. She had often discussed health matters with her mother. She clearly remembered one time when the doctor examined a young man who had threatened his mother with a knife because there were voices in his head telling him to do so. Her mother explained to her that the voices were real to him and that he had schizophrenia. She shuddered remembering that shortly before she died in 1939, her mother had told her that German psychiatric patients were being sterilized and murdered.

It was obvious to Judy that Becky was suffering from mental illness—and her illness needed to be treated as the disease that it was. But how could she suggest that Becky get help if Faye never acknowledged it? She knew Faye cared about appearances. It was a stigma and a giant elephant in the room. She became more and more frustrated—even angry—that Faye continued to ignore it.

Although she had secretly become more alarmed after the New Year's Eve incident, Faye was still not willing to confront her daughter's condition directly nor to discuss it with anyone. But lately Becky had taken her strange behavior to new levels.

One night, with a blizzard predicted, Becky had gone outside and stood under the streetlamp. As the snow began to fall, Faye peered from the kitchen window at her detached and disheveled daughter. There she was—with no hat, no coat, no gloves, no boots. What was she thinking? What demons inhabited her mind? She watched as Becky appeared to mumble to herself, examining her fingers.

The twins were upstairs in their room, getting ready for bed.

"They're predicting a blizzard," said JoJo. "I hope school will be cancelled for tomorrow."

Bronka ran to the window to see if the snow was starting to accumulate, and she spotted Becky standing under the streetlamp and panicked.

"Aunt Becky is standing out in the snow. I have to go outside and bring her in."

"Bronka, let the grown-ups handle it," said JoJo. "Mindy says she belongs in Creedmoor with all the other crazy people. She shouldn't be living here. And if she stays, I told Mama I want us to move."

"Oh no," said Bronka, crying. "She has to stay here with us. She is family. I don't want her sent away. And I don't want to move. I have to help her. I feel so sorry for her."

"You're nuts. I feel sorry for *us*. She's spoiling everything. Everyone can tell she's crazy. Pretty soon, no one will want to be friends with me anymore."

"If those are the kind of friends you have, why would you even want them?"

Bronka ran down the stairs while JoJo yelled, "Stop it, Bronka. She's ruining our lives. Stay out of it."

"Mama, Tante Faye," Bronka screamed hysterically as she went to the coat closet, frantically pulling out Becky's coat and hat and gloves. "Aunt Becky is going to freeze to death out there. I'm going to go outside."

"No, Bronka," said Izzy. "I'll take care of it. Give me those."

"Bronka," Aron chimed in. "I do not allow you to go outside in a blizzard. I will go with Izzy. This is not something you can fix."

Bronka reluctantly handed Becky's things to Izzy, while Faye was already putting her coat and boots on.

"I will talk to her; give me the coat," said Faye as she walked out the door with the two men following her. "Let me handle it."

Faye approached the shivering and mumbling Becky. She was looking aimlessly at her fingernails, a blank stare on her face.

"Here, sweetheart, I brought you your coat; you must be freezing,"

Becky did not respond, so Faye tried to drape the coat around her, but Becky knocked it off.

Izzy was neither a gentle nor a subtle man and he grabbed Becky's arm, hard.

She started screaming. "The snow is upside down. It's on its head, on my head. The men all have knives—icy knives. They are coming here tonight."

With his sixth sense, Irv Rosen was soon on the scene. And when Lenore saw Irv and the commotion from her window, she joined the group.

For all of Lenore's faults, she was a good friend to Becky. She found her interesting and intelligent, although unstable.

"Hi, Becky, what's the matter, honey?" Lenore said. "Are you drunk?"

"No way; not me. Don't you hear them? They're warning us about the knives. Hide the sterling silver."

Irv put his arm around her. "Becky, let's go in the house. It's freezing out here."

"My head is full of knives. Don't hit me with a stick or a bat or a rock."

"Becky, you must come inside now. We are all going to freeze to death."

"It's not safe, and now we can't hide, and they're going to kill us all."

"The three of us can try to carry her into the house," said Irv.

"Why don't we just call an ambulance?" Lenore suggested. "I'm telling you she needs medical attention. They'll know how to handle this. I'm going inside to call."

No one stopped her; after all, Lenore was Becky's one friend, and she worked in a hospital. Five minutes later, the wailing of the police car and ambulance sirens further agitated Becky.

As the ambulance came to a stop, Becky lay down in the snow. She ignored the pleas of the medical attendants and the police. Finally, she was taken away in a straitjacket. Faye rode in the ambulance with her daughter.

The twins observed the entire scene from their second-floor window.

~

When Faye hopped into the ambulance, she told Izzy not to bother following her in his car. She preferred to go to the hospital by herself. Izzy would just be restless and annoyed.

It was normally less than five minutes from 253rd Street to JHNQ, but the roads were slick and as yet unplowed, so it took significantly longer. Becky alternated between screaming, groaning, and babbling unintelligibly.

When she arrived at the hospital, she was placed on a metal table and her body strapped with leather restraints. She thrashed and yelled and howled.

"It's a good thing that you called an ambulance, and your daughter is in the hospital," the young doctor in the emergency room told Faye. "Her condition is extremely serious. I believe she is exhibiting signs of acute paranoid schizophrenia. We will keep her here for a few days for observation, call in a psychiatrist, and probably administer some medication. After that, we will consult with you and make a decision."

Schizophrenia. The very word struck fear and recrimination in Faye. She was not only devastated but wracked with guilt. The truth attacked her like a newly sharpened knife. She was relieved she was alone. She could not bear to face Izzy's annoyance or even Judy's well-intentioned sympathy.

What could she have done to prevent this? Faye had believed if she'd just listened to, comforted, and coddled Becky enough, she would be okay. No, not really. She had been deluding herself. She knew her daughter was getting worse, not better. She had sought to sweep Becky's issues under the rug, but she feared they were no longer within her control. Now, what would she tell people? What would she tell herself?

The blizzard lasted for two days. Faye spent two nights in the hospital, and once the snow stopped, returned home. She visited her daughter every day. A week after Becky was admitted, Faye was called to a meeting with a medical doctor, a psychiatrist, a nurse, and a social worker.

"There is no question that Rebecca has schizophrenia," said the psychiatrist. "Her symptoms are classic—disorganization of thought, hallucinations, voices in her head, speaking in nonsensical gibberish.

You must understand that this is very real to her. She is living in a state of terror.

"We believe we have alleviated some of the symptoms, both through shock therapy and a fairly new medication. There is a new drug, chlorpromazine, which is now being used to alleviate symptoms of schizophrenia.

"Ten years ago, chlorpromazine did not exist, so the timing is good. If she stays on it, her condition should improve. But many people with schizophrenia stop taking meds once they feel better. Also, there are side effects to chlorpromazine. These include movement problems, sleepiness, dry mouth, low blood pressure upon standing, and weight gain. There are also some more serious side effects, but those are rare. That is why we are strongly recommending that you agree to institutionalize your daughter, at least for the near future.

"Our recommendation is for you to commit her to Creedmoor. As her mother, you have the authority to sign the papers committing her. Her condition will be carefully monitored there, and she will be in a safe and secure setting."

Faye was well aware of Creedmoor. It was the seventeen-story, sandstone state mental hospital that sat on two hundred acres of flat grass and trees on the edge of Alley Pond Park, only two miles from her home. In stark contrast, it was bordered by neighborhoods of small one- and two-story homes. For people who lived in northeast Queens, especially children, the very word Creedmoor evoked mystery, dread, and dark humor. No one knew what went on there, but there was always a fear that some of the patients would escape and drift through the community, wreaking havoc.

This was a lot for Faye to absorb. It seemed like only a few months ago Becky was buying the twins Ginny dolls, launching them on a reading project, and going on blind dates. She could not stand the thought of putting her daughter in an institution, especially one that had the reputation of being a crowded madhouse.

"Is there no alternative but Cree—?" the word stuck in her throat. She could not even get out the word, *Creedmoor*. She was exhausted and angry and defeated.

"Well, if you want to consider a private mental facility, Lakeville Hospital shares a campus with us," said the social worker. "It's tiny compared to Creedmoor, and she'll get much more personalized attention there. They have meaningful activities for the patients too, like gardening and arts and crafts. I can set up an appointment for you to go over there now, if you like. They'll show you around and discuss the fees with you. If you can afford it, it's a good alternative."

"I want to see her first before I decide," Faye said.

An hour later, Faye had signed on the dotted line. Becky would be a patient at Lakeville for the foreseeable future. To Faye's mind, if her daughter had to be institutionalized, she had at least placed her in an elite setting.

Once that was done, she took the bus home and started thinking of a cover story. It was hard enough for her to accept that her only daughter had schizophrenia, but she knew she could not bring herself to say the word to others—certainly not to Izzy. She racked her brain but could not think of anyone she knew who ever admitted that they had someone with mental illness in their family. She felt ashamed, responsible, disgraced, as if it were a reflection on her—her genetics, her parenting skills, her personality, her very being.

When Faye arrived home, the whole family gathered around her.

"Where's Aunt Becky? Is she okay?" Bronka said in an agitated voice.

"Of course," said Faye. "You know, she's just very tired and needs to rest."

"Why can't she rest here?"

"She needs some medicine and treatments to help her recover, which they can only administer in the hospital. Lakeville is a very beautiful place, with lovely rooms and trees and gardens."

"Okay, that's enough questions," Judy said. "Faye looks so tired. Let her take her coat off. I'll make you some tea, Faye. Girls, why don't you bundle up and go outside and make a snowman? Then you can come in and I'll make you some hot cocoa."

Bronka was beginning to detect a pattern to her mother's behavior. She shooed her and her sister away whenever the real story was about to be revealed. She could see that she did not want them to know about certain things. But Judy's actions had the opposite effect on Bronka. She yearned for the unvarnished truth in all things.

As the girls started to scurry away, they heard Judy ask Faye about the nature of Becky's illness.

"Oh, she had a nervous breakdown," Faye said casually.

"How long will she be there?"

"Oh, for the foreseeable future. And then I'll look into a nice, long-term facility. The social worker told me there are several out on Long Island, where she can stay, and I can visit." Faye began choking up.

Judy didn't say a word. She knew that treatment for a nervous breakdown did not require the sort of long-term care Faye was describing. She realized Faye was too embarrassed to tell her the truth, and that made her sad.

1960-1961

———————◉————————

BELLEROSE, NEW YORK

IN JUNIOR HIGH SCHOOL, THE twins became preoccupied with *American Bandstand*. They liked to watch the teenagers from Philadelphia dance to rock 'n' roll records and enjoyed hearing Dick Clark introduce the teen idols, like Frankie Avalon and Fabian, who appeared on the show. They especially enjoyed singing and dancing along. Faye was less than enchanted with the commotion emanating from her living room.

"This is not real music; it's just loud noise," Faye complained to Judy. "Not to mention . . ."

"Not to mention what?"

"Come with me," said Faye. "I want to show you something."

Faye led Judy into the living room and pointed to a spot in front of the TV where the girls did their dancing. There was a big patch of rose-colored carpet that had rippled into what looked like a small mound. Then she pointed to another spot where the carpet was so worn, you could almost see the padding underneath.

"You remember when we got this carpeting?" said Faye. "It's not even three years old."

"I'm sorry, Faye. I should have noticed."

"I'm only bringing this up for their own good. The kids on American Bandstand look like juvenile delinquents, the way they dress and wiggle to the music. The girls are so innocent; it's not good to expose them to all of that. And the loud, bawdy music is giving me headaches and raising my blood pressure. They were doing the twist along with Chubby Checker, and I couldn't believe it. That's considered dancing nowadays? That's what the young people call music? And what kind of name is Chubby Checker? What is this world coming to?"

"I'm sorry you're so upset, Faye. I'll tell the girls they can't watch anymore."

Humoring Faye was the price Judy paid for living in her house. She had tried to move when Becky began disrupting the household, but she had given in to Aron's desire to stay. "Just ignore her," was his response. That was easy for him to say. He had the personality and life experience to do just that. He was, after all, a survivor. A man who survived by hiding from the Nazis was highly practiced in over-looking unpleasantness. But not his American daughters, who in his eyes led pampered and entitled lives. "What do they have to complain about?" he would say to his wife each time she suggested moving. "They have their own room, they are fed, clothed, go to school, and have friends. They are not being persecuted for their religion. I wish my sister and brother could have had their lives."

At the height of JoJo's insistence that she did not want to live in the house with Becky, Aron had flatly refused to move. Judy had been torn. One daughter wanted to move; the other wanted to stay. The path of least resistance had been to give in to Aron. And that was Judy's comfort level—acquiescing to him at every turn. She figura-tively stood on her head to please him in the present. And she had literally risked her life for him in the past.

And then there was the pressure Faye exerted on her to stay. Once Becky was out of the picture, JoJo had abandoned the constant lobbying to move. But the idea of starting fresh in her own home still appealed to Judy. For two springs in a row, Judy and Aron had gone house hunting. But every time they got close, Faye would manipulate Judy into staying—with pleas, tears, and even physical illnesses. Judy loved Faye and appreciated all she had done for her and her family, but she wondered if she would ever be able to take control of her own life.

Unlike her mother who was a people pleaser, her daughter JoJo was adept at getting her way. Despite Faye's tantrum about *American Bandstand*, she had no intention of giving up her favorite program.

So after school, she now headed over to Mindy's house to catch the program and to hang out with Mindy and her friends. Lenore was at work, and Jennie was pre-occupied with taking Harry to doctor appointments. He had recently been diagnosed with leukemia. In the absence of the three adults, Mindy and her friends had free reign of the house. They sang and danced along with the show and had chips and soda. They looked through the teen magazines to peek into the lives of the kids on *Bandstand*.

Mindy and her friends, Susan and Linda, fascinated JoJo. Mindy painted her nails coral. Linda alternated between pale pink and white lipstick. Susan used an eyelash curler and tweezed her eyebrows. All three girls taught JoJo how to apply makeup, as well as the latest dance steps. She was trying out for the school play, and they wanted her to look and perform her best.

Bronka, on the other hand, was literal and compliant. Her mother had told her that she could no longer watch *American Bandstand*, so she now spent her time either with Tina Rosen—with whom she shared a fascination for current events—or with Esther Zilberman, her Hebrew School buddy and fellow Holocaust sleuth.

Bronka was amazed that Esther's prediction on the first day of Hebrew School that she would have a bas mitzvah ceremony turned out to come true. She was the first girl in the synagogue's history to have one. Her father had relentlessly pressed Rabbi Herbert to allow it, and he had finally acquiesced. It was a simple Friday night affair with Esther, in a blue party dress, chanting a haftorah portion and speaking about the responsibilities of a Jewish woman. A special Oneg Shabbos of cold cuts, rugelach, and a sheet cake that said "Mazel Tov, Esther," followed the service.

As Bronka took in the ceremony and the refreshments, she felt wistful that she had not done the same. But it was already several months past her thirteenth birthday. *Too late,* she thought. Besides, she would have been too afraid to even broach the subject with her father. And after the service, Faye commented to her mother that she thought it was an unnecessary strain to put on a young girl. Bronka overheard her mother agreeing, saying, "Yes, especially for Bronka; she's so shy. I'm glad we didn't put the girls through it."

The focus on bas mitzvah was short-lived. The presidential election of 1960 between Richard Nixon and John F. Kennedy captured their attention, not only the adults in her home, but Bronka as well.

The very first time Bronka heard John F. Kennedy speak, he immediately replaced the teen idol Ricky Nelson as the object of her affection. Both Bronka and her friend Tina fell in love with the young politician's looks, his vigor, and the soaring cadences of his speech. They started dreaming about joining the Peace Corps or marrying a politician. They signed up for the school newspaper in the hopes of grooming themselves to follow Jackie Kennedy's career path. When Tina shared that her father had been present at the convention and had photographed the young, dynamic candidate, Bronka spent many afternoons in the Rosens' basement, exulting in the photos that Irv had shot of Kennedy, his beautiful wife, and his adorable toddler, Caroline. Bronka started a Kennedy scrapbook, which she maintained until his assassination. On her bulletin board, she replaced magazine clippings of Ricky Nelson, Fabian, and Neil Sedaka with JFK and his young family—and of course, the articles she penned for the school paper.

With Esther, she shared her passion for investigating the Holocaust. Her mission was expedited by the capture of Adolf Eichmann on May 11, 1960.

Beginning the following April, Bronka glued herself to the television every weeknight at 6:45 to watch highlights of the Eichmann trial, which was televised on Channel 7. The two girls began to spend hours listening to Esther's dad, Jakob, recount his experiences and observations at Auschwitz-Birkenau. For the most part, his wife, Eva, held her silence. And while Bronka's parents watched the Eichmann proceedings with pained expressions, they added little information about their own story when she asked them questions.

~

A couple of weeks after Kennedy won the election, Jackie Kennedy gave birth to a baby boy, John Jr. And a week after the Inauguration on January 20—after years of trying and heartbreaking miscarriages—Connie Rosen gave birth to a son. Faye called him a "change of life" baby since the new mother was past forty and Tori was already fifteen, Christina thirteen, and Toni twelve.

Irv went up and down the street giving cigars to the men, exulting, "It's a wonderful thing to have a man-child at last."

The new baby, Thomas James, or TJ as the girls called him, quickly became the darling of the block. He was an adorable little pudgy baby with a round face and big brown eyes. People said his face should be on jars of Gerber's baby food. The Rosens hosted a party in their home to celebrate his baptism. Lenore begged off, telling Connie her father's illness would prevent her from coming.

Lenore was a person who could tolerate ambiguity in her long-term relationships, first with Al and now with Irv. She knew that she could have settled down with an average accountant or lawyer years before; she'd had no lack of suitors. But Lenore craved a certain cachet in the men she made part of her life. Unfortunately, the price of those relationships was secrecy, dishonesty, and ultimately disappointment.

Irv had told her that he could not divorce Connie because she was a strict Catholic, but that he adored Lenore. Some other woman might have been bothered by the fact that he had three daughters, a wife, and mother-in-law living in his home, but not Lenore. She chose to believe that it was merely a marriage of convenience.

But the new baby and Irv's concomitant enthusiasm made her question her own judgment. Everyone knew TJ's birth had not been an accident. It was common knowledge that the Rosens had been trying to have a son for years. Why hadn't she put two and two together? Had she been duped again? She was forty and not getting any younger. *I'm just an idiot where men are concerned,* Lenore berated herself.

Now she wondered whether she should have more seriously considered some of the other men she had dated. In the past, she had viewed them merely as props she used to camouflage her relationship with Irv. Becky, her one friend, was in a mental institution. Her father had a fatal illness, her mother was getting older, and Mindy was becoming a typically difficult teenager.

Lenore's neglect, coupled with the absence of a father, had made Mindy not only very attached to her grandparents, but more and more resentful of Lenore as she became an adolescent.

Now—with Harry so ill, and Jennie preoccupied with him—there was no one to supervise Mindy or even to find out what was going on in her life. Harry had been her steadfast companion, surrogate father, and friend. Jennie was her substitute mother and soothing confidante. Now, Harry was absorbed with dying, and Jennie had put all her wifely energies into his care and comfort.

Mindy would sit at his bedside and choke back her tears. He sometimes managed a wan smile, but she could see that he was wracked with pain. She began singing to distract him and also to drown out his moans. Although she had grown up with the acceptance that her father had died, she had never seen dying before.

One day when she was visiting, she spotted Jennie standing at the door. "It's so sweet of you to entertain Grandpa. But I think he should rest now."

Mindy got up from the bed and began sobbing. She fell into her grandmother's arms.

A week later, Harry was admitted to the hospital. Jennie asked Mindy to help her make his favorite mushroom barley soup, which she brought and spoon-fed to him in his hospital bed. Two months later, the love of Jennie's—and Mindy's—life was gone. He was seventy-five.

~

Visitors packed Jennie's house for the shiva, the seven-day period when people come to the home of the mourners to pay their respects, offer a sympathetic ear, and share memories. As custom required, Lenore and Jennie each sat on a low wooden bench and wore a ripped black ribbon pinned to their clothes to signify their loss. People took turns sitting with them and chatting, and milling around the rest of the small house, schmoozing.

Never having participated in a shiva before, Mindy and her peers were intrigued with the mirrors in the house, covered with white sheets, as well as with the huge volume of food that continued to pour into the modest home. They absorbed the smells of smoked fish, cream cheese, and bagels, which alternated with corned beef and pastrami and potato salad and roast chicken. Jennie explained to them that mourners must refrain from their normal daily activities, so the Jewish community had ensured that they would be fed.

Izzy and Aron had provided trays of cookies and rugelach, but that didn't stop many of the visitors from bringing cake too. Linda whispered to Susan that it almost looked like a clown car, with one guest after another walking through the door with their box of cake or pastries.

On the third day of shiva, right before the dinner hour, there was a lull as visitors began leaving. Only Faye and Judy, Bronka and JoJo were left. Faye and Judy were setting the table for dinner as Lenore and Jennie perused the guest book from the funeral.

"Oh, my," Jennie called out, startled. "Did you see Al at the funeral?"

"Mom, this is not a time for cruel jokes. Have you lost your mind? I'm upset enough without you mentioning him."

"Well, either he was there, someone else signed his name, or it's a different Al Springer," said Jennie as she passed the book to Lenore and pointed to Al's signature.

"How did he know? Why did he come? This is too much," said Lenore.

Just then, the doorbell rang, and the girls ran to see a deliveryman with a grandiose, wicker basket, the largest basket they had ever seen. It was piled high with fruit and other delicacies wrapped in plastic and tied with ribbons. The display was stunning, and included kiwis, mangos, pears and plums, red and green apples, oranges and grapes. Also included was a box of assorted chocolates, a container of cocoa mix, chocolate truffles, fruit preserves, and mixed nuts.

"Bubbie, Mommy," yelled Mindy. "Come and see this humungous basket. Who sent us this?"

"I'll get it," said Judy. "You don't need to get up; you're not supposed to do anything—you're sitting shiva."

Judy retrieved the basket and placed it on the table in the dinette, where Faye was laying out silverware. The girls, Faye, and Judy stood there in awe, admiring it. Lenore and Jennie soon joined them.

Jennie opened the little envelope attached to the basket and pulled out a small white card.

She tried to hide the pleasure she felt by stifling a smile as she read the message to herself: *To my girls, Lenore, Mindy, and Faye, With love and sympathy, Al Springer.*

"It's from Al," said Jennie.

"Who's Al?" everyone but Lenore asked at once.

~

The presence of ten Jewish men was required to enable the mourners to say Kaddish, so each night of shiva, there was a minyan in the Mandelstern home. But on the fifth night, there were two more families in the synagogue who had lost loved ones, and they also required a shiva minyan in their respective homes. Rabbi Herbert said he would conduct the service at the home of the Bronsteins, for whom he had officiated at a funeral that morning. And Cantor Yudenfreund was going to cover the shiva minyan for the Weiss family. The rabbi and cantor had left the Mandelstern shiva minyan in the capable hands of the reliably pious and knowledgeable Aron Lubinski. It was scheduled for seven thirty.

On the evening in question, the Mandelstern home was filled with visitors—but they weren't all necessarily Jewish men.

Lenore had cringed when Irv and Connie Rosen walked in at 7:25. Jennie was standing near the front door when they entered. Lenore sat on the low shiva bench next to the couch as she watched the scene play out. She looked as first Irv, then Connie, gave Jennie a hug.

"How's the baby?" Jennie asked.

In response, Irv whipped out some photos from TJ's baptism to show her.

What a hypocrite, Lenore thought to herself, as she observed the scene from her perch on the shiva seat. *The nerve of him—he is here at my father's shiva, showing off pictures of his new baby.* She almost felt sorry for clueless Connie, who was chatting with Jennie.

Lenore kept looking at her watch, so excruciating was the sight of Irv invading her own house of shiva. She was hoping the minyan would start before Irv made his way over to her—if he dared.

It looked like Irv was babbling to Jennie about the baby, so Lenore averted her eyes in the direction of Aron, the minyan leader, who was consulting with Jakob Zilberman. She could tell from the expression on his face that he was starting to get worried. He was looking around the room, counting. He was trying to determine whether there were enough Jewish men present to constitute a minyan. He counted six— without Irv Rosen. Could he count him?

Whispering, Aron asked Jakob Zilberman.

"I don't know; he goes to Yizkor on Yom Kippur," said Jakob.

"But he just had his son baptized. He and his wife are showing off pictures from the christening."

"That's the eternal question—who is a Jew?" Jakob said. "Hitler would have considered him a Jew. He has two Jewish parents."

"*Shoin genug.* That's enough with the Hitler," Aron barked at Jakob. "Just knock it off. If we don't hurry up, we could lose some of the people we already have. Do you want to make some phone calls? Or perhaps I will go ring the doorbell of a couple of the neighbors. But I think all the Jewish men from the block are here already."

"Okay, I'll make some calls," said Jakob. "I'll call Murray Lesser."

Aron rolled his eyes. He had hoped to manage without Murray, the financial savior and perpetual president of the Northeast Queens Jewish Center. He, like many others, had hoped that when Murray moved to Manhasset Hills, it would be the end of his bragging and bullying family. But unfortunately for Murray, the tonier community did not embrace him in the same way as had the congregation in Queens.

Unfortunately, his move to the suburbs coincided with the exposure of the TV quiz show scandals. As a former winner and now key witness, Murray testified to Congress that the answers had been fed to him week after week on *Man on the Street Genius.* As other contestants corroborated his testimony, everyone impli- cated—contestants, producers, and hosts—took a big hit to their reputations. So when Murray first moved to Manhasset Hills, he brought with him the baggage of not being a real genius, but merely a fraud.

After he was exposed, he was hardly a sought-after superstar in his new community. So he continued to maintain his family membership in the Queens congregation, where he was a founding member and financial supporter. Those who had known him for a long time were willing to look away from the cheating. By Bellerose standards, Murray was a rich man, and the synagogue was glad to have his resources. Even though his celebrity faded, he was still elected president of the shul time and again. Aron feared that Murray was going to keep that position for life.

"Sure, call him; he's the president," said Aron, who at this point was left with no other option. "He can drive here in five minutes. And ask him to bring his sons."

While a few other women circled Jennie and Connie and began admiring photos of the beautiful baby boy in his christening gown, Irv took the opportunity to make his way to Lenore. He bent down to hug her, but before he could, she raised her hands to push him away.

"How dare you come to my house? What are you doing here? Take your wife, your baby pictures, and get out now before everyone knows what a phony, cheating lowlife you are."

Irv turned beet red. He was surprised by Lenore's violent reaction. She had known him for more than a decade. She knew full well that he was a married man with a family. *Women are so emotional*, he thought. *Perhaps she's getting her period.* Or perhaps he could chalk it up to her losing her father. He headed over to the conversational circle of baby admirers to retrieve Connie.

"Come on, Connie," he said.

"You're leaving so soon?" Jennie asked.

"Yeah, we have to get home and check on the kids," Irv said. "It's a school night, and we want to make sure the girls have finished their homework. And TJ needs to be fed. We just wanted to stop by and pay our respects."

As they walked outside, Connie said, "I thought you said we were going to stay at least a half hour."

"I forgot that they have a religious service at seven thirty. You might be uncomfortable."

"Irv," she said, "why would you say such a thing? You know that as a religious person myself, I respect other traditions. I would have been curious to see it."

"Well, maybe another time."

Minutes later, Murray Lesser walked in with his two sons—Randy, the Hebrew School bully, and the older boy, Kenny. Both boys had a cockiness that disgusted Aron. On the other hand, Aron was relieved that he now needed only one more man for the minyan.

Randy and Kenny made a beeline for Mindy and Bronka and JoJo, who were standing by her side. Randy had seemingly developed amnesia about how he had belittled and terrified the girls in Hebrew School. And why wouldn't he? They were now attractive teenagers with pretty faces and cute figures.

Kenny, who was eighteen and a student at C. W. Post College in Brookville, had his hands all over Mindy, ostensibly in an attempt to comfort her. Vulnerable and grieving, the rather plain-looking Mindy clearly relished the attention.

By 7:45 Aron began to panic about Jakob's lack of success in recruiting one more man to the minyan. But just then, the door opened and in walked an incredibly well-groomed, well-dressed, middle-aged man. He donned a yarmulke as he entered the house of shiva. His physical features might have been described as nondescript, but his demeanor screamed prosperous and sophisticated. No one in Bellerose had the means or the inclination to pay so much attention to their appearance. As all eyes turned to the stranger, Lenore gasped.

Still reeling from her encounter with Irv, she had not seen Al for ten years. But she would recognize him anywhere. He looked like a male version of Mindy. Moreover, her interaction with Irv had sapped all her anger and hatred. She was surprised that she was not unhappy to see him.

Aron went to shake his hand, while Jakob started distributing the prayer books.

"I'm Aron Lubinski, and you're the tenth man; you make the minyan."

~

Immediately, Aron began the service, first announcing which way was east, the direction Jews traditionally face when they pray—toward Jerusalem. Prayer books in hand, the ten men, Lenore and Jennie, and those guests who chose to remain in the living room gathered around Aron. A few of the women retired to the kitchen, including Faye, but Judy stood with Lenore, whose face had lost all its color and whose hands were shaking. Lenore could sense that Al was standing behind her. They had not yet acknowledged each other, and she willed herself not to turn around and glance at him. But she knew he was there. The familiar scent of tobacco comingled with the light, musky, powdery fragrance of Canoe wafted over her and filled her senses with aching and desire.

Unlike the rabbi or cantor, Aron raced through the evening prayers. He did not announce the pages until he got to the Mourner's Kaddish. This he recited slowly so that Lenore and Jennie could keep up with him. At the end of the service, he asked Lenore to read aloud from Ecclesiastes. Her body shook and her voice cracked as she read:

To everything there is a season,
And a time to every purpose under heaven:
A time to be born and a time to die,
A time to plant and a time to reap,

A time to build up and a time to tear down,

A time to laugh and a time to weep,

A time to dance and a time to grieve,

A time to gather and a time to throw stones,

A time to embrace and a time to refrain from embracing,

A time to seek and a time to lose,

A time to keep and a time to cast away,

A time to love and a time to hate

A time for war and a time for peace.

At the conclusion of the service, Aron intoned the traditional words of consolation—in Hebrew and in English—"*May God comfort you together with all the other mourners of Zion and Jerusalem.*"

No sooner had these words been spoken than Lenore felt Al's hand on her shoulder. She turned around and instinctively threw her arms around him.

"Thank you for coming, and also for that gigantic basket," she said.

He laughed, pleasantly surprised by her friendly welcome, as he embraced her.

"You look frozen in time," he said as he gazed at her with the look that brought back a flood of memories. "You haven't aged a day."

"Actually, I've never looked worse," she said.

"I'm sorry about your father. How is Mindy handling it?"

Mindy—her daughter's name suddenly jolted her back to reality. Mindy, the sad, entitled teenager, who was grieving for her grandpa, her best friend. For a moment in Al's arms, she had almost forgotten about her daughter, Al's child—the one he had never seen. The daughter who thought he was dead.

"I can't talk about Mindy now."

Al was not only smart, but also strategic. He had played his cards well up to that point. He knew when to fold them.

"Perhaps we can catch up another time, Lenore."

"Sure," she said. "You can reach me at JHNQ. I work in the accounting office. I'll walk you to the door."

As Al opened the front door, she walked out onto the porch with him. He knew not to say another word, but instead, simply took her hand and kissed it.

"I'll call you," he said, as he headed toward a big black Cadillac Fleetwood that was parked in front of the Lubinski house. Lenore saw him get into the back seat with the easy grace of a person who was accustomed to a lifestyle that included a limousine and a chauffeur.

~

After the week of shiva, it was time for the Mandelsterns to resume their regular routines. The lack of the constant company of solicitous and chatty people was a welcome relief, but also an inescapable trigger that signified Harry was truly gone.

While Jennie found the steady flood of people exhausting, once the shiva was over, she was overwhelmed with feelings of loss and loneliness. She was now without the love of her life. She had known Harry since she was a teenager, and together, they had weathered everything life had thrown at them with dignity, courage, and good humor. Jennie wasn't sure how she would go on without him. She knew she needed to—at least for Mindy and Lenore—but her husband had been her rock, and she suddenly felt weak and vulnerable and bereft—and every bit her age.

Mindy was sad and angry. She truly missed the love and company of her grandfather, but as adolescents are prone to do, she worried about the upset in her own life. Not only had she lost her companion and confidant, but she had also lost the chauffeur who took her to school and shopping and parties at a moment's notice. That's why she was so delighted when Kenny Lesser called her shortly after the shiva and invited her to the Spring Ball at his school. She had never even known, let alone dated, a college boy, one who not only drove but had his own car.

After the week of shiva, Lenore returned to work. Her colleagues greeted her with hugs and condolences. She was confident that Al would call her, but when a week went by without her hearing from him, she began to despair.

Her coworkers were more solicitous than usual. They brought her buttered rolls and coffee when she arrived at work. They picked up the phone on the first ring, only handing it off to Lenore when someone requested her, or if it was a matter specifically requiring her attention.

Ten business days after her return to the office, she finally heard from Al. The phone rang five times and no one else answered it.

"Accounting Office," Lenore said as she finally picked up the phone on the fifth ring.

"Lenore, is that you? It's Al." Her heart raced as she heard the ebullient voice on the other end of the phone.

Dammit, thought Lenore. She had been anticipating his call and had hoped someone else would answer. She imagined how he would think she was so valuable and professional to have someone else answering her phone for her. *Why couldn't she even catch one little break? And why had he waited a whole ten days to call?* But the sound of his voice stirred her with excitement. At that moment, she yearned for Al to be back in her life, no matter what the cost.

They made plans to meet at the Silver Spoon Diner on Union Turnpike, a few blocks from the hospital. She glowed with feelings of pleasure and possibility. Al was back.

By the time Lenore actually met Al in person a week later, she was having second thoughts about him. She had swung back and forth so many times in her mind that she was losing sleep and developing headaches. The very thought of Al still excited her. She had to admit that she was still attracted to him on a visceral level. But what about the Al who had forsaken her when she was arrested? And, despite his financial success, he was a convicted felon.

Of course, she told herself, Joe McCarthy had been discredited, and many innocent people had also gotten swept up in the Red Scare of the 1950s. But if you believed J. Edgar Hoover, the head of the FBI, the communists were still a major threat to America. What's more, Al had ended up in prison because he'd lied. She, on the other hand, had told the truth.

Yes, she had listened to her attorney and told the whole truth about her relationship with Al and with the Greenglasses. The lawyer had been right. Once she told the truth, the charges were dropped. The messy, ugly truth had set her free.

On the other hand, she had not told her daughter the truth about her parentage. She had deprived her, not only of a relationship with her father, but of the knowledge of her family history. Now that he was back in her life, Al might try to persuade her to tell Mindy that he was her father. How could she tell her the truth now? But then again, how could she not?

Although she didn't have to be at work until nine o'clock, and she was meeting Al for lunch, she began applying her makeup with the skill of a runway model at 6:45 a.m. Then she doused her hands with Elizabeth Arden's Eight-Hour Intensive Moisturizing Hand Cream, should Al take her hand. She sat and listened to the radio for a half hour in order to let the cream soak in.

She wiped off the residue and sprayed herself from head to toe with her signature Shalimar perfume. Then she freshened up her bouffant hairdo, courtesy of Cindy, her hairdresser. She had kindly kept the shop open the previous evening just to accommodate her.

Lenore gazed at herself in the full-length mirror from several angles. *Not bad,* she said to herself. Turning forty had been hard for her, and she was determined to look as young and fashionable as she possibly could.

At eight o'clock, she headed downstairs to the kitchen.

Jennie was seated at the kitchen table, having a cup of coffee.

"Well, good morning, Mrs. Kennedy. Don't you look young and lovely?"

"Thanks. Do you really think I look like Jackie?"

"A dead ringer."

"Mom, where's Mindy?"

"Oh, you just missed her; she left for school about five minutes ago. Do you want something to eat, some coffee?"

"No thanks. I'm going to head over to work early. I'll grab something there. Al asked me to meet him for lunch, and I'm not sure how long it will go."

Jennie said nothing but gave her daughter a knowing smile. She had long thought that Lenore should have let Al tell her his side of the story. Lenore wasn't getting any younger; she could do a lot worse.

～

The Silver Spoon wasn't one of the old-fashioned greasy spoon diners located out of the way in a small town, but a spanking new spacious eatery with bright lights and upholstered booths with jukeboxes. Al was already waiting for her when she arrived at 11:45, right before the lunchtime crush. Impeccably coiffed and dressed, he looked a bit out of place standing beside the revolving glass dessert showcase.

Lenore was also overdressed for the diner. She wore her favorite red silk suit with pearls. Although she had a matching pillbox hat, she had decided to skip it. No one wore a hat to the Silver Spoon; it would have attracted too much attention, and besides, it might have messed up her hair.

Al and Lenore sat at a booth in the back, and the waitress brought them each a menu.

"This menu is the size of a phone book," Al joked. "Do you know what you want?"

"I'll just have some poached eggs, toast, and coffee," said Lenore. She was really not hungry at all and didn't want to eat anything that would upset her stomach.

"Breakfast for lunch, eh. You're a cheap date. Well, I'll have a turkey club and a Coke." When the waitress appeared moments later, Al ordered for both of them.

As they waited for the food to come, Al began. He was painfully aware that Lenore had never given him a chance to explain. Her mother had turned him away, and Lenore had hung up when he called her. He was determined to finally tell his side of the story.

"You abandoned me," Lenore said. "Did you know Jerry sent Lester, a first-year associate, who was wet behind the ears and couldn't stop babbling about how concerned you were about your wife and your children?"

"Well, I was concerned about them. But I was also concerned about you and Mindy. I always have been, and I always will be. That's why I tried to speak with you, but you wouldn't let me. That's why I never stopped sending Mindy gifts. What did Lester know? He was an inexperienced lawyer. He was just repeating what Jerry told him. Why did you put so much stock in what he said? You never gave me a chance to explain."

"And what's to explain?' Lenore asked.

"I was fighting for my reputation and the welfare of my family. I told Jerry to take care of you. I didn't edit what he told Lester or what Lester heard him say. I was distraught. I trusted Jerry to do the right thing by you. Do you really think I told him to stick you with an inexperienced lawyer?"

"Well, apparently you never thought to ask him how he was taking care of me."

"Lenore, my whole world fell apart. The case and the time in prison led to the end of my marriage. And of course, my wife felt betrayed when she found out about you. It took me a long time to get back on my feet again. Thank God, my partner, Max, is a genius, and we had a winning product at the right time. But my personal life was in shambles for many years. My children wanted nothing to do with me for a long time."

"And now?"

"Well, my son is at MIT getting a PhD in chemical engineering. My daughter got married last year, and she's living in Philadelphia with her husband. The kids talk to me now, and I see them from time to time. I went to my daughter's wedding, but my ex-wife refused to speak to me or to acknowledge my presence. She and her new husband walked my daughter down the aisle. That really hurt."

On the one hand, Al was making a compelling case that he needed and wanted her. But Lenore couldn't help thinking that was because he was now alone. She had to wonder what had engendered his wife's extreme rage and need for revenge, where she wouldn't even let him accompany his daughter down the aisle. She wanted desperately to believe Al. But she couldn't help but think of the dictum, "There are three sides to every story—his side, her side, and the truth." She would never know the truth.

"So, Lenore, I come to you alone. I am unencumbered, and I am a changed man. It was never the right time before, and I was afraid you would slam the door in my face. I admit I've made a lot of stupid mistakes, which I regret. I know I hurt you, but I need your forgiveness. I want you in my life. I want Mindy in my life. I'm prepared to shower you with a lifestyle that you've never imagined. I will take care of your mother. By the way, has Mindy started looking at colleges?"

"She'll go to Queens College. She has the grades to get in, and it's free. The kids in our neighborhood who could go to Ivy League schools go to Queens."

"And why is that?"

"Because their parents can't afford it, and Queens is a great school."

"I'm sure it's a good school. But you don't get the connections you can get in a really top school with cachet."

Lenore was warring with herself. This sounded too good to be true. And it probably was. Al really had a lot of nerve to suddenly reappear after ten years and dangle a carrot in front of her like this. What's to say he wouldn't break her heart again if someone younger and more exciting walked into his line of vision?

"So, what do you say, Lenore? Let's start by taking Mindy and Jennie to dinner."

Al was no fool, Lenore thought. And his proposition was fraught with huge risks for her. He would charm and wine and dine her daughter and mother, and they would fall in love with him. But where would that leave her? In learning the truth about her father, Mindy would discover that her mother had perpetuated a colossal lie. Mindy was a teenager, angry and rebellious. Lenore had not been the most attentive mother. What if Mindy ended up hating her and loving Al?

"I really have to absorb all of this. I have to think about the ramifications. I'm not ready to make a decision now."

"I understand fully," said Al, as he took her baby soft hands in his own.

"You have a lot to consider. Take your time. But in the meantime, can just the two of us have dinner together soon? Surely, there's no harm in that."

"I guess that would be okay," Lenore said, as he kissed her hand.

1962

————◦————

BELLEROSE, NEW YORK

THERE WAS NO QUESTION THAT Faye and Izzy had performed a mitzvah when they initially provided a home, shelter, sustenance, and support to the refugee family right off the boat. But as Judy and Faye's relationship developed over the succeeding years, it became a symbiotic one. Faye liked to brag to her neighbors and friends about how essential she was to the life of the younger family. By 1962, the truth was that she probably needed them more than they needed her, but that didn't stop her from praising herself.

"I manage the household," she would say, "and I plan and cook all the meals. I'm a built-in babysitter. So Judy is free to work in the bakery and do anything else she needs or wants to do during the day."

Judy would wince whenever she heard Faye's spin. Although it was largely true, except for the babysitter part—the girls were old enough to be babysitters themselves—she didn't like that Faye had to share their personal arrangement. And, of course, in Faye's version, there was no mention of the older woman's overbearing and controlling behavior. The toll that Becky had taken on the entire household was never acknowledged. Neither was the emotional support and camaraderie that Faye wanted and got from Judy. Judy was not only compassionate, but she could see beyond the surface. She knew that Faye meant well. Faye just couldn't help being loud and bossy.

It seemed to Judy that Faye no longer needed to be so defensive. She was now prosperous and an integral part of the bakery business. She not only took care of the household expenses, but she also managed the books for the two shops. In fact, Faye signed Aron's generous weekly paychecks. Judy did her bidding.

One frigid winter day, Faye slipped on the ice as she was leaving the bakery.

Judy happened to look out the bakery window and saw Faye on the ground.

"Izzy! Aron! Come quick," she yelled, "Faye fell on the ice. It looks like she's hurt."

Izzy ran out first.

"Faye, come on, get up," he said.

"I can't get up," she said as she winced in pain. "I think I broke my knee. I can't feel or move my leg."

By then, both Aron and Judy had joined them outside, as well as Morty, who had also witnessed the scene from his shop.

"We can call an ambulance," said Judy.

"I don't really want an ambulance," Faye said.

"I have my car in the parking lot," said Morty. "I'll drive it around to the front and take you to the hospital if you don't want to call an ambulance."

Faye thought she probably needed an ambulance, but the memory of the ride to the hospital with Becky conjured up unpleasant feelings. As she allowed the two men to help her into the car, she suspected she was doing even more damage to her knee.

By the time the orthopedist arrived in the emergency room, she was in such pain that she'd convinced herself her knee was broken.

"I've reviewed the X-rays, and your patella is broken in three places," he said. "I need to do emergency surgery right away."

"I don't want to be put to sleep," she said.

"I won't do the surgery if you're awake, and we need to do it right away."

Writhing in pain, Faye had no choice but to agree.

As Judy sat with Izzy in the waiting room during the surgery, she began to realize that things were about to change at home—at least in the short term. She knew that she would be the one to take care of Faye, and she imagined what it would be like to be supervising instead of taking orders.

When Izzy brought Faye home from the hospital a few days later, she was confined to her bedroom. The doctor had used small screws and plates to secure the broken bones. She was ordered not to bear weight for a month and to keep her leg elevated as much as possible.

Cranky Faye replaced bossy Faye. She could only walk with the assistance of crutches in the small house. She called for water, for ice, for pain medication. Judy almost yearned for the return of the capable, domineering woman she had come to know.

Judy had no choice but to take over the household. She bought the groceries, planned and prepared the meals, did the laundry, and straightened up before the cleaning woman came. She learned that she was fully capable of being in charge. And she enlisted the twins to assist by giving them specific tasks.

Since JoJo was the more outgoing of the two, she gave her the job of answering the phone and taking messages. She tapped Bronka for the task of looking through the voluminous mail and assigning it to piles for Faye to later review—bills, business correspondence, get well cards, and circulars. Bronka rather liked her job of mail clerk, being innately curious. But because Bronka was a helper by nature, she was quick to do more than the mail. She fetched ice for Faye's knee, brought her meals on a tray, and chatted with her.

About a week after Faye returned from the hospital, Bronka went into Faye's room and announced cheerfully, "It looks like you got six get well cards today."

"I didn't know I was so popular," Faye gloated. "Who are they from? Read me the names on the envelopes."

Bronka enjoyed studying the cards Faye received, examining the handwriting and the return names and addresses. She sat on the side of Faye's bed and they opened them together. They read the greeting and the personal note that often accompanied it. And Faye told Bronka anecdotes about the people who had sent the cards.

A week later, Bronka worked up the courage to ask about Becky. It seemed as if she had disappeared from the planet. Faye assured her that Becky was well cared for and that she had taken up painting. When Bronka asked if she could accompany her when she resumed her visits to Becky, Faye replied, "We'll see. But why don't you write her a letter; I'm sure she'd love to hear from you."

Bronka wrote a letter later that evening and mailed it the next day. Thereafter, each day she looked for a response from Becky.

A few weeks into this routine, Judy was preparing dinner and Bronka sat at the kitchen table going through the mail.

As Bronka put the mail into piles, she said, "Mostly bills and bakery-related business today, and only two get well cards."

"Well, they're bound to taper off after a while," said Judy. "It's been more than three weeks since the surgery."

Bronka eyed a thin, blue, lightweight letter that she had missed in the first sorting. It said *Aerogramme* on it, and it appeared to be in one piece, folded and glued. The handwriting looked strained and deliberate, much like her father's, whose penmanship had a foreign flavor to it. It was post-marked Jerusalem, Israel. It was from someone named Naomi Ben-Zvi and it was addressed to Edyta Wozniak, c/o Lubinski.

"Who is Naomi Ben-Zvi?" Bronka asked.

"I have no idea."

"And who is Edyta Wozniak?" Bronka tested her mother, knowing full well that her father called her mother Dyta.

She had always believed that her mother's real name was Judyta. Everyone called her Judy, but her father, referred to her by his pet name for her, Dyta. But who was Edyta? And she did not recognize the name *Wozniak*. Bronka's antennae were aroused.

Bronka saw the color rise in her mother's cheeks. And her sky-blue eyes, usually cheerful and twinkling, had become pools of fear.

Judy averted her gaze from her daughter. She had never heard of Naomi Ben-Zvi, but if she was addressing her as Edyta, she must have some connection to her past. She felt trapped; she had feared this moment for years. She knew she had been exposed.

"I imagine that would be me. We'll open it and see what she has to say," she said, realizing that it was time to face the truth. "Let's read it together."

My dear Edyta,

I have been trying for years to locate you. You probably don't remember me, but I remember you. I was an eight-year-old girl when you rescued me and two other children in the darkness of night from the Kielce Ghetto. You covered us with blankets and smuggled us in a Red Cross lorry out of the ghetto. You brought us to the convent where Mother Mary Martha and your own sister, Sister Mary Krystyna, welcomed us into the Convent of the Blessed Virgin Mary. Although I never saw you again, Sister Mary Krystyna often referred to you as her little sister, Edyta, and told us you were the angel who had rescued me and numerous other children. And we always prayed for your health and safety. We were well cared for in the convent and when the war ended, I was reunited with my aunt, who lives in Israel. All of my Polish family perished.

I now work in the office of Aryeh Kubovy, who is the chairman of Yad Vashem. Ever since the capture of Adolph Eichmann, he has been receiving letters saying that it's not enough to focus on the atrocities committed by the Nazis. Israel must also honor those who risked their lives to rescue Jews during the Shoah. I agree. By honoring people like you, we shine a light on what is best in humanity, and teach young people the importance of kindness, respect for differences, and for acting against evil.

The Avenue of the Righteous was dedicated at Yad Vashem on Yom HaShoah this year. Trees will be planted in honor of the rescuers. An independent public commission will meet soon to decide who will be the first virtuous and praiseworthy Gentiles to be honored. As soon as the program seeks nominees, I wish to submit your name—with your permission, of course.

All the words and honors in the world are not enough to thank you for saving my life and the lives of so many others. But, if in some small way, I can pay tribute to you, I would like to do it.

Respectfully,
Naomi Ben-Zvi

Judy was caught off guard. She should have been proud to receive such a letter, but she was ashamed. She had been unmasked. She had never found the right time to tell her daughters that she had been born a Christian and had embraced Judaism after the horror of the Kielce pogrom in 1946—after the war. It was because of Aron; he acted as if it were a dirty little secret, not a noble and beautiful gesture, as with Ruth in the Bible. This hurt her every day of her married life.

She believed she was a good Jew. And under Faye's tutelage, she had become an even better one—learning all the customs that were lived out in a Jewish home. But now, Bronka, for whom there were no shades of gray, would demand an explanation. And she wasn't sure she could give her a satisfactory one. Aron had forever stalled her, and now she had to explain to her literal-minded daughter, not at a time of her own choosing, but right now.

"I don't even know what your real name is," Bronka blurted out, seeing her mother's pain, but not able to conceal her own. She felt betrayed. She did not focus on her mother's heroics, but rather that she had concealed the truth. Who was this mother she thought she knew?

"My birth name was Edyta Wozniak. My family called me Dyta, and that is what Papa has always called me."

"I thought your real name was Judy."

"Izzy called me Judy when I first came to America, and it stuck."

"And who is Sister Mary Krystyna?"

"She is my older sister."

"You have a sister, and she's a nun?"

"Yes."

"Have you been in touch with her since the war?"

"We've exchanged letters, but Poland is behind the Iron Curtain, so we've not seen each other."

"Does Papa know your sister is a nun?"

"Yes, he does."

Bronka's head was reeling. How could this be? The Lubinskis were the super Jews of 253rd Street. Papa went to shul every day. Mama did everything a Jewish mother was supposed to do. If she told Christina Rosen that her mother had been born Catholic (which she had no intention of doing), she would probably say Mama was going straight to hell.

"Bronka, people are allowed to change. We are all changing all the time. I had good reason to abandon my childhood faith and embrace Judaism. I am a Jew now, and Papa and I have raised you and Johanna to be good Jews."

"Why did you lie about your background? You're reprehensible."

"You are calling me reprehensible? I didn't lie; I just didn't tell you the whole truth. I'm hurt and shocked that you are totally ignoring the point of the letter. I saved many Jews during the Shoah, including Papa. This woman says I am righteous. That means nothing to you?"

"She is nominating you as a Righteous Gentile. You can't be Mrs. Super Jew and a Righteous Gentile at the same time."

"I made a mistake; I should have told you sooner," Judy said, smarting from her daughter's disdain as tears streamed down her face.

"And how many times did I ask you, did I beg you, to tell me your story?"

"I thought you were too young to understand."

"And when do you think I would be old enough to understand?" Bronka began to cry.

"I wanted to tell you, but the time was never right." Judy sobbed.

As curious as Bronka was, she had heard enough for now. "I'm going out," she said as she slammed the front door.

Sobbing, Bronka ran across the street and rang Mindy's doorbell. Jennie came to the door.

"What's wrong, *Bubbelah*?"

"I have to talk to JoJo. Is she here?"

"Yes, the girls are upstairs in Mindy's room."

Bronka, still in tears, tore up the staircase and found them sitting on the bed, perusing *Glamour* magazine as Mindy told JoJo all about Kenny Lesser.

"Bronka, what's wrong?" Both girls said at once as they saw her tearstained, bloated face.

Jennie followed Bronka up the stairs; she was concerned that something terrible had happened. Perhaps Faye had taken a turn for the worse, or someone else was sick or had died. She stood in the door as Bronka blurted out, "It's Mama."

"What's wrong?" JoJo asked again.

"Mama has been lying to us all along."

"About what?" JoJo asked. "What could she possibly lie about?"

"About who she is."

"What are you talking about?" JoJo asked.

"Let's go downstairs and discuss this around the kitchen table," said Jennie, making a snap decision that as much as the teenage girls thought they knew everything, some adult intervention was needed.

Jennie put some cookies and fruit on the table, along with a pitcher of lemonade and some glasses, and sat down with the girls.

"So who is Mama?" JoJo asked in a whimsical way.

"It's not a joke, JoJo. There was a letter from Israel from a woman who Mama saved during the war."

"So that's a good thing," said Jennie.

"Well, I guess it's good that Mama saved her, but I found out that Mama didn't used to be Jewish and she never told us about it."

"What was she?" JoJo asked, incredulously.

"She was Catholic; she even has a sister who's a nun in Poland, and Mama rescued children from the ghetto and brought them to the convent where her sister was."

"What's her sister's name?"

"Sister Mary Krystyna."

"Wow—what would Tina, Toni, and Tori Rosen think about that?" JoJo said.

"Don't you dare tell them!" Bronka barked.

"So what's the problem?" JoJo asked. Always eager to be a genuine American, she kind of liked the idea that she had an aunt who was a nun and that her mother had not been born Jewish. She also was intrigued that her mother, who rarely went farther than the bakery, had risked her life to save Jewish children.

"Mama has been lying to us all of the time," said Bronka.

"Well, she didn't really lie," JoJo said. "And besides, not for nothing, she's a hero. Who knew? Maybe she was just being modest."

"You think?" said Bronka.

"Sometimes parents don't tell children the whole truth because they believe they can't handle it," said Jennie.

"That's not lying; it's protection. Your mother just thought she was protecting you. And sometimes we tell white lies, harmless fibs to avoid hurting someone's feelings or upsetting them. I don't know whether your mother told you white lies along the way, but everyone does from time to time. They're a good thing because they are done out of compassion."

"This doesn't sound like a white lie to me," said Bronka. "It might not be a technical lie, but it feels like a big fat deception."

"I understand what Bronka is saying," Mindy said. "Ever since Grandpa died, I've been thinking that I don't know anything about my father—what he was like or even how he died. I bet you know, Bubbie."

"It's your mother's truth, and she is the only one who can tell you."

"I have a feeling she never will."

"Our mother has no choice now but to tell us the truth," Bronka insisted. "And that goes for Papa too. He's not so innocent either; he participated in the cover-up."

"Bronka," said JoJo. "Everything's not a conspiracy. Maybe there's more to our parents than meets the eye."

"It's six-fifteen, girls," Jennie said. "Don't you have dinner at six every evening?"

∾

When the girls walked into their house, although they could smell the meatloaf and potatoes in the oven, the table was not set for dinner. Usually, you could set your watch by the Lubinskis' six o'clock nightly dinner.

Instead, Mama and Papa and Izzy were in the living room, sitting on the green sofa covered in plastic. And Faye had actually left her bedroom. She sat on the beige chair with her leg elevated by two pillows on the matching hassock. Judy and Aron were looking very grim. Faye and Izzy were silent. The television was off, and the only sound was the whirring of the fan coming from the kitchen.

Bronka began to panic. For fifteen years, she had tried to be perfect and now—in one fell swoop—she had disrespected and deeply wounded her mother. She could not imagine what punishment was in store for her. JoJo, on the other hand, was slightly amused at the sight of the somber adults. She had not been a party to the discussion, so she was curious about what would transpire next.

Izzy spoke first. "Sit down, girls."

The girls sat close together on the piano bench, which faced the couch.

"Now, I understand there was an argument earlier," Izzy said.

Bronka's mouth was uncomfortably dry, but she didn't dare get a glass of water. She would have to face the inquisition without one, she thought.

"Izzy," challenged Faye in her booming voice. "Don't call it an argument. It was a misunderstanding. And Aron and Judy are here to clear it up once and for all. They want you girls to know how much they love you."

"Why can't they tell us themselves?" JoJo asked. "Why are you speaking for them?" She'd had enough of Faye's meddling. *Was Faye acting as the emcee here or the judge? Why was it that Faye had to control and interject herself into every situation?* She could believe her mother loved them, but Papa, not so much.

"They will speak, but I want you to be respectful," Faye continued. "All parents make mistakes and learn from them. Think about it, parents are just human beings who are a generation older than their children. There's no school that teaches parenting."

At that moment, Bronka realized that Faye and Izzy knew what was coming.

"Okay, Faye, that's enough," snapped Izzy. "Let Aron speak."

"It's my fault; I didn't want your mother to tell you," Aron explained. His voice cracked with emotion. "The time was never right. I didn't want you burdened by the past. No, I was not like Jakob Zilberman, who tells everyone in his line of vision what happened. Who is to say what is right? Is it better to be completely open and honest or to protect my children? I did not want to share my personal darkness with you. I thought I was protecting you. I wanted you to be carefree Jewish-American girls, released from the demons of Europe, safe from the graveyard of Poland. But I have to say, Bronka, I am very disappointed that you spoke to Mama in such a disrespectful manner."

Bronka did not say a word. All she saw was a brooding, melancholy man. Who knew if he was even capable of love? He ordered her mother around as if she was his servant, and he was constantly annoyed by Faye's big mouth. He was only pleasant with strangers—in the bakery and in the shul. She had wanted to know what made him so miserable. But he was mum. Her mother had given her clues here and there, but her sixth sense had always told her there was more. Did he really think he had been protecting his children? They could see his despair; they could feel his depression, even if he did not say a word.

"Bronka was just shocked." Her twin rose to her defense, knowing her sister would not have the nerve to defend herself, and generally being disdainful of her father. "She takes Judaism very seriously. And you know, she is very honest. She never liked fake things. Remember, how she even thought Tiny Tears was phony? Of course, she was stunned to hear that Mama was being nominated as a Righteous Gentile. I, on the other hand, can tolerate shades of gray. I think it's neat that we have Christian blood and our aunt is a nun—"

"*Shoin genug*," Aron said. "Stop it this minute. What a mouth on you. You sound like Hitler. Religion is not about blood. It's about belief and *kavannah*."

"Don't you dare compare me with Hitler. I'm an American girl, and I'm proud of it. You'll never be a real American because you're buried in the past."

"You and your sister are both impossible," Aron yelled as he got up from his seat. "How dare you upset your mother like this?" He was screaming as he raised his hand and slapped JoJo across her face.

Her face smarted from the slap, and she started to cry. Aron had never hit either of the girls before. But so close were the twins, that Bronka felt the sting, the humiliation, and the anger too. The twins sobbed in unison.

This is not going well, Izzy thought. He needed to be the adult in the room. "If you guys keep this up, it's only a matter of time before Irv Rosen and his pal, Detective Sergeant Moe Solomon, will be snooping around here, trying to find out who's disturbing the peace. Let's make up and have a civil conversation."

"I am ready to talk if the girls want to hear," Aron said. "But I don't want to be interrupted with snide remarks."

"Do you want to hear the story?" Izzy the peacemaker asked. "And do you promise to just listen, and not comment?"

"Yes," said JoJo, still furious, but tremendously curious about the man who had just slapped her, and the mother who had not yet said a word.

"Sure," Bronka said. At that moment, she could not imagine that anything her father would say could possibly soften her aching heart.

"My father was a respected doctor in Kielce, Poland," Aron began. "He was admired not only for his medical skills, but also for his kindness and generosity. He treated both Jews and Christians. We lived in a big stone house; my father's office was on the main floor. I was the oldest child; I had two sisters and two brothers. My grandfather was a rabbi. We were a religious family, observing Shabbos and *kashrus*. Most of the Jews—about seventy-five percent—were Orthodox.

"Before the war, the families of Jewish doctors, lawyers, and factory owners, like our family, lived in wealth. Other Jews lived in poverty. Most were neither rich nor poor and were involved in trade and crafts. Jewish merchants accounted for more than half of Kielce's shoemakers, tailors, bakers, butchers, haberdashers, shoemakers, and saddlers. There were also the teachers who taught in Jewish schools, and rabbis who served the Great Synagogue and more than thirty other prayer houses in Kielce. One of these was my grandfather. During the war, the entire Jewish community became poorer and poorer.

"Before the war, we had a maid and a cook and also a nanny for the two youngest children, who were fifteen and seventeen years younger than I. We went on vacations to a resort at Karlove Vary. On Sundays, we went on outings to the forest of the district *stadion*, where there was a rifle range, swimming pool, and tennis courts.

"We learned about the outbreak of war on the radio and that bombs were falling on the army barracks on Bukowka. We were shocked during the first days of the war. Bombs destroyed Mr. Sobelski's tannery and Mr. Breiner's sawmill. The drone of the German airplanes frightened us. We saw Polish troops leaving, and refugees started moving east. At the beginning, we thought this could not last long.

"I was supposed to go to medical school and become a doctor and go into practice with my father. But Hitler ended all that. When the Nazis invaded Poland in 1939, my life changed. Jews were persecuted, barred from education, and eventually driven from their homes and murdered. Instead of becoming a prosperous doctor like my father, I became prey for the Nazis. If I did not wear the Star of David, I could be arrested or shot. Poles who used to be our friends and neighbors turned against us. We did not know who we could trust. It was very confusing. I went out of the house as little as possible. My plans and dreams were shattered.

"Still, we could not have imagined how much worse things would get. When the Nazis occupied Poland, many Jews, including my parents, could not believe that the Germans—a nation of great intelligence and culture—could treat the Jews in such a cruel and sadistic way.

"They confiscated and plundered Jewish property and businesses. The Germans took over Jewish factories. They gave Jews the dirtiest jobs, making them clean toilets with their coats. I saw them beat up a man and set fire to his beard.

"The Great Synagogue in Kielce was plundered and closed, as were the smaller prayer houses. Still with the hope things would get better soon, I married Sarah Rabinowicz, whose father was also a doctor. We were married by my grandfather in our house because religious weddings had been banned. At first, we lived in the big house with my parents and siblings. Over time, the Nazis forbade Jews from practicing medicine, law, and other professions and from engaging in business. Businesses were confiscated, and we were driven from our homes.

"In 1941, the Germans established a ghetto in Kielce, where all the Jews were forced to live. At first, my mother thought that since my father was a well-known doctor, and we were such a fine family, we would be treated better than the ordinary Jews and not have to go there. Especially because he also treated and was friendly with many Christians. But my family was sent to the ghetto anyway, along with all our *lantzmen*. Our entire extended family was stuffed into a tiny two-room flat. The ghetto was in a very small area, which was enclosed with a fence and barbed wires. There were signs: 'Closed area. No entrance. Jewish Ghetto.' It was the poorest district of Kielce. The buildings did not have running water, and sewage flowed in the gutters. Even though we were forced from our beautiful home, my parents thought the war would end and we would return. They left their valuables with a Polish doctor who was a colleague of my father.

"Believe it or not, at first some of the Jews actually were happy at being sent to the ghetto. They thought the Jews would be left in peace and joked it would be like Tel Aviv. But that soon proved wrong. We were hungry all the time, and we were closed in like a prison. After a few weeks, some Poles started bringing us food and other supplies, like medicine.

"Your mother was one of those Poles. I first met her when she was a young girl. Her mother, Bronka, was a nurse who assisted my father in his office. It is only because of your mother that I am alive today. Dyta, tell them the story of how you saved my life."

"Why don't you tell it?" Judy suggested. She was not sure if he was deferring to her because he wanted her to tell it in her own words and was afraid he would not do her justice. Or was he incapable of giving his wife her due? Was he still ambivalent about what had happened? Or was it just too painful? She would never know.

"I want they should hear it from you," he said.

Fine, she thought, *if that's what he wants, I'll tell it myself.*

"Before the Nazis came, Poles often did business with Jews or used Jewish doctors," Judy said. "Papa's parents were very kind and generous to my family. When I was little, I sometimes accompanied my mother to work, and Papa and his family were always very nice to us. As I got older, I worked as a nursing assistant in the office. I, too, had my plans cut short by the Nazis. I wanted to become a nurse like my mother. But my mother died right before the German invasion, and my father began drinking heavily. My sister left home and became a nun. Once the war broke out, my father, who was a Polish policeman, started voicing anti-Semitic remarks. I didn't know if it was the drink, political expedience, or if he really believed these things. I spent less and less time at home, and I began working with the Polish resistance.

"When the Jews were herded into the Kielce ghetto, I first began to bring them food and blankets right outside the ghetto walls. Then in 1942, the Germans decreed that the penalty for leaving the ghetto illegally was death. It was then that I thought about doing more. One day, while I was in church, a friend from school approached and asked me to come with him. To my surprise, there was my sister, Krystyna, in the mother superior's office. In front of my sister, the mother superior, and the parish priest, he asked me if I wanted to save children. I said yes, and he told me they had a plan, but first I had to agree to join the Polish Underground. I agreed.

"The plan was that I would put on my mother's nurse's uniform and pretend I was a Red Cross nurse, going in and out of the ghetto. The Nazis were terrified of typhus, and my story was that I was going in to check for disease. I endured the ogling—and even groping—of the Gestapo and the Polish police. They whistled at me and blew me kisses. And I blew kisses back, even though they disgusted me. The Resistance provided me with a truck and a driver. They had painted a Red Cross on it, so with the uniform and the truck, I looked official.

"Along with the driver, we smuggled in food and medicine, clothing, blankets, and supplies. On our way out, we took babies and children. Naomi, the woman who wrote the letter, must have been one of those children. Her last name was different then. We first went to the parents and got permission from them to take their children and promised we would try to reunite them when the war was over. It was always a very painful discussion. No one can see the future. Some agreed, but many did not. They still clung to the hope that the situation would get better. For those who gave us permission, we hid bigger children under blankets and towels and medical supplies. We smuggled out babies in tiny coffins with holes in them so they could breathe. I placed the babies in friendly Polish homes. I brought the older children, like Naomi, to the Convent of the Blessed Virgin Mary, where Krystyna was. Her mother superior, Mother Mary

Martha, took them in and shielded them. The convent was the safest place for Jewish children during the war.

"One day on my rounds, I spotted Papa. I told him that I had heard that the ghetto was going to be liquidated soon, and that I would like to take his little sister, Hannah, and his brother, Yosef, with me to safety in the convent. He said he would ask his parents. But they did not want to let the children go. They said they and their family were protected because his father was a doctor and the Germans had told them they needed doctors, and so they were safe. This part is Papa's to tell, and I am only mentioning it because it is part of the story. He argued with them, but they would not part with the children because they were sure their family would be spared.

"Then, the next day, I even went to visit them myself in the tiny flat in which the whole extended family was living, and begged them to let me take the children," Judy continued. "They knew me, and they had known my mother. They knew I had only their best interests at heart. But they refused. Although I feared the children would end up dead, I also understood how unbearably difficult it must be to let your children go.

"But your papa was logical and believed me. He got very angry with his parents, and everyone in the tiny flat started yelling and screaming, and the children began to cry. I tried to tell Papa's parents that time was running out; the Nazis were going to liquidate the ghetto soon. I even appealed to his grandparents. But Aron's mother still was convinced that they would not harm a doctor's family. Aron finally realized that his parents were not going to let Hannah and Yosef go with me. But he believed me when I said there was trouble coming very soon. So he said that he and his wife would go with me instead of the children.

"I had never smuggled adults out of the ghetto before, only children. So I improvised. I snuck them onto the truck and covered them with everything that was there—blankets, sacks, towels, and supplies. I waved at the policeman and blew a kiss as he motioned to let us go through without stopping."

"I will tell you the information I found out after the war from a Kielce survivor," Aron interjected. "The liquidation of the ghetto took place during five days in August 1942. It happened only a few days after your mother warned us. The Nazis shot about a thousand people, mainly children, pregnant women, and the old and sick, including little Hannah, my brother, Yosef, and my grandparents. The rest were taken to the death camp, Treblinka, where my older sister and brother were killed.

"The Jews who were left in the ghetto, including the doctors and skilled workers, were about fifteen hundred, crammed into fifty flats. They eventually shot or deported all of them except for the doctors and their wives.

"Finally, on April 24, 1943, at noon, my parents met their fate. The Germans ordered all the doctors to get ready for a long trip. They were told that the camps did not have enough doctors and they were bringing them there. They told them they could bring their wives. The doctors and their luggage were packed into two trucks. At the Jewish cemetery, my mother and father, along with the remaining doctors and their wives, were undressed and shot. After throwing the dead and injured people into pits, the Nazis threw grenades at them. There was blood-curdling screaming and shouting."

Judy then spoke as tears streamed down her face. "You want the whole truth; well here it is." She sat upright, now emboldened. She had finally found her own voice and wanted to tell the story herself. As she spoke, she began to realize how much the subterfuge and the secrecy had cost her during all these years. Once, she had been an outgoing, proactive, and courageous young woman, but ever since fleeing with Aron, she had been shy and withdrawn, afraid to take any initiative. Her secret past had paralyzed her. She fought back a flood of tears, but she was determined to go on, sensing that her forthrightness would free her. Why was she so afraid of Aron? He would not be alive if it were not for her.

"In the cover of night, after I smuggled Papa and Sarah from the ghetto, I brought them to my house. Now I was taking my activities to a new level. I had been prepared to find hiding places for children, not adults. I had never hidden anyone in my own home before. But I could not think of another option, so I hid them in our attic. I was very nervous. My father was becoming a belligerent drunk and an outspoken anti-Semite. Aron and Sarah were right under my father's nose, and I was petrified that he would discover them.

"After a few days, a German officer banged on the door. I went to answer it. My father was fast asleep in his room. The officer said he had information that there were Jews hiding in the area, did I know anything? I said of course not, but I would let him know if I heard or saw anything. My heart started to race. It occurred to me that perhaps my father had tipped him off. A few days before, he had attacked me and insinuated that I was helping Jews. I'm not sure if he knew then that they were in the house, but he had figured out for sure that I was helping Jews in some way.

"Then the German officer looked me up and down with a lascivious look and touched my face and brushed my lips with his mouth. I was terrified. Poles were being hanged and shot and sent to concentration camps for helping Jews. It was illegal and punishable by death. And I did not want Papa and Sarah caught. He pressed me closer and thrust his tongue into my mouth. Although he disgusted me, I did not resist. When he left, he said he would be back again soon.

"The next morning, when the truck came to my house, I told Papa and Sarah to get in and placed blankets and clothing and medical supplies on top of them. We drove them to the forest. Another member of the underground was a forester there, and his job was to help the Jews who were hiding. I brought them to him, left in a hurry, and said I would be back. He gave them tools and shovels to dig a bunker.

"It was still summer, so I knew they would not freeze to death. I periodically returned to the forest with lumber, food, and medicine. In the fall, I brought warm clothing and a tarpaulin so they could build a roof on their hiding place for winter. I knew they were better off than the Jews I had seen being herded onto cattle cars and taken to death camps. But I knew their lives were in constant danger because Germans were known to patrol the forests. I had gotten beyond the point of being frightened for myself as I saw Poles hanging from trees for daring to help Jews."

Aron then said, "So it was, Bronka and Johanna, that only because of your mother, Sarah and I survived. But right after the war, she did not know we were still alive, and I had no idea where she was. Then we found each other again in Kielce."

The anger was gone from Papa's voice. He spoke his daughters' names softly. Was that actually affection Bronka heard? But she was still confused and afraid to speak. She had been ordered not to question, but the churning questions in her mind were giving her a headache. Papa had another wife? What happened to her? She dared not ask—yet. But as the tension mounted in her body, she knew that she would ask the question if the answer was not revealed. She had no choice but to wait and see if he would tell the entire truth.

"I wanted to go back to Kielce to see if any of my family members were alive," he continued, "and also to see what happened to our home and property.

"When I returned, the wife of my father's colleague, who was supposed to have safeguarded our belongings, looked me in the eye when I knocked on her door and said simply, 'You are still alive; I thought your whole family was dead.' She claimed she had no knowledge of our things. I could hear disappointment and annoyance in her voice.

"I found also that our beautiful stone house, the scene of so many childhood memories and which had housed my father's medical practice, was now a police station. During the war, it had served as a hotel for German officers.

"After these heartbreaking disappointments, we made our way to 7 Planty Street, where the Jewish Committee was located. At that point, we had no home and no family. And Sarah was pregnant. We had no choice but to stay there until we were sent somewhere else, such as Palestine.

"There was only one bright light in this situation. You can imagine how surprised and pleased I was to find out that your mother was working there. Her heroic rescue of Jewish children had gained her the respect of the Jewish community, and she was now working to help survivors of the Shoah come back to life after the war."

Suddenly, Faye interrupted. "I smell smoke!"

Izzy jumped up and ran into the kitchen. Smoke was pouring from the oven. He immediately turned the oven off and pulled out the meatloaf and potatoes, which were black and hard and burned to a crisp.

"Stick a fork in it," Faye called from the living room, dismayed that her special meatloaf recipe—with vegetarian vegetable soup and a hard-boiled egg in the middle, that she had taught Judy to make— was now ruined.

"It's hard as a rock; even a dog wouldn't eat it."

"No one is hungry," said JoJo. "Please, Papa, finish the story."

"Perhaps we should finish the story another day," he said.

"How can it be any worse than what you've already told us?"

"Sometimes things get worse before they get better," Judy jumped in. "It's Papa's story to tell. It's up to him. I think it's time for you to know the truth."

She turned to her husband. "Aron?"

Aron's eyes filled with tears. "I can't. It is just too painful." He began to cry.

"Then let me tell it," Judy said, sitting up straight and looking right at her daughters with laser-sharp focus. She displayed a strength the girls had never seen in their mother before. She spoke from her heart, not looking for approval from Aron—or even Faye.

"The time is long past due for the girls to know. In understanding, there is forgiveness. But first, Bronka and Johanna, you must go over to your father and give him a big hug. He is the only father you have, and he needs a hug."

The telling of the story had dissipated the girls' anger. Their heads were spinning with all the new information they had yet to fully absorb. They dutifully walked the few steps from the piano bench to their sobbing, newly vulnerable father, who stood up to receive them. Together, they embraced him, and soon Judy walked over and put her arms around the girls in a group hug.

After a few moments, the girls went back to the piano bench and Judy sat down next to Aron.

"On July first, 1946 an eight-year-old boy from Kielce named Henryk Blaszczyk went missing," Judy began. "When he returned home two days later, he told his parents he had been kidnapped. This was a lie. He had actually hitchhiked to his former neighborhood because he wanted to get cherries that were grown by one of the neighbors there. When he came back, his father, who was very drunk, took him to the police station to complain. On their way, the child made up a story about a Jewish man in a green cap who he said had kidnapped him. He said the man had held him in the basement of 7 Planty Street, where the Jewish Committee was housed, where I worked, and where one hundred eighty refugees were living.

"By the next morning, vicious rumors started spreading among the Poles. They said Jews were kidnapping Christian children for ritual sacrifice and were holding them in the basement of 7 Planty. A violent mob assembled to get revenge against the Jews. These were out-and-out lies; the building did not even have a basement. The Jews who lived there were sick, tired, downtrodden refugees; almost all of their *lantzmen* had been murdered by the Nazis. They were waiting there to start new lives.

"The police and militia were called in, supposedly to keep the peace. But instead of calming things down, they began shooting and dragging Jews from the building into the courtyard, where the local Poles viciously attacked them. They even threw some Jews from the second floor. It was pure chaos. Police, soldiers, and ordinary citizens were attacking Jews with stones and clubs and pipes. Others were taking aim with guns. Everything was drenched in blood. The violence lasted for hours."

Judy closed her eyes for a moment, covered her mouth with her hands, and took a deep breath. She braced herself for the worst part.

"I am ashamed to say that my father was among the Polish policemen that day," Judy continued. "He may have been drunk, but that is no excuse for what happened. Forty-two Jews were killed, and more than forty were injured, including a mother and a newborn baby."

Judy began to cry again.

"And a woman who was six months pregnant was murdered," she continued. "That woman was Sarah, Papa's first wife. And that is how Papa lost his wife and his unborn child in the Kielce pogrom, which took place more than a year after the war was over.

"I watched the scene from the window where I was holed up with twenty Jews, where I had tried to barricade the door. I saw that Papa was hysterically crying and bent over his wife. I ran outside to him, and I could see she was dead, so I pulled him away. I brought him back into the building for shelter until the massacre was over. The two of us went to the morgue to identify Sarah, and we remained in Kielce for the burial and shiva of the forty-two Jews.

"After the Kielce pogrom, we were both done with Poland. Papa realized that Poland was no place for Jews. He had survived the war but lost his entire family. He thought he was about to start a new family and a new life, but that too was lost. He did not want to go on.

"I knew in my heart that Kielce was no place for decent human beings. It wasn't just the instigators that troubled me; there are always troublemakers. I was not only appalled by the mob that participated, but also by those who stood idly by and watched as passive bystanders. I am deeply ashamed that my father—my own flesh and blood—was an anti-Semite. I will take that shame to my grave. After I witnessed the Kielce pogrom, I could no longer stay in Poland. I had to renounce my country and my family. And I had to save Papa. There was no other choice for me.

"I told Papa that we would leave Kielce together and I would forsake my country, my family, and my religion. I wanted to become a Jew. I spoke the words of Ruth in the Bible: '. . . for whither thou goest, I will go; and where thou lodgest, I will lodge; thy people shall be my people, and thy God my God.'

"In Germany, the Allies had set up displaced persons camps for the survivors. I told Papa I would go with him there. But my friends in the Jewish Committee told me I could not go to a Jewish DP camp as a Christian. I said, 'There must be a way.' And there was a way. There is always a way. My friends said to me, 'You helped so many Jews during the war and saved so many lives, now it is our chance to help you.'"

"They dyed my blond hair dark brown, and they gave me identification papers with the alias of Judyta Abraham. Papa and I boarded a train to Warteplatz, Germany. We vowed to put Poland behind us. I asked him many questions about Judaism, and he answered them patiently. He taught me the Shema and other prayers.

"When we arrived at the camp, I was accepted as a Jew. Papa and I got married by a rabbi in a group ceremony with six other couples under a *chuppah*. And a year later, you beautiful twins were born.

"You must believe me that this was the happiest day of our lives.

It was also happy for all of the people in the camp. It was a double mitzvah—a sign from God that Jewish life would go on with the birth of two little girls who would one day become Jewish mothers. It was a sign that Hitler had been defeated. It signified the resilience of the Jewish people. I know you wish that Papa would be more affectionate with you, but maybe now you understand what he has been through. Why he does not want to speak of it. We love you more than words can ever say."

The truth—the messy, difficult, complicated truth—was now out in the open. In the moment, it cleared the air. There were tears and apologies and hugs and kisses on all sides. For the first time in their lives, the twins had a window into the trauma and the pain that both of their parents had endured.

As Judy made peanut butter sandwiches for the drained and exhausted family, no one said a word. Everyone suddenly realized that they were hungry and downed their sandwiches in a few minutes. Then the girls went upstairs, leaving the adults alone.

"I think that went pretty well," said Faye.

"I hope so," said Judy. "I feel like a weight has been lifted from me."

"But you know down the road there will be more questions," Aron said. "Bronka will want to get to the bottom of every single thing."

"Let's worry about that when the time comes," Judy said. "It might not happen for a long time."

"Or ever," added Izzy.

"What about the Jewish identity issue?" Aron asked.

"It's not an issue for me," Izzy said.

"Nor me either," said Faye. "Judy is the best Jew I know."

"Okay, I guess if it ever becomes an issue, I can speak to the rabbi," Aron said.

But Judy was thinking about other issues. In telling their story to her daughters, she had revealed secrets, lies, and cover-ups, not to mention the anti-Semitism of their biological grandfather. She had made it seem like the choices she made at the time were the right thing (the only thing) to do—to renounce your family, your religion, your country. Surely, this was a clear case of right and wrong, she told herself. *What choice did she have?*

But how would Bronka and Johanna analyze and internalize their parents' story, now that it was out in the open? How would it affect them as they grew up? That was a concern for another day.

For tonight, despite her weariness, she knew for sure that she was strong and resilient. She felt cleansed by the truth, awash in forgiveness and family harmony, alight with tranquility and reconciliation.

GLOSSARY

Balabosta – Efficient Jewish homemaker.

Bashert – Destiny. It is often used to refer to one's divinely preordained spouse or soulmate.

Bench – To recite blessings.

Bissel – A little.

Challah – Ceremonial braided egg bread used on the Sabbath and Jewish holidays.

Chuppah – Marriage Canopy

Conservadox – A synagogue that is affiliated with the Conservative movement, but leans toward more traditional Orthodox practices.

Dayenu – Traditional Passover hymn, literally meaning: "It would have been enough."

Gay avek – "Go away."

Gottenyu – "Oh, God!"

Gezuntah – Big, large.

Gut Shabbos – "Good Sabbath."

Haftorah – A selection from one of the books of the Prophets read after the Torah reading on the Sabbath and holiday mornings.

Mourner's Kaddish – Prayer recited by mourners.

Kashrus – The Jewish dietary laws and the rules of keeping kosher.

Kavannah –Intention.

Knesset – Israeli Parliament.

Lashon hora – Gossip.

Machar – Important person, big shot.

Machberes – Notebook.

Mach Schnell – "Hurry up!"

Mazel Tov – "Good luck!"

Mechitza – Partition in an Orthodox synagogue to separate men and women during prayer.

Meshuggene – Crazy, mad, insane person.

Mikveh – Ritual bath, representing spiritual cleansing.

Minyan – Quorum of a group of at least ten Jews required for a prayer service.

Modeh Ani – The first words of a prayer that observant Jews recite daily upon waking.

Morah – Teacher.

Oneg Shabbos – Literally, "Joy of the Sabbath." It usually refers to the refreshments following Friday night services.

Oy vey iz mir – "Woe is me!"

Pareve – Neutral food that is neither meat nor dairy.

Rachmonos – Compassion, mercy, pity.

Shechechiyanu – Prayer of thanksgiving.

Shalom Bayis – Peace in the home.

Sheket b'vakasha – "Quiet, please."

Shema – Seminal Hebrew prayer that acknowledges the oneness of God.

Shiksa – Non-Jewish woman.

Shiva – Seven-day mourning period.

Shoin genug – "That's enough!"

Shul – Synagogue.

Siman Tov u Mazel Tov – Sung on happy occasions, the literal meaning is "Good Sign and Good Luck!"

Smicha – Rabbinical ordination.

Sukkah – A temporary shelter, used for meals during the Jewish festival of Sukkot.

Tachlis – The heart of the matter.

Tallis – Prayer shawl.

Tefillin – Cubic black leather boxes containing Torah texts on parchment that observant Jews wear on their head and their arm during weekday morning prayers.

Treyfe – Non-kosher food.

Undzer Hofenung – Our Hope.

Vaz is das?– "What is this?"

Warteplatz – Waiting place.

Yad VaShem – The World Holocaust Remembrance Center in Israel.

Yahrtzeit – Anniversary of the day of death of a loved one.

Yenta – Busybody.

Yichus – Pedigree, ancestry, family background.

Yizkor – Prayer Service in Commemoration of the Dead.

Yom HaShoah – Holocaust Remembrance Day in Israel.

A NOTE FROM THE AUTHOR

THE CHARACTERS AND EVENTS OF *The Takeaway Men* are all figments of my imagination. But the settings of the story are real.

Warteplatz is a name I chose for the Jewish Displaced Persons camp in which the twins were born. It means "waiting place" in German. Many survivors of the Holocaust lived in DP camps after the war because they were unwilling or unable to return to their home countries—or were unwelcome by the non-Jews who had moved into their homes and those who had been their neighbors. The bulk of the Jewish survivors later immigrated to the US or Israel.

The term *Holocaust* did not gain traction until well after the years covered in this book. Instead, Jews often used the Hebrew word *Shoah* when referring to the murder of European Jews by the Nazis and their collaborators. It means destruction and is a word that had been in use since the Middle Ages.

I liberally used Yiddish and Hebrew words to give flavor to the dialogue. In the '50s and '60s, Jews of European background used the Ashkenazic pronunciation of Hebrew. Later, the Sephardic pronunciation, popularized in Israel, became standard. For example, the Lubinskis and their peers would say "Shabbos," while today the common usage is "Shabbat."

The story of the Kielce pogrom is true. More than a year after the war ended in Europe, forty-two Jews were killed and forty others injured by an angry mob of Polish civilians and policemen. The casualties included a mother and a newborn baby and a pregnant woman.

In the decade following the end of WWII, many survivors did not speak about their experiences. Nor was it mentioned in the curriculum of public schools—and not in Hebrew Schools, either. Thus, the scenes in Deborah Cohen's Hebrew School class, as well as the aftermath of her actions, are invented.

The Bellerose/Floral Park area of Northeast Queens developed in the postwar era. The names of churches, synagogues, and schools are made up. Some of the stores on Union Turnpike actually existed, such as May's, Dan's Supreme, and Barry's Stationery Store, while others were renamed.

In the 1950s, American foreign policy was focused on the communist threat and the Cold War with the Soviet Union, not with capturing Nazis. Those Nazis who slipped into the United States were not exposed until decades later, if ever. The story of Rudolf Schmidt is totally imaginary.

Senator Joseph McCarthy conducted hearings to expose communist infiltration. People lost their jobs for having joined the Communist party when they were in college, others because they were falsely accused. The hysteria reached a fever pitch with the arrest and trial of Ethel and Julius Rosenberg. It is true that David Greenglass testified against his sister, Ethel Rosenberg, and her husband. The story of Lenore and Al and their influence on the Rosenberg case is entirely fictional.

The Rosenbergs were the only Americans to be executed as spies during peacetime. Although the judge and lawyers were Jewish, many Jews viewed their treatment as a manifestation of anti-Semitism.

The extent of Ethel's role in her husband's spying activity remains in dispute. Years later, Greenglass admitted that he lied about her involvement to save himself and his wife, Ruth.

Students in public schools in the fifties participated in "duck and cover" drills. They also sang religious Christmas carols.

In 1939, Hitler gassed German psychiatric patients.

In the fifties and sixties, mental illness in the United States was still stigmatized and rarely discussed in public. Chlorprozamine, discovered in 1950, was the first anti-psychotic drug. In 1960, Creedmoor had seven thousand patients. The names of the other hospitals in the book are fictitious.

Until 1979, the question of who was a Jew was determined by the mother's religion and conversion. If your mother was Jewish, you were Jewish. But that year, the Reconstructionist Rabbinical Association declared that a child would be considered Jewish if his father alone was Jewish and the child was raised as a Jew. In 1983, Reform rabbis adopted the same position.

In all movements, a rabbi must perform conversion, which requires a course of study and, depending on the rabbi, immersion in a mikveh. Judy Lubinski was, therefore, not a Jew according to Jewish Law. Because this story took place in the forties, fifties, and sixties, neither were her daughters. In Orthodox and Conservative congregations, women were not counted as part of a prayer service; that is why they needed ten men to conduct a prayer service at the shiva for Lenore's father.

The deodorant business grew and thrived in the fifties and sixties, but there was no company named SpringPearl.

Most married women with children did not work outside the home.

In 1962 Yad Vashem called for nominations for *Righteous Among the Nations*.

I have been researching this topic for most of my life, so the resources I found helpful constitute a book themselves. I would like to give special mention to: Menachem Rosensaft's, *God, Faith, and Identity from the Ashes;* Jan T. Gross's, *Fear;* Helen Epstein's, *Children of the Holocaust;* Raul Hilberg's, *The Destruction of the European Jews;* Keith Lowe's, *Savage Continent;* Irene Gut Opdyke's, *In My Hands;* and Michał Jaskulski and Lawrence Loewinger's film about Kielce, *Bogdan's Journey.*

I would like to also express my appreciation to Boris Chartan, a founder of the Holocaust Museum and Tolerance Center (HMTC) in Glen Cove, New York, and to Robert Meeropol, a son of Julius and Ethel Rosenberg. Both offered their recollections for my previous book, *The Living Memories Project: Legacies That Last,* which proved invaluable in writing this book. Thanks also go to Robert Meeropol and his brother, Michael, for their book, *We Are Your Sons: The Legacy of Ethel and Julius Rosenberg.* Thanks also to Ivy Meeropol for her documentary, *Heir to an Execution;* to Sam Roberts for his book about David Greenglass, *The Brother;* and to Miriam Moskowitz for her book, *Phantom Spies, Phantom Justice.*

While my husband Stewart, an identical twin, has been my live-in expert on the subject, Abigail Pogrebin's book, *One and the Same,* helped me better understand female twins. And Jenna Bush Hager and Barbara Pierce Bush's *Sisters First,* gave me valuable insight into fraternal twin girls.

ACKNOWLEDGMENTS

———◦———

THE TAKEAWAY MEN IS THE result of my lifetime thirst to learn more about the Holocaust, first as a sixth-grade student after I read *The Diary of Anne Frank* for the first time, then as a history teacher, and later as a reader and researcher. I would like to thank all those from whom I have personally learned, especially the survivors and children of survivors.

I am deeply grateful to Brooke Warner, Lauren Wise, Crystal Patriarche, and everyone at SparkPress for believing in my book and for making my dream of publishing a novel come true.

I truly appreciate everyone who supported me in the endeavor that resulted in this work of historical fiction. Thank you especially to my cherished friends, family, and beta readers, who encouraged me from the very beginning and made valuable suggestions: Audrey Atlas, Jennifer Feingold, Arthur Fischman, and Rabbi Jonathan Waxman. I am sorry that Howard Sorgen, who enthusiastically and perceptively read the manuscript in the last months of his life, did not live to see its publication.

Thank you to my daughter-in-law, Beth Ain, who enthusiastically supported my undertaking and put me in touch with her writing instructor, Rachel Sherman. Rachel edited my first draft, and her edits and recommendations helped me craft a better book. Beth also connected me with the kind and generous Amy Blumenfeld, who led me to SparkPress. I also appreciate the input of my daughters-in-law, Alana Joblin Ain and Halie Geller, who supported me and shared their thoughts throughout the process. And of course, my three sons—Jonathan, Daniel (Rabbi Dan), and Michael (Morty)—empowered me with hope, strength, and support, as always, and spurred me on to complete the project.

My chief cheerleader, my husband Stewart, was a dynamic and consistent presence from the very beginning. His helpful suggestions, praise, and criticism—not to mention his correction of my comma usage—helped make this a better read.

I wish that my parents, Helen and Herbert Fischman, could have lived to savor this milestone, but I know they would be proud that their legacy—not only of love and kindness, but also of critical thinking, writing, and speaking—lives on. My mother would also be delighted that I found yet another "project."

Finally, I hope that when they are old enough, my grandchildren will read *The Takeaway Men*, and ponder the questions and issues raised. May they understand that history is today's current events, and that no matter how dire a situation seems, individuals still have the power and responsibility to make a difference.

ABOUT THE AUTHOR

© Diana Berrent

MERYL AIN'S ARTICLES AND ESSAYS HAVE appeared in *Huffington Post, MariaShriver.com, The Jewish Week, The New York Times, Newsday,* and other publications. In 2014, she coauthored the award-winning book, *The Living Memories Project: Legacies That Last,* and in 2016, wrote a companion workbook, *My Living Memories Project Journal.* She is a former history teacher and school administrator. She holds a BA from Queens College, an MA from Teachers College, Columbia University, and an EdD from Hofstra University. She and her husband, Stewart, live in New York; they have three sons, three daughters-in-law, and six grandchildren. This is her first novel.

SELECTED TITLES FROM SPARKPRESS

SparkPress is an independent boutique publisher delivering high-quality, entertaining, and engaging content that enhances readers' lives, with a special focus on female-driven work. www.gosparkpress.com

Child Bride: A Novel, Jennifer Smith Turner
$16.95, 978-1-68463-038-7
The coming-of-age journey of a young girl from the South who joins the African American great migration to the North—and finds her way through challenges and unforeseen obstacles to womanhood.

Seventh Flag: A Novel, Sid Balman, Jr.
$16.95, 978-1-68463-014-
A sweeping work of historical fiction, *Seventh Flag* is a Micheneresque parable that traces the arc of radicalization in modern Western Civilization—reaffirming what it means to be an American in a dangerously divided nation.

Sarah's War, Eugenia Lovett West
$16.95, 978-1-943006-92-2
Sarah, a parson's young daughter and dedicated patriot, is sent to live with a rich Loyalist aunt in Philadelphia, where she is plunged into a world of intrigue and spies, her beauty attracts men, and she learns that love comes in many shapes and sizes.

Trouble the Water: A Novel, Jackie Friedland
$16.95, 978-1-943006-54-0
When a young woman travels from a British factory town to South Carolina in the 1840s, she becomes involved with a vigilante abolitionist and the Underground Railroad while trying to navigate the complexities of Charleston high society and falling in love.

The Year of Necessary Lies: A Novel, Kris Radish
$17, 978-1-940716-51-0
A great-granddaughter discovers her ancestor's secrets—inspirational forays into forbidden love and the Florida Everglades at the turn of the last century.

About SparkPress

SparkPress is an independent, hybrid imprint focused on merging the best of the traditional publishing model with new and innovative strategies. We deliver high-quality, entertaining, and engaging content that enhances readers' lives. We are proud to bring to market a list of *New York Times* best-selling, award-winning, and debut authors who represent a wide array of genres, as well as our established, industry-wide reputation for creative, results-driven success in working with authors. SparkPress, a BookSparks imprint, is a division of SparkPoint Studio LLC.

Learn more at GoSparkPress.com